DATE DUE		
4-25			
		MAY	2001

The Indian Sign

Also by Les Roberts

✲ ✲ ✲ ✲ ✲ ✲ ✲

Other Milan Jacovich Mysteries

✲ ✲ ✲ ✲ ✲ ✲ ✲

THE BEST-KEPT SECRET

A SHOOT IN CLEVELAND

THE CLEVELAND LOCAL

COLLISION BEND

THE DUKE OF CLEVELAND

THE LAKE EFFECT

THE CLEVELAND CONNECTION

DEEP SHAKER

FULL CLEVELAND

PEPPER PIKE

The Saxon Mysteries

✲ ✲ ✲ ✲ ✲ ✲ ✲

THE LEMON CHICKEN JONES

SEEING THE ELEPHANT

SNAKE OIL

A CARROT FOR THE DONKEY

NOT ENOUGH HORSES

AN INFINITE NUMBER OF MONKEYS

The Indian Sign

LES ROBERTS

Thomas Dunne Books
St. Martin's Minotaur
New York

THOMAS DUNNE BOOKS.
An imprint of St. Martin's Press.

www.minotaurbooks.com

ISBN 0-312-25217-X

First Edition: August 2000

10 9 8 7 6 5 4 3 2 1

For
Holly Albin,
with love

ACKNOWLEDGMENTS

The author wishes to thank, as usual, Dr. Milan Yakovich, who patiently and cheerfully endures all the questions and wisecracks that are his lot for having a fictional private eye named after him. He's a real-life superstar.

A bow to Diana Yakovich Montagino, who many years ago casually mentioned her brother's name and planted the seed for my own particular cottage industry.

Much love and gratitude to Lisa Wasoski, who was asked a simple question and promptly came up with a hundred pages of careful research on the indigenous Native Americans of Michigan, without which I could not have written this book.

Appreciation to Karen Anderson of the Bellfaire Jewish Children's Bureau in Shaker Heights, Ohio, who must have thought my questions frivolous at best and crazed at worst.

And to Cynthia Garman of Lancaster, Pennsylvania, for supplying valuable background material which inspired while it informed.

Hugs to my editor, Ruth Cavin, from whom I learn more of my craft every year, and for my longtime agent and friend, Dominick Abel, whose only fault is his execrable taste in baseball teams.

Cross Village, Michigan, is a real place. But just as I fictionalize Cleveland, so I have used and changed Cross Village and its people, businesses, and institutions for my own nefarious fictional purposes.

I have used the terms "Native American" and "Indian" interchangeably in this novel, preferring to be guilty of political incorrectness than of bad and awkward writing.

The characters herein are fictitious, and any resemblance to persons living or dead is just one of those bizarre coincidences that sometimes happen to writers of fiction.

The Indian Sign

Chapter One

It was snowing hard the first time I saw the old Indian. A gentle, Currier and Ives Christmas card kind of snowfall, with big fat flakes whose facets catch the light as they drift downward, pirouetting madly in the eddying currents of the warmer air closer to the earth.

When people speak of Indians in Cleveland, Ohio, they usually mean the kind who wear protective athletic cups, politically incorrect Chief Wahoo caps, and red socks pulled up to the knee, who terrorize American League pitching by batting 311 for the season with 115 runs batted in or win Gold Gloves for fielding prowess.

This particular Indian was the real deal, though—a Native American. He was broad-shouldered and deep-chested, and though he was seated I got the idea that he might be almost as tall as I am; the black high-crowned, wide-brimmed hat atop his head added to the illusion of height. He appeared to be at least sixty years old, and his iron gray hair was done up in two long braids that fell to his waist. He was wearing a hip-length jacket that looked like it was made from a colorful wool tribal blanket, with bone toggle buttons. His work-faded Levi's were tucked into soft-looking leather boots.

It was just before nine o'clock on a morning that was February-bitter, dark and gray. He was on the bench across the street from my apartment building at the crest of Cedar Hill, in the little mini-park in front of the Baskin-Robbins ice cream shop on Fairmount Boulevard where it forms a triangle with Cedar Road in Cleveland Heights. Snow frosted his eyelashes and mini-drifts were collecting in little piles on his hat and shoulders, but if he noticed it, he didn't seem to be bothered by it. Next to him on the bench was a small paper sack that could have contained his lunch. He was sitting so motionless that I had to take a second look to make sure he wasn't dead. Only his eyelids flickered.

Although there are no longer any Indian tribes living in Ohio on reservations, there are plenty of Native Americans just going about their business. But most of them dress the way everyone else does, so his decidedly eccentric clothes made him very noticeable. His back was ramrod-straight against the back of the bench, his hands were at rest on his thighs, and his eyes were riveted on the row of three-story apartment buildings across the triangle on Cedar Road. His mouth was a thin slash in his mahogany-colored face and his jaw was thrust forward in an attitude that could have been described as pugnacious.

He looked like an R. C. Gorman oil painting.

I didn't give him much more than a second glance as I climbed into my car; I had other things to do that morning down at my office in the Flats on the west bank of the Cuyahoga River in downtown Cleveland. Still, for some reason he stayed in my mind all that day like a bad song that gets stuck between your ears and drives you crazy.

The funny things you see, as my father used to say, when you haven't got your gun.

And I didn't have mine. Either of them. I keep one on a high shelf in the guest closet in my apartment, and the other—the big one that means business, the .357 Magnum—in the top drawer of the desk in my office. I didn't think I'd need them for my nine-thirty appointment with a prospective new client.

"Client" meaning a customer for my security business. I deal with industrial security, mostly. Employee background checks, electronic surveillance systems, damage control, that sort of thing. Milan Security, I call the company. I gave it my first name, Milan, because my last one, Jacovich, is too tough for anyone except another eastern European to try to pronounce. I'm the owner, field operative, secretary, receptionist, and part-time janitor. I only recently turned the bill-paying over to an accounting firm, otherwise I'm pretty much a one-man band.

I like it that way. I spent three years on Uncle Sam's payroll in the early seventies as a sergeant in the U.S. Army military police, wearing the combat greens he so generously provided, mostly in a Southeast Asian garden spot called Cam Ranh Bay. After I came back from Vietnam I served for a few years as a Cleveland police officer, and those two hitches in the uniforms of my country and city developed in me an aversion to saluting and chains of command that was strong enough for me to know I wanted to be my own boss and run my own business.

It's not that I have such an entrepreneurial spirit. I just don't play well with others.

I also have a private investigator's license—but that's the part of my job I like the least. Nobody comes to a private investigator unless they're in trouble. And that usually means I sign on for their trouble, too.

Everyone was having trouble this particular season. After El Niño had blessed us with two years of mild, snowless winters it was payback time, and we hardy Clevelanders, who normally button our top buttons only when the thermometer starts sinking into negative readings, had grown soft and spoiled and almost resentful of the icy temperatures and relentless snowfall that had been visited upon us since the very first day of January.

The cold front, one of several that annually blow down on us from western Canada, was turning the snow slick and slippery on the streets, especially heading down Cedar Hill from Cleveland Heights into the city, and I concentrated even more than usual on keeping my car within the lane lines. On the radio, John Lanigan and Jimmy Malone kept me alert with their own particular brand of craziness on WMJI, Majic 105. A lot of Clevelanders who drive to work couldn't make it to their desks in the morning without the company of Lanigan and Malone in the car with them.

The Indian was nagging at me. I couldn't imagine what he was doing sitting in front of the Baskin-Robbins shop at nine o'clock in the morning, staring off into space while the snows of a midwestern February piled up on the brim of his hat.

But there are all sorts of things in this world that I don't know and will never understand, and after a few minutes' musing I decided he was simply one more on that long list.

The graveled parking lot outside my office building was dusted white by the time I arrived, and when I wheeled my nine-year-old Sunbird into my reserved space next to the door, the tires took the virginity of the morning snow. It's an old building; I bought it for less than one might imagine a few years back when my Auntie Branka died and left me some money. I have a tenant downstairs, a company that makes wrought-iron gates and grilles, and they are noisier than I'd like, hammering and clanking, the roar of the acetylene torch frequently floating up through the floor. The owner, Tony Radek, habitually bellows around his ever-present cigar at his hapless employees, most of whom seem to be his younger brothers. My other tenant, sharing the second floor with me, is a surgical supply house, and the best I can say for them is that they're nice and quiet, and pay their rent on time.

The combined rental income more than covers the mortgage, and I have myself a free office—*and* an investment.

The world headquarters—the *only* headquarters—of Milan Security is one very big room and one very small one, with hardwood floors, exposed brick walls, and windows that arch gracefully from near the floor almost to the ceiling, affording me a fabulous view out over the hairpin twist of the Cuyahoga River known, from the days of the six-hundred-foot ore tankers who used to regularly engage in aquatic fender benders, as Collision Bend.

The office features a small closet, a spacious unisex bathroom with a shower stall, and the smaller, windowless utility room where I keep my copying machine and store a lot of the electronic toys I was talked into buying but rarely use: the micromini cameras that look like fountain pens, the microphones that can pick up the rumblings of a kitten's gastric juices from three blocks away, the tape recorders and illegal telephone bugs, and some of the database software I'd had specially designed that can supply amazingly detailed information about anyone in America short of what they had for breakfast this morning. Not to make anyone nervous, but that includes *you*.

There was a fire in here a year or so ago, courtesy of a well-thrown Molotov cocktail, and although thanks to the insurance company everything had been repaired or redone, in some cases to the betterment of the original, there is still a hint of smoke odor, not entirely unpleasant, that prickles the hairs inside your nose on cold mornings and will probably never go away.

I hung up my parka—I had worn the heavy black one this morning that had come with a tag affixed informing me that it wasn't a parka at all but a "cold-weather system." I made a pot of coffee, my second of the day. I'm an addict; I had drunk four large mugsful before leaving the house and I figured I would share this batch with my nine-thirty visitor.

He was a few minutes shy of prompt; at about 9:46 he came through the door, wearing a white silk scarf and brushing the snow off the shoulders of his cashmere overcoat and onto my hardwood floor.

"Mr. Jacovich?" he said, erroneously pronouncing the *J*. Properly it's YOCK-o-vitch. And the first name, while I'm on the subject, is MY lan. Long *i* sound and the accent on the first syllable. Milan Jacovich. I am by heritage a Slovenian, and if you're unsure as to just where Slovenia is, join a big crowd of geography-challenged Americans. It's the northernmost republic of what used to be Yugoslavia; we're the quieter and more peaceable neighbors of the Serbs and Croats, and fortunately were not part of the nonsense that ripped the Balkans apart at the end of the twentieth century.

I repeated my name correctly for my prospective client and clasped his hand. He took off his gray cashmere coat, shook it out hard, leaving more droplets on the hardwood, and gave it to me to hang up on the brass coat tree by the door. It was soft, luxurious—just handling the damn thing was sensory overload. Everything about him was expensive—his haircut, his tie, his suit, his shoes, and his attitude, which was wave-to-the-masses-from-the-carriage-but-don't-let-them-touch-anything.

And yet there was a bulldog-hard droop to his mouth, augmented by a formidable set of jowls I was willing to bet he'd sported since his early twenties.

His name was Armand Treusch, which he had pronounced TROYSH when he made the appointment by phone. You'd think he'd have a certain sensitivity for pronouncing other people's names properly.

And he played with toys.

Very profitably, too.

Treusch was the CEO and founder of an outfit called Troy-Toy, Inc.—evidently an easier-to-spell variant of his last name. TroyToy was headquartered in the southeastern suburb of Solon, where it occupied most of a large, modern industrial park and enjoyed a national reputation. One of their dolls, a pinch-faced, frizz-haired female moppet with an anatomically correct pubis that sprayed mock-urine on command, had been something of a craze a few Christmases earlier. Not as big as Tickle Me Elmo or Beanie Babies, but TroyToy had made its professional bones on it, anyway, and was now the third-largest toy manufacturer in America.

I had done some checking on Armand Treusch before the meeting, thanks to my handy-dandy computer database, so I not only knew about his very viable, growing company, but that he himself lived on a forty-eight acre estate in Hunting Valley and was worth somewhere in the vicinity of twenty-four million dollars.

He declined my offer of coffee and seemed a trifle irritated when I chose to have some without him, staring with undisguised curiosity at my coffee mug. I didn't bother explaining it to him, but it used to belong to my best friend, and had his name on it, and a replica of the gold lieutenant's shield he'd carried from the Cleveland Police Department LT. MARK MEGLICH, it said, and beneath the shield number 7787. I'd staked my claim to the mug after Marko caught a fatal bullet the year before trying to back me up in a murder case that was actually outside his jurisdiction, and from that day forward I drank my coffee from it every morning.

I'd had a chronic heartache ever since then, too.

After I'd settled behind my desk, Treusch took out a solid brass card holder and gave me one of his business cards. It was embossed with his name and title, the name of the company, and the TroyToy logo—a bright blue cartoon of a helmeted Trojan warrior wearing a kind of loopy, dreamy-eyed grin that made him look like he was zonked on quaaludes.

"I've got an ulcer," Treusch announced, patting his Santa Claus stomach. I had to admit it was a unique gambit with which to begin a conversation with a stranger. "It comes with the territory in my racket. There's no more competitive field anywhere than the toy business. As a result, there has been quite a lot of industrial espionage going on in the last few years. Stealing secrets."

I nodded.

"It doesn't really matter whether or not our product is *better* if someone beats us to the punch. You understand what I'm saying?"

I lowered my eyelids once. Nothing irritates me more than for someone to ask whether I understand what they're saying. I have a master's degree from Kent State, and I guess I can understand English all right.

"I know it sounds silly to an outsider," he said without apology. "Like the CIA or something. But if somebody swipes an idea and beats the other guy to the marketplace, it could be a swing of several million dollars.

"So we have to be damned careful. Careful who we talk to, careful who we let inside the gates of Troy." The heretofore dyspeptic Treusch here flowered into a grin that spread from corner to corner; it was evident he was monstrously pleased with his little double-edged pun.

I decided to go with it. "And you feel there's a Trojan horse inside?"

"That's exactly right," he said. "I feel it. Here." He stuck a gentle finger into his ample gut, and grimaced; maybe the ulcer was kicking up. "I live my whole life on my instincts."

"I see," I said.

He suddenly turned somber. "Here's the thing, Mr. Jacovich." He pronounced it correctly this time; Armand Treusch was obviously a fast learner. "My comptroller—chief accountant—died about three months ago. Embolism in the brain. Went like that!" And he snapped his fingers to illustrate just how quickly *that* was.

"I'm sorry," I said.

"Yeah. He'd been with me since the very beginning. He was practically my first hire. Well, no, my fourth, actually. . . . Anyway, I'd have trusted him with my life. He was more than an employee, he was a friend."

I didn't say anything; I'd already expressed my condolences once, and figured that was enough. After all, he wasn't talking about his mother.

Treusch leaned forward earnestly to drive the next point home. "And he was well compensated for his loyalty. I take good care of my top people. Not only salary, but built-in bonuses, stock options, medical-dental-optical, company car phone. All the bennies."

His shoulders rose and fell in a jerky twitch. "Hey, it was sad losing him, but life goes on, you know what I'm saying?"

I sighed. I knew what he was saying, but I resisted the urge to tell him so; he was, after all, a paying client, and I *was* in business to make money.

"I mean, hey," he went on, "you gotta have an accountant . . ."

Life without one was indeed inconceivable. I nodded.

"So I hired a new guy. His name is David Ream. Kind of a wimpy, nerdy little guy, but what do you expect from an accountant?"

I sipped at my coffee; I make it strong and like it black, but my guest was making it taste bitter. I don't have the luxury of only working for people I was crazy about, and I had not lucked out with Armand Treusch.

"Anyway, I've got this funny feeling about him. Ream."

"How long has he been working for you?" I said.

"Not quite a month."

"And why do you have this funny feeling?"

Treusch ran his right thumb delicately over the balls of his other fingers as if he were getting ready to crack the combination of a safe. "I can't say, really. . . ."

"Has he *done* anything?"

"Not exactly, no. . . ."

I lifted an eyebrow and waited. I generally find out a lot more when I keep my mouth shut and listen; I've learned to be comfortable with the silences. Most people haven't.

Treusch fidgeted and eventually rewarded my patience. "Well, he asks too many questions."

"Questions?"

"Yeah. Asks our production people and the guys in the marketing department a lot of things about the various products we make. Stuff an accountant doesn't really need to know."

"Maybe he wants to learn as much as he can about the company he's working for," I suggested. "I should think that would be a plus."

"Normally I would think so, too. It's just this *feeling* I've got," Treusch said. "I mean, he's new and all . . ."

"That doesn't make him a bad guy."

"I know, I know. But our most recent hire before him was—I don't know, five years ago, six. And my people are as loyal to me as they are to the flag."

I put my coffee mug down on its warmer, watching the little red light flicker on. "What do you want me to do about it?"

"Check him out for me," Treusch said. "David Ream. His background."

"I should think hiring somebody that highly placed in your company, you would have investigated him before you offered him the job. Thoroughly."

"I did," Treusch said. "Or I should say my human resources director did."

"I'll probably want to talk to him, then."

"Her. Her name is Catherine McTighe. But I'd rather no one else at TroyToy knew what was going on."

"Why?"

"Like I said, this is a sensitive industry. Need-to-know and all that."

"I'll be very discreet in my inquiries," I said.

He stuck out his jaw again. "What does that mean?"

"I'll lie if I have to."

That seemed to please him, because he almost smiled. "Well, Ream's bona fides vetted out." He opened the expensive briefcase and extracted a file folder. "Here's his personnel file, his references, everything."

I reached across the desk and took it from him. "I'll make a copy."

"Don't bother. That *is* a copy. You can keep it."

Armand Treusch had it all figured out. Or partway, anyhow. Actually it was kind of refreshing; most clients don't think of such details until they're prompted. I put the file down without opening it. "And what would you like me to do with this?"

Treusch's eyes rolled upward as he searched the old, restored stamped-tin ceiling of my office for answers. A lot of people have looked up there for the same reason. "I'm hiring you to tell *me*."

I decided to help him out. "I think I can. You want more personal stuff than what's in this file."

"Exactly," he said.

"Deep background."

"Uh-huh."

"You want to know what kind of beer he drinks and what kind of music he likes and what he had for supper."

Treusch beamed, nodding enthusiastically; I think he was getting into the spirit of it. "Right, right."

"And most of all, you want to know if he has any connection whatsoever with any other toy company."

He lit up like the scoreboard of a pinball machine when the little steel ball hits a million; I could almost hear the bells. "Now you're talking!" he said. "You're a bright guy, Jacovich. I'd heard you were a bright guy. That's why I came to you in the first place."

"Mr. Treusch," I pushed the file back across the desk at him. "You're wasting your time."

His inner light went out and he slumped in his chair, a kid who'd been promised a pony for Christmas and got a cheap ukulele instead. "Why?"

"Right now, all you have about David Ream is a completely unfounded suspicion."

"I'm going on gut instinct," he said. "I told you, my gut has never let me down yet."

"Maybe not. But what you're talking about—that kind of thorough probe—your gut is going to cost you a hell of a lot of money."

He lowered his head, and the bulldog look darkened his heavy features again. I got the idea Armand Treusch was no one to be trifled with. "What do you care?" he said. "It's my money."

I sighed. I'd met clients like Treusch before; they come in with a set idea in their head and nothing anyone can say talks them out of it. I opened the bottom drawer of my desk to extract one of my standard contract forms. "Yes," I said, "and it looks like some of it is going to be mine."

I didn't much like it. It was Armand Treusch's paranoia that was sending me out on a witch-hunt, and I had the sinking feeling that if I discovered David Ream to be squeaky clean and bleeding TroyToy blue, Treusch was still going to be dissatisfied and suspicious.

It's the way some people are sometimes. They get an *idée fixe* and won't let go of it. I figured no matter what the results of my investigation, David Ream was not long for TroyToy. That made me feel kind of bad for the guy, but I'd learned—from Marko Meglich, actually—that you can't take on the world's troubles as your own. From that comes ulcers, disappointment, frustration, and eventually failure. And I have enough failure in my life without going out hunting for it.

Maybe Treusch had another agenda, another reason for digging up David Ream's buried treasures that he was loath to tell me about. Nevertheless, I'd taken his money, and now I owed him my complete attention. Although I make noises like I'm as independent as hell, I do need to earn a living, and don't have the luxury of turning down a couple of thousand dollars for a few days' easy work, even though I held no affection for Armand Treusch or his cause. Industrial security is, after all, what my little company is about.

So I'd make the proper inquiries, rattle some cages, and at the end of a week tell him he had indeed wasted his money.

Unless of course I found something.

But that didn't seem likely. Success had made Treusch overly wary of any change. Apparently he hadn't yet come to the realization, as I had, that life is about nothing if *not* change.

I spent the rest of the morning reading through David Ream's personnel file. It didn't tell me much. The vast brigade of crusaders who set up a hue and cry about people's "rights" have made it illegal for an employer to ask about age, marital status, or even gender—although there was a photocopy of the applicant's picture that made it highly unlikely he was a female. His sand-colored hair was sparse, his eyes pale blue behind nerdy, unfashionable glasses, and he had a receding chin and no lips to speak of at all. In a crowd of three he would completely disappear. He was one of the vanilla people.

Other than that, personal information was sketchy. He lived in Shaker Heights, on a street just off Van Aken Boulevard that was neither high end nor depressed, at an address commensurate with the sixty-five-thousand-dollar annual salary he was getting from TroyToy. So if he was indeed in the employ of a rival toy company, he was keeping his ill-gotten gains where no one could see them.

According to his application, he was a 1984 graduate of Case Western Reserve University's Weatherhead School of Business, which would probably place him in his late thirties. Right out of college he had gone to work as a bookkeeper at a health spa in Aspen, Colorado, where after three years he had risen to the title of comptroller. His most recent job had been as chief accountant with a digital analog company in Strongsville, a southern suburb of Cleveland.

If I ever got to meet David Ream, I'd have to ask him what in hell a digital analog was.

Interestingly enough, there was an eight-month gap between his leaving the Strongsville firm and hooking up with TroyToy. I was sure that Armand Treusch's in-house watchdogs had asked about that and been satisfied, but I decided I needed a little reassurance.

I called the company in Strongsville and asked to speak to the personnel department. A mistake, apparently, because the operator rather stiffly informed me that she'd connect me with *human resources*, and leaned on the two words so I wouldn't make such an egregious error again. For a guy like me who regularly thinks of a sofa as a davenport and a refrigerator as an icebox, the new terminology comes hard. I'm Newspeak-challenged.

The person who answered the phone had a husky, matronly voice, and I pictured her as slightly chubby, curly-haired, a jolly earth-mother type. She told me her name was Mrs. Ver Planck, and after I identified myself as being with a nonexistent credit bureau, she did some hemming and hawing and "calling up" records on the computer, and indeed verified that David Ream had worked there as their chief bookkeeper until the past June.

"Was he terminated?" I asked, uncomfortably aware of what that word meant in certain government circles. But I had to prove I could talk the new, politically correct talk with the best of them; five years earlier I would have inquired right out whether Ream had been canned.

"Oh, no. He resigned," Mrs. Ver Planck said.

"I see," I said, not seeing. "Did he give a reason?"

"There's nothing in the records. But I just happen to remember when he came in to clear the company on the last day. When he turned in his ID badge and his keys, he said he was leaving for personal reasons."

"You mean a higher-paying job?"

"I think he characterized it as personal fulfillment."

Things are indeed different nowadays. I'm quite certain no one even asked my father, when he was toiling in the hellish pits of the steel mills south of the city in the temperatures that often reached more than one hundred and twenty degrees, whether or not his career fulfilled him personally.

I thanked Mrs. Ver Planck and put the telephone down, forgetting to ask her about digital analogs, and thoughtfully drummed my fingers on the receiver. After "clearing the company," David Ream hadn't worked for eight months. And after that, his personal fulfillment had taken the shape of working a similar job to the one he'd left, only at a commercial manufacturer of toys instead of digital analogs.

Curious, I thought. Not suspicious, certainly not damning. But curious nonetheless.

I opened a new file on my computer, titled it *treusch.doc*, and typed in my notes on my initial meeting with him and my thoughts on the conversation I'd had with Mrs. Ver Planck. I copied it onto a floppy disk, and then made a hard-copy folder of my own—I still prefer paper I can hold in my hand to an electronic version that is in constant danger of disappearing—and placed the copies of David Ream's personnel records from TroyToy inside.

I'd eaten a big breakfast, so I wasn't really hungry for lunch and decided to skip it. I've reached that age where weight goes on easily and comes off with the utmost difficulty. Besides, I was having dinner that evening with my lover, Connie Haley, and since she usually has a very healthy Irish appetite, I wanted to be sure I was hungry enough to keep up with her.

I flipped through my Rolodex and found Rudy Dolsak's name. Rudy and Marko Meglich and I had gone to high school together and then reconvened at Kent State. Chubby, myopic Rudy had never realized his dream of playing big-time college football, but he'd plodded and plotted and worked his way up to varsity equipment manager and quietly idolized Marko and me for actually putting on the pads and getting bruised and dirty out there. After grad school, I'd gone to Vietnam—not the norm for young men from Kent State in the early seventies—and Marko had become a police officer. Rudy got a job in banking, and just as at Kent, had doggedly risen through the ranks until now he was the senior vice president at Ohio Mercantile Bank, downtown on Euclid Avenue. It was generally acknowledged that he was next in line for the presidency.

Providing he didn't get caught feeding confidential financial information to his private-investigator friend.

I was a little ashamed to call him, to tell you the truth. As close as we had been, as close as I felt to him, I find myself only contacting him when I need some information. Maybe it was because he's a family man and I have been divorced and single for many years. Maybe it was because we moved in very different circles. Sometimes the people we care most about get short shrift because of the pressures of career and family and just plain old living.

Rudy is relentlessly cheerful, however, and didn't hold it against me. He wasn't too thrilled that day, however, when I asked him to poke into David Ream's financial records.

"Aw, Milan," he said, and it came out perilously close to a whine. "Not again, okay? I hate it when you ask me to do things like that."

"Come on, Rudy, you can do whatever you want—you're the boss."

"I won't be if anyone gets wind that I'm giving out confidential records to private detectives."

"Don't let me down now, pal. You've always been there for me. When I'd catch a blister, or get a shinsplint, you were the one who always patched me up, right? You were my go-to guy." I chuckled to cover my guilt at the outrageous wheedling. "Nothing's changed—you're still covering my butt."

He laughed in spite of himself. "Don't manipulate me, Milan, I'm not seventeen years old anymore."

"Good," I said, relieved he had caught me. "I wasn't doing it very well."

"What is it you need?"

"All I want to know is what went on from June of last year to the present. Whether Ream was making any deposits."

Rudy sighed. "I don't suppose you're going to make it any easier on me by giving me a social security number."

I flipped open the personnel file. "As a matter of fact I am." I read it off to him.

He buzzed and hummed and made little grunting noises as he scribbled it down. Then he said, "I'll do what I can for you."

"Thanks, Rudy. I owe you dinner."

"Dinner my Aunt Fannie! If I get burned for this and lose my job, you're going to have to support me."

I laughed. "As long as it isn't in the style to which you're accustomed."

I hung up and reflected on what a good thing it was to have friends. Old friends. Like Rudy, since we were kids. A couple of other childhood chums like Alex Cerne and Sonia Kokol, who generally saw to it that I didn't spend Thanksgiving or Christmas alone in my apartment. Louis Vukovich, who ran Vuk's Tavern on St. Clair Avenue and had ceremoniously served me my first legal drink of alcohol—a Stroh's beer, right from the bottle. And Ed Stahl, the curmudgeonly op-ed columnist for the *Plain Dealer*, who's been my comrade, confidant, drinking partner, and information source since I was a raw police rookie, and who can always be counted on to scrounge up Indians tickets for my sons and me on selected weekends even though the games have been sold out for the last six years straight.

Thinking of friends reminded me of Marko, and I winced involuntarily as the sharp wolf-bite of regret dug into my gut. Everybody loses friends, loved ones—it's the cycle of life, and we usually go on. But Marko, whose nose I bloodied the day I met him in the fifth grade and who had gone on to be my friend for more than thirty years, had died for me. And that doesn't go away so easily.

Marko was dead because he covered my ass when he didn't have to, and here I was, relentlessly hunting down a man suspected of spying on toys.

Well, I thought, going on the defensive against myself, so what? That's what I *do*. It's not my job to preserve peace in the Balkans, find a cure for cancer, or stomp out hunger and poverty. It was my job, at the moment, to keep the world safe for Armand Treusch and the TroyToy empire. Did that mean I wasn't worthy enough to mourn my friend? Would it be better if he had sacrificed himself to save a welder, a salmon fisherman, a flight attendant, or the old guy who shines shoes in the lobby of the Halle Building instead of me?

I shook it off as I had so many times before. As Marko would have wanted me to. I'm sure he would have leveled one of those long, strong, pass-catching fingers at me and narrowed his eyes, and his mustache would have twitched as he ordered, "Milan, get over yourself!"

So I got over myself. I read Ream's file again, looking for some clue, some irregularity, but I couldn't find one. Then I made a few more calls, locked up the office, and headed eastward on Carnegie Avenue toward Cleveland Heights before the homeward-bound traffic turned University Circle into gridlock. The snow had stopped, for all intents and purposes. It was still in the air, but in tiny, almost invisible flakes that dissipated as they hit the ground. The homeowners of Greater Cleveland were spared additional shoveling tonight—except for those souls up north in Lake and Geauga Counties who live in what is commonly termed the snow belt.

I got up to the top of the hill at about a quarter to five.

The old Indian was still on the bench in front of the ice cream shop, looking for all the world as if he hadn't moved since nine o'clock that morning.

Chapter Two

The only difference was that the paper sack that had been beside him on the bench that morning was gone, so I assumed he had eaten his lunch and dutifully disposed of the trash in the nearby receptacle. But was it possible he had been sitting on that bench all day without otherwise moving, keeping who knows what kind of vigil?

The temperature was somewhere in the low teens and the wind brisk. He must have been very cold, but he didn't show it. He sat there impassively, chin jutting proud-high, staring across the street, apparently unmindful of the late-afternoon traffic bound for the eastern suburbs now snaking its way up around the curve of Fairmount Boulevard, tires hissing on the wet pavement.

He certainly had my curiosity piqued, and for a moment I was tempted to stroll across the street and talk to him, ask if there was something I could do to help. But I'm sure he would have found that patronizing; in these days when a gentleman opening a door for a woman is sometimes perceived as an insult, the best of intentions can turn poisonous.

Besides, unless I'm getting paid for it, I've found it's wiser to mind my own business. So as far as I was concerned, the old Indian could sit out there until the birds came and covered him with leaves.

I parked my car, collected the pack of mail from my box in the vestibule, and went upstairs to the second floor. My apartment was chilly; I turn the heat down to fifty-five degrees when I'm not there during the day. Slovenians are by nature what might charitably be called "thrifty."

I reset the thermostat at sixty-eight, riffled through the mostly junk mail and threw it all away unopened except for my Illuminating Company bill. Then I headed to the refrigerator for a Stroh's.

I've been drinking Stroh's beer ever since I started drinking anything, and its recent sale to a larger beer company hadn't dampened my ardor one whit. I suppose my fondness for it would earn me disdainful looks at some of the boomer fern bars downtown and on the west side, but then again I rarely go to such places to drink, so it doesn't matter. I wrenched off the cap and quaffed it straight from the bottle, the way I always do. I think it tastes better that way.

I wandered into my den, where I keep my only TV set, and watched the early news on Channel Twelve. Vivian Truscott, the elegant, tall, blond, and much-beloved anchorwoman who, unbeknownst to everyone in town but me, used to be a high-priced call girl in Las Vegas, was frowning as she talked about a plane crash in Canada. I riffled through a *Sports Illustrated*—not the swimsuit issue—and thought about David Ream and Armand Treusch.

I knew that the toy business was cutthroat, more so in the electronic age, when computer games were taking a big share of the market and plagiarism and secret-stealing were rampant. But it seemed to me that Treusch was being unreasonably suspicious about his new comptroller. If he became this agitated over every new employee, it was no wonder he had an ulcer.

I also wondered if his suspicions meant that Treusch had something in particular that he was trying to keep secret himself. I held out little hope that he'd tell me if he did. He was obviously a very cautious man. I supposed that was why he was worth twenty-four million bucks.

I finished my beer and stood up, glancing idly out the window as I did so; I always leave the blinds open in the wintertime during the day, on the off chance there will be even a moment or two of random sunlight to perhaps lend its stingy warmth to the apartment.

Across the street, the Indian still kept his place on the bench.

Winter brings early darkness, and the passing headlights of eastbound cars illuminated him briefly, then plunged him back into shadows the way they would a motionless scarecrow on a country road. The onset of evening didn't seem to affect him one way or the other. The snow had stopped now, but the wind had gotten serious, a brutal, biting gale swooping from off Lake Erie to the north, and I think he was hunching his shoulders a bit more than he had been earlier. That was his only visible sign of discomfort, and he didn't seem inclined to leave, either.

I wondered whether he was going to sit there all night, or even if he'd been there the night before, though I hadn't noticed him until morning. I've spent enough crushingly boring hours on surveillance to know the difficulties and discomforts, and my practical mind wondered what he was doing for bathroom facilities. The Mad Greek restaurant was right next to the ice cream shop, and perhaps he had been popping in there every so often to use their men's room.

There was something about him, though, about the way he sat so still, that made me question whether he ever *had* to.

I went into the kitchen and dropped my empty into one of the two blue recycling bags I keep handy—one for glass and one for plastic. I sometimes can't help questioning whether it makes a damn bit of difference, whether the city just dumps it all into the same landfill as our chicken bones and our junk mail and laughs at us for our pains, but it makes me feel better to maintain the *illusion* of doing my part for the planet.

From the refrigerator I took two steaks I'd bought the day before from Mister Brisket on Taylor Road, loaded them with pepper and garlic powder—never garlic *salt,* I had learned from Connie's chef brother, because it breaks down the fibers of the meat—covered them loosely with plastic wrap, and left them on the counter. Then I went into my bedroom, stripped the bed, and set about putting on clean sheets. Company was coming.

I'd been seeing Connie Haley for almost a year. She and her father and brothers own an upscale restaurant on the west side called the White Magnolia, and all share a big rambling house in

Rocky River, too, so when we wanted to be together and alone, Connie had to make the trek to the east side. That's a bigger deal than one might imagine, although it isn't much more than a twenty-five-minute car ride; in Cleveland west siders rarely come east, and vice versa, as if the Cuyahoga River, twisting its crooked way through the middle of downtown, was an international border separating two mildly hostile nations.

Connie and I had great times together, and there were moments when I thought about making it a more permanent arrangement. The thought of lovely, lusty, laughing Connie being around on a full-time basis was an appealing one. But I have been divorced for many years, and have been through a few damaging relationships, and I think I'm more than a little gun-shy. Commitment-phobia is harder to combat than a heroin addiction or the fear of high places.

Since Connie didn't seem particularly anxious to accelerate our relationship to another level either, I was biding my time and enjoying what is, rather than speculating on what might be. And yet there was a niggling worm of doubt in my belly; why didn't she seem to care about taking that next step?

The mattress was bare, now, and I had to make some decisions. The floral sheets, or the solid blacks? No, the blue and white stripes tonight, I thought, with the light blue extra pillowcases. And I made sure there were several fresh long-burning candles on the dresser, thick-columned white ones scented with vanilla. Connie likes making love by candlelight.

So do I.

I showered and shaved for the second time that day and put on a pair of freshly pressed khakis and a soft black pullover sweater with no shirt. I opened the box of homemade chocolates I'd bought for Connie from Mitchell Fine Candies on Lee Road in Cleveland Heights; she is a chocolate lover, although I can take it or leave it alone. I guess chocolate is a "girl thing."

I made sure there was a bottle of chenin blanc chilling in the refrigerator, massaged the outside of a couple of baking potatoes with olive oil (I like the skins crispy) and popped them unwrapped into a slow oven. Then I got a second Stroh's and went back into the den to wait.

I couldn't resist another quick peek out the window. It had begun snowing again, but the Indian was still there.

Maybe it was precognition, but I found myself a lot more interested in him than I should have been. Anyone who has spent a winter in Cleveland knows that whiling away the day sitting on a bench outdoors in the snow and the wind is not the most felicitous way to experience February. And if the Indian had been white or black or even Hispanic, I might not have paid any attention to him at all. But Cleveland is not New Mexico or Arizona, and a colorfully clothed Native American is more noticeable here than in many other places in the United States.

But even beyond that, I had a funny feeling about the Indian.

I didn't have time to dwell on it, though, because Connie arrived promptly at seven. One of her most appealing qualities—and there are many—is that, like me, she is scrupulous about being on time. I don't do well with waiting.

Her blond hair was in its usual adorable pigtail, her eyes sparkled as they always did, and her two remarkable dimples deepened and danced as she smiled when I opened the door.

"Hey," I said, and then I couldn't say any more because I was getting kissed. Thoroughly, royally, dizzyingly. Our mutual ardor had not diminished since the first time we looked at each other, and we seemed to live in a constant and delightful state of sexual tension.

The kiss heated up after a couple of seconds, and I did manage to kick the door shut with my foot so as not to scandalize Mr. Maltz, my neighbor from across the hall; he's in his nineties and can't take too much excitement.

It wasn't until we broke the kiss, me gasping for air; that I noticed the bottle of St. Emillion in her hand. She thrust it at me. "You said you were going to cook steaks, so I raided Leo's wine cellar." Leo was her father. "Open it and let it breathe."

Still quivering from the kiss, I said, "I'm worried about *me* breathing right now," and took the bottle into the kitchen, wrenched out the cork, and left it to stand guard over the steaks. When I came back out she had already taken off her coat and was hanging it in the closet by the front door. Connie and I had arrived at that place where she was no longer exactly a guest—but she didn't live there, either.

"Traffic was yuck-o," she said. "You'd think people here would learn how to drive in the snow."

"You managed to get here on time, though."

"You know me. If I'm more than ten minutes late and I haven't called, start checking the hospitals."

"Don't even say that," I scolded. "Not even in fun. I chilled some chenin blanc for before dinner. Interested?"

"I'm fascinated," she said. "By everything you do. But if you're asking whether I want some—no. I don't want to mix white and red."

"Smart girl. A vodka, then?"

"No, I think I'll just wait till we eat."

"Me, too," I said, and we sat down on the sofa together.

"I'm not waiting on these chocolates, though," she said, and delicately plucked one out of the box and put it in her mouth. I took her hand and licked a tiny smudge of chocolate residue off her thumb. We are a touchy-feely kind of couple, I'm afraid, hand-holding and putting our arms around each other's waists in public—and more. We've had sex in the car, after-hours in the tiny office in her father's restaurant, and wherever else we thought we could get away with it.

I've always been the conservative type, a good Catholic son of immigrant parents whose frivolity extended only to the occasional glass of homemade *kvass* on a Saturday night, but Connie had brought out a wilder side of me I'd never known existed before. I was almost to the point of not being embarrassed about it anymore. I liked it.

We spoke of our respective days. She had engaged in a dissing match with the produce delivery man that had ended in raised voices, bringing Leo, an ex-Marine, out of his office with balled fists. I told her a bit about Armand Treusch and TroyToy without mentioning any names. I trusted Connie's discretion, but I am, after all, in a business where clients expect, and deserve, confidentiality.

She listened, nodding occasionally. "It's the same in the restaurant business," she said, "only on a smaller scale. One chef stealing another one's recipe."

I laughed.

"Really. That's why, on the rare occasions when a good chef gives out a special recipe, he'll always leave one key ingredient out."

"You're joking."

"I'm very serious," she said. "There are trade secrets in every business, and they're damn valuable. I can see why your client might be in something of a flop sweat right now."

I had to agree with her. Everyone plays their cards somewhat close to the vest; in the investigating business I certainly had my sources, like Rudy Dolsak, whom I wouldn't want to share with anyone else.

After a while I went into the kitchen and put one steak into the electric broiler on the countertop. I like mine medium, a lot more done than Connie does; with a fine chef for a brother, she has been indoctrinated into the supposed joys of blood-rare beef. As far as I'm concerned, I don't want to eat anything that might possibly talk back to me during the process. From the other room I could hear that Connie had inserted a Bill Evans solo piano CD into the player. I emptied a block of frozen peas into a saucepan and dosed it with a pat of butter, and finally put the second steak in to join the first.

I walked back out into the living room, and casually drifted by the window, looking out at what I knew would be there. Nothing had changed. "Connie, when you were coming in tonight, did you happen to notice that big Indian on the bench in front of Baskin-Robbins?"

Her brows knit for a moment as she tried to recall. "Yes, now that you mention it. Why?"

"I think he's been camped there since early this morning. He was there when I left for the office and he looks as though he hasn't moved."

"And your point is?"

"Why would anyone sit on a bench outside all day in weather like this?"

"Maybe he's homeless," she said.

"I thought of that. But he's pretty well dressed, pretty healthy looking. He seems to be waiting for something."

"Probably."

She came over to stand beside me, throwing an affectionate arm around my waist, and together we studied the motionless figure on the bench; if he noticed us framed in the bay window, silhouetted against the light, he gave no indication. "My inquiring mind wants to know," I said.

"Milan . . ." She gave it an upward, warning inflection.

"Well, I do. A healthy curiosity is one of *my* trade secrets."

"The operative word there is healthy."

"Okay, I know about how it killed the cat . . ."

"Last time it almost killed *you*." She pinched the flesh over the waistband of my slacks rather painfully.

"Ow."

"More where that came from," she threatened. "It's none of your affair. Stay out of it."

"I am out of it. I'm just naturally nosy."

She stood on tiptoe, pulled my head down to her, and kissed my nose. "You have better places to put that nose than in somebody else's business," she said.

"Mmmm."

"Or are you just a glutton for punishment?"

To Connie's annoyance and concern, I had absorbed some pretty bad punishment on my last case that fall, my cheek still bore the faint, faded scar left by a burning cigarette. I was not anxious to enjoy any more. "I'm a glutton for *you*," I assured her. "I can't ever get enough." I pulled her close and turned the nose kiss into something more serious.

She responded eagerly for a moment, then pushed me away. "Not before dinner," she said. "My stomach is growling."

"I heard that, but I thought it was passion."

The dimples winked at me. "Dare to dream."

We ate at the coffee table in front of the sofa; for years I had used this room as an office before moving down to the Flats, and I hadn't yet gotten around to buying a dining table and chairs.

The steaks were perfection. Connie attacked hers with obvious delight, flirting outrageously as she cut it into bite-sized pieces, and the way she rolled the bright green peas around on her tongue while staring fixedly into my eyes was nothing short of erotic. The St. Emillion she'd brought from her father's cellar was superb, and she dipped the end of her tongue into it before each sip, making even the drinking of wine teasing and sensual. It was an Oscar-caliber performance of confident seduction, and it really got me stoked when she reached over and patted some butter from the baked potato off the corner of my mouth. Before we were finished eating, we were ready for dessert, each other being the featured creations, and I didn't even bother taking the dirty dishes back into the kitchen.

The lovemaking that evening will surely find its way into the highlight film. We didn't even get around to lighting the candles.

The alarm went off at seven the next morning, but we'd gone to bed very early and were both feeling rested and frisky. We showered together joyfully, each making sure the other was *really* clean. And it saved water, too—one more victory for the environmentalists.

While Connie put her makeup on, I made a pot of coffee, and she had time for a quick cup before she was off to brave the rush-hour traffic heading westward from the Heights.

I kissed her good-bye in the doorway at the precise moment. Mr. Maltz came out to collect his newspaper, wearing his ratty old bathrobe that looked like the carpeting in a 1930s downtown hotel. He shook his head in disapproval over the excesses of flaming youth for which neither Connie nor I qualified anymore, and went back into his apartment muttering.

I watched Connie as she walked down the hall toward the stairs, enjoying the fluid roll of her hips beneath the long denim skirt she was wearing. She had the kind of body that was enticing under any type of clothing, her various components moving almost independently from one another. I retrieved my own paper and went back inside to read it. I put the lid back on the still-uncovered chocolates and hoped they hadn't grown stale overnight. Then I finished my coffee and devoured two English muffins.

At a quarter to nine I donned my cold-weather system that was not a parka, and went downstairs to my car. As I was climbing in, I glanced across the street at the bench.

The Indian was not there.

❊ ❊ ❊ ❊ ❊ ❊ ❊

Chapter Three

❊ ❊ ❊ ❊ ❊ ❊ ❊

The day was just as bitingly cold as the previous one, but at least the sun was shining brightly, one of those almost astonishing mornings in winter when northeastern Ohio gets a break from the cloud cover. Sometimes it seems that when we get a rare sunny day in the middle of February, it's even colder than when the sky is gray. I imagined that the Indian had finally capitulated to the elements and sought shelter. At least I hoped so.

I didn't head downtown to my office; instead I turned southward to Shaker Heights to take a look at the home of David Ream, slowing to a suspicious-looking creep as I drove past it. I don't know what I hoped to learn, but sometimes I can get a better feel for someone I've never met if I know where they live.

The house was a brick Georgian, two brownish-red stories, with a small front lawn and lace curtains covering the casement windows in the front. It was a bit smaller than the other homes on the street, and I estimated that it was a three-bedroom. A straight, wide driveway with a four-year-old Dodge Caravan parked in it led back to a detached two-car garage with a basketball hoop affixed over the door. Unremarkable, solidly middle-class, and in that particular neighborhood of Shaker probably worth about $190,000.

I made a note of the Caravan's license, but I was almost sure it was driven mostly by Ream's wife. Even though prospective employers are not allowed to ask marital status, Treusch had included Ream's health insurance papers in his personnel file, and the co-beneficiaries on the medical policy were Audrey, Todd, and

Caitlynn Ream—same address. And my guess was that Audrey was Mrs. Ream, and Todd and Caitlynn were their two children. Certainly no one over the age of fifteen is named Caitlynn, at least not spelled *that* way. The days of children being christened Bill, Bob, Mary, and Janet were long gone—those names seem as archaic today as Homer, Phineas, Agatha, and Jerusha did when I was a kid.

I didn't get much of a feeling about my subject from seeing the house, one way or the other. I know that otherwise unremarkable people can sometimes lead remarkable lives, but nothing about the Reams' house struck me as being anything out of the ordinary, much less sinister or suspicious.

I dialed Rudy Dolsak from my car phone and was told he wouldn't be in until ten o'clock. I guess it's true what they say about "banker's hours."

I drove to a place on Chagrin Boulevard in Woodmere Village called Coffee and Creations, and killed half an hour looking at the well-turned-out suburban matrons enjoying a quick breakfast of fancy pastry before heading off to the elegant mall shops at the nearby Beachwood Place. I had a large cup of the house coffee, but passed on the creations—as tempting as pastries all looked, needless calories are an indulgence I can no longer afford.

At ten past ten I finished my coffee, went out to my car, and called Rudy again. I had to admit that even though I had battled against the notion of a telephone in my car, having heard of too many accidents caused by someone paying more attention to their chatting than to driving, it was turning out to be a lot more efficient than running around looking for a pay phone, most of which, in wintertime Ohio, are outdoors and deadeningly cold.

This time Rudy was in his office, and from the eager tone of his voice I could tell he had some eyebrow-lifting news for me. Rudy moans and complains, but the truth is he *loves* playing detective. Even if it's not completely ethical.

"Those dates you gave me for David Ream?" he said. "That eight-month period? Looks like all that time he was depositing eight hundred dollars into his account about once a week."

"Regularly?"

"Pretty much, yes."

"He was supposed to be out of work all that time."

"Eight hundred a week is a pretty hefty chunk of unemployment."

"He wasn't eligible for unemployment benefits," I said. "He quit his last job voluntarily."

"Well, he was getting it from somewhere. *And*—and I think you'll find this even more interesting, Milan—*and* he's *still* depositing those eight-hundred-dollar checks every week."

"Eight hundred dollars even?"

"Right."

I cleared my throat. "I don't suppose you'd be able to tell me who drew the checks?"

"That I'm afraid I can't do," he apologized. "My power to work miracles is somewhat limited."

"What you gave me is great, Rudy. Thanks."

"Milan, I hope to hell that if I ever need *your* services I can count on you."

"Rudy," I told him, "I hope to hell you *never* need my services." But Rudy was right; he knew good and well he could count on me. For anything. That's what you do with friends.

We spent another two minutes in chitchat about families and sports, and then I broke the connection. I found myself frowning. David Ream had been drawing some sort of regular paycheck all the time he was supposedly out of work, and had given no indication of it on his job application. Even though everyone does to one extent or another, you're not supposed to lie on those things. Maybe Armand Treusch wasn't so paranoid, after all. That Ream was still drawing those checks wasn't exactly damning, but it did lend credence to Treusch's imaginings.

Instead of heading back downtown, I pointed my car in the opposite direction, squinting into the blaze of morning, then turned southward toward Solon and the offices of TroyToy.

The logo of the silly-looking Trojan warrior was eight feet high on the face of an otherwise undistinguished industrial building. I half expected a security guard on duty at the entrance to the parking lot, but there was none, and I cruised inside slowly.

Company protocol had made it easy for me; the executive parking spaces were clearly marked with black lettering on white plastic signs: MR. TREUSCH, MR. RENDER, MS. MCTIGHE, MR. REAM. Ream's sign looked newer than the others. In his assigned space was a luminescent green two-year-old Bonneville.

I eased my car into an unmarked slot, and emerged in the teeth of a biting wind as I crossed the lot to the double glass doors. And then I found out why there was no need for a security guard in the parking lot; the outside doors were locked solid. A red button bearing the plastic admonition to ring was set into the wall. I pushed it, and through the doors and another layer of glass, a young woman craned her neck to see me, and then buzzed me in. Not really great security if she was going to allow me entry just on the basis of my appearance, but I suppose I should have been flattered that I don't look like a serial killer, a disgruntled ex-employee with an Uzi, or whoever else TroyToy was trying to keep from entering. Nonetheless, I made a mental note that if things worked out well with my probe of David Ream, I would try to sell Armand Treusch on creating a new security system.

Having been admitted through the front door, I found myself in a small vestibule, with still another locked door in front of me. The woman who had buzzed me in was behind a waist-high glass partition, and was regarding me with supreme indifference.

"Yes?" she said.

"I'd like to see the human resources director."

"You have to go around to the side door," she said. "Just turn left and around the corner."

Sighing with annoyance, I went back out into the winter and around the side of the building. It was a big building, and by the time I got to the entrance marked HUMAN RESOURCES OFFICE the wind had painted my cheeks rosy. If I had to stand outside another locked door in the cold, begging for admittance, I was going to become seriously irritated.

But the knob turned, and I found myself inside still another tiny vestibule. This time the woman behind the glass, an older one with frizzy Chico Marx hair, buzzed me in without interrogation.

It was a typical hiring-office waiting room, complete with apple green industrial paint job and ugly utilitarian furniture, and along the walls were several school chairs, the kind with the built-in writing surfaces blooming off the right arm. Five of them were taken up by job applicants, laboriously filling out their preliminary forms, heads bent close to the desk like third graders, clutching their ballpoints in deep concentration. One of them even had his tongue protruding from the corner of his mouth as he frowned over the paperwork.

The woman at the human resources desk was marginally less chilly than the one at the front entrance. She didn't exactly smile, but she didn't regard me as though I were bearing the plague, either. "Good morning," she said, holding a clipboard out to me at arm's length. "If you'll have a seat and fill out this application, we'll try not to keep you too long."

"I'm not here for a job," I explained, "but I would like to see Ms. McTighe."

Her eyes opened a little wider in surprise.

"Ms. McTighe?" she said. "Um—did you have an appointment?"

"No," I said. I handed her one of my business cards. "I'm a private investigator."

She accepted that news the way one would a lobbed artillery shell. It usually gets people's attention. Not that of cops, or attorneys, or bail bondsmen or mob muscle—for them a PI is business as usual. But to everyday working people, people whose brushes with danger rarely involve anything more harrowing than rush-hour construction delays on southbound I-77, I suppose a private detective is pretty exotic.

She gulped. "Oh. Um—is anything wrong?"

"No," I said. "But I'd really like to discuss it with Ms. McTighe. Could you tell her I'm here, please?"

She reassessed me; I was clearly outside the normal flow of her workday and she didn't know how to deal with it, which made her cordiality vanish like Indians playoff tickets in September.

"Just a moment," she said frostily, and picked up the telephone receiver.

I stood there while she talked to her boss, helped her with the pronunciation of my name as she repeated it, listened while she mouthed "private detective" as if it were a synonym for something loathsome, and finally followed her directions into an inner office toward the back of the reception area. The waiting job applicants glowered at me resentfully.

Catherine McTighe was a tall, attractive woman with long, straight brown hair, and she rose pleasantly to extend a hand of greeting to me, even though I could tell she was a trifle worried. "Private detective" does that to some people. She did, however, invite me to sit down.

"I'm a freelance investigator working for an insurance company, Ms. McTighe," I lied, offering her my business card. "We're doing a follow-up on a Mr. David Ream, who I understand is employed here."

"That's right," she said. "He's our comptroller. Is there a problem?"

"Not at all. But there is a gap in his employment record, just before he began working here, that we'd like to get cleared up." I had a twinge of remorse; Catherine McTighe seemed like a very nice person, and was far too pretty to lie to.

"Why don't you just ask him?" she suggested.

I smiled conspiratorially. "That wouldn't really be responsible investigating, would it?"

She smiled back, albeit reluctantly. She had a nice smile. "Maybe not. But you must realize that our personnel records are completely confidential."

I nodded. "Of course. But I have no doubt you noticed that gap when you were processing him, and asked about it."

She didn't answer.

"He was hired less than a month ago. Surely you would remember?"

"I remember." Reluctantly.

I served up my most sincere smile. "No one is trying to hurt

Mr. Ream. And certainly not to hurt you. You'd be helping him as well as me."

Her fingernails were long, orange-red, and probably acrylic, and she drummed them nervously on the top of the desk, making little staccato clicks. "I'm not comfortable with this . . ."

"Mr. Ream will never know we've talked," I said. "Nor will anyone else." I showed her my empty hands. "I'm not taking notes. And I haven't got a tape recorder running in my pocket. This is just a routine check, that's all."

She considered it for almost half a minute. Then she sat up a little straighter, and I felt she'd come to a decision.

"I hope I'm doing the right thing here," she said. "It could mean my job, you know."

I couldn't tell her that I was employed by her own boss and her own company and that her cooperation would hardly jeopardize her position. So I just said, "You have my personal guarantee."

She smiled. "Personal, hmm?"

"For what it's worth."

"I wonder just what it *is* worth," she mused, and I tried to look my most innocent. "Well, Mr. Ream told me he had taken that time off because of a medical problem. Not his—but someone in his family."

"Ah," I said, and scribbled a note.

"Yes."

I nodded, and waited a few moments to see if she would volunteer any other information. She did not. She just looked at me. Pleasantly. She was really very pretty, with *big* brown eyes.

"Do you have any idea how he supported himself during that eight-month period?"

"I didn't ask and he didn't volunteer," she said. "Those kinds of questions go well beyond the purview of the type of information we are allowed to ask for on a new hire."

"Why? He could have been selling heroin, or knocking over gas stations and convenience stores. Wouldn't that go right to the heart of a potential employee's character?"

She regarded me with some amusement. "You're a very suspicious man, aren't you, Mr. Jacovich?"

"I guess it comes with the job," I said.

She leaned back in her chair, and folded her hands in front of her on the desk like a third grader, and her jaw took on a determined look that told me I wasn't going to get much more out of her. I looked back for a while and then decided the staring contest was a waste of time.

I broke the stalemate by standing up. "You've been very helpful, Ms. McTighe. I appreciate your cooperation."

She took my outstretched hand, her smile widening. The little smile line, at the corners of her eyes were kind of sexy. "Anytime. Feel free to call me, Mr. Jacovich." And then she added some extra emphasis. "If you need *anything* further."

I went back out into the cold smiling. I'd gotten the information that I wanted, and I think I'd been flirted with in the process. That always makes a guy feel good. Catherine McTighe was very attractive, and if not for Connie I might have taken her up on the invitation to "feel free to call."

But that wasn't going to happen. Connie and I weren't formally committed—we never really discussed exclusivity. But we did have an "understanding" of sorts, and I think it was assumed.

I climbed back into my car and thought about David Ream. Certainly taking time off to care for a sick child was a reasonable excuse for staying out of the workforce for eight months. What troubled me, however, were the regular deposits Ream had made to his bank account all during that period. Where had they come from?

Since I had decided to hang out there in the TroyToy parking lot until the lunch break, I had some time to think about it.

At about two minutes past twelve it seemed as if the entire building exploded, disgorging people singly and in groups from every exit, all of whom rushed through the wind with heads lowered to get to their cars. The parking lot was filled with the rumbling coughs of cold engines coming to life.

A few minutes after that, David Ream came out of the double doors alone.

I recognized him from the photo in his personnel file. He was wearing a nondescript gray tweed coat, knit gloves, and on his head was a black lamb's-wool Astrakhan cap that made him look like an old Soviet apparatchik. His glasses were fogged from the cold as he hurried to his Bonneville and, with trembling fingers, unlocked the door.

Was he going to lunch alone? I wondered. Maybe he hadn't been employed at TroyToy long enough to have earned a slot in a regular go-out-to-lunch bunch, or maybe he just didn't make friends easily. Or perhaps he wasn't going to lunch at all but was heading off on some secret espionage mission. I chuckled at that option, but decided to follow him anyway.

After a ten-minute drive, he ended up at the Winking Lizard Tavern, the original one on Miles Road in Bedford Heights. A popular pool hall and sports bar that has expanded to several locations, including one downtown and another on Coventry Road very near my place, the Lizard's lunchtime clientele ranges from construction workers, truck drivers, and unemployed layabouts to elegantly suited executives and clusters of professional women from the neighboring industries. They have a great selection of sandwiches and beers, and I was hungry anyway, so I followed David Ream inside.

He found a small table against the wall, and took off his hat and coat, revealing a suit that looked very much like it was made from the same fabric as his overcoat. I perched on a bar stool, ordered a Stroh's and a roast beef sandwich with fries and onions, and watched him through the mirror behind the bar.

When his lunch arrived he ate quietly, earnestly, his head down; for all intents and purposes he might have been dining in a small room all by himself. He was a number cruncher, I had to remember, and often they are not people persons, so he did no observing of his fellow diners, no girl-watching, and seemed to take no joy in his temporary reprieve from the confines of his office. His face was more sour than bland, and I got the idea he was someone who took little joy in anything—one of those people one simply cannot imagine ever having sex. And true to my word to Treusch, I *did* discover what brand of beer he drank. Amstel Light, as if it mattered.

My sandwich was delicious, and I hoped the onions wouldn't exact payment later that afternoon. I quelled the heat with the beer, then ordered another one. The petite bartender, as did all the servers, wore a Winking Lizard polo shirt.

After a time, Ream looked at his watch, signaled for his bill, and paid for it with cash, I noticed. Then he stood up, put on his coat, and hat in hand headed not for the front door but toward the back. He bypassed the men's room, instead going straight for the pay phone on the wall.

Curious, I thought. Armand Treusch had told me he had the use of a company vehicle and car phone. Could it be that he was calling a number he didn't particularly want to appear on the TroyToy phone bill?

He spoke intently for about three minutes. I'm a pretty good lip-reader, but he frustrated my efforts by turning his face to the wall as he talked. Then he hung up, looked nervously around the restaurant to see whether he had been observed by anyone he knew, shouldered his way hurriedly through the crowds waiting to be seated, and headed out the front door.

I got down from the bar stool and walked back to the telephone, taking my notebook and a pen from my pocket. When I picked up the receiver and put it to my ear, it was still warm. I put a quarter in the slot and punched the REDIAL button, then waited for five rings, shifting my feet. I dislike waiting for the phone to be answered; it makes me nervous.

Finally, a woman with a low, mellow voice like a tenor saxophone answered. "Consumer Watchdog, good afternoon," she said. She sounded just slightly out of breath, as if she'd had to run from somewhere to answer the telephone.

"I'm sorry," I said, scribbling the name in my notebook. "I dialed the wrong number."

Chapter Four

Why does a man who has a perfectly good office and a cellular of his own make a furtive call from a pay phone in a neighborhood bar at one o'clock in the afternoon? I was going to have to ask someone about that before I was done with Armand Treusch and what might now *not* be manifestations of his bizarre paranoia.

Maybe David Ream *was* running some sort of a game on TroyToy. But who and what was Consumer Watchdog? And did it have anything to do with Armand Treusch's suspicions of industrial espionage?

I groped for the tattered Ameritech White Pages dangling from a chain beneath the telephone, looked up Consumer Watchdog, but didn't find it. I dialed up information, but they had no listing, either.

I went back out to my car. By checking the number he'd called, I had lost any chance of picking up Ream's trail; he was long gone. There didn't seem to be much point to surveillance, anyway; the odds were pretty fair that he was simply going back to his office, which would be a waste of my time and gasoline.

I activated my car phone and tapped out the number of Ed Stahl's direct line at the *Plain Dealer*.

Ed Stahl is as much a fixture in Cleveland as Indians baseball, the Terminal Tower, and the Old Arcade. His acerbic, opinionated, thoughtful, and sometimes very funny column appears five times weekly, alternately tickling and outraging his readers and often sending local politicos and bigwigs scurrying for cover—or for the offices of their lawyers. Ed never talks about the Pulitzer he won several years ago for investigative reporting; he used the cash prize that came with it to remodel his sprawling old house in Cleveland Heights. But other than that, it was all in a day's work to him. A decorated veteran of the late and much-lamented *Cleveland Press,* back in the days when our town had two competing dailies instead of just one paper, he's one of the last of the classic newspaper guys. He has an ulcer that he feeds with Jim Beam, tortoiseshell glasses that make him look like a debauched portrait that Clark Kent might keep in his attic, and he smokes a pipe so malodorous it could clear coughing workers out of the room in a rendering plant in five minutes flat.

Now that Marko Meglich is gone, Ed Stahl is just about my closest friend.

"Ed, I haven't seen you in two weeks," I said after he had barked his typically terse, almost annoyed "Stahl!" into the phone.

"Not my fault, laddie," he said. "I just sit here all day in my office. You're the one who runs around breaking heads."

I had to laugh at that one. I hadn't "broken heads" in quite some time, and Ed was well known for getting out on the street and wearing out his shoe leather in pursuit of his stories.

"Well, it's about time we lifted a jar together, don't you think?"

"Milan," he said, "you're Slovenian and I'm German. What's this 'lifting a jar' crap? Are you hanging around with that Irish girl too much?"

"In her case, there's no such thing as too much, Ed. Want to get together after work?"

"It just so happens I'm having dinner at Johnny's Downtown with a very high-ranking city official this evening," he said, "and I hope you're suitably impressed."

"Who's buying?"

"We're going Dutch, I imagine. The press is incorruptible—and of course you *know* our civic leaders are, too."

"Yeah, right," I said.

"We're not meeting until seven, though. Want to have a quick drink beforehand?"

"That sounds fine, Ed."

I disconnected and started up the car. Even though I'd finally capitulated about getting the car phone, I still try to avoid using it while actually in motion. I'd been rear-ended a few years before, right in front of the entrance to Lakeview Cemetery, by a baby boomer in a Volkswagen Golf who was so busy talking on the phone he didn't notice that I had stopped for a light. I considered the fact that my shock-absorbent bumper had taken the impact with no damage whatsoever and he had totaled his car some sort of cosmic justice.

It took me a little better than half an hour to get down to the Flats. It wasn't snowing today, but the salt trucks had been by during the night, and the plows had pushed all the snow off the street into piles up on the curb, which were now freezing into dirty gray bunkers of ice. I love Cleveland, and it's a good thing. During the winter one almost *has* to.

While I was driving, hoping the tires of the Sunbird would bite into the ice and not skim across them like Tonia Kwiatkowski, my beeper quivered on my belt and I checked the readout. It told me the number belonged to TroyToy. Armand Treusch, checking up on me, I imagined. Well, he could damn well wait until I got back to my office.

I passed the First United Methodist Church on East 30th and Euclid. By night it serves as a shelter for the homeless, and even during the day there are always several people huddled up on its steps and in its doorways, seeking respite from the wind and cold, all their worldly goods surrounding them in trash bags, shopping carts, or simply in large bundles. And that reminded me of the Indian who had sat across the street from my apartment on the bench all the previous day. If he was out in the elements again today, he was bound to be shivering. It was none of my business, but I hoped he was somewhere more cozy.

Back in the office, I checked my voice mail to see what message Treusch had left, but there was none. I found that mildly curious, but then Treusch was a no-nonsense kind of guy who might consider it a waste of his valuable time talking into a telephone when there was no one on the other end to hear it.

I brewed up half a pot of coffee to get me through the afternoon. My doctor, Ben Sorkin, with whom Rudy and Marko and I went to Kent State, despairs of all the coffee I drink. But then, he also despairs of my smoking cigarettes, my consumption of klobasa sandwiches and beer, and my profession, which frequently necessitated calling on him for a quick patch-up job.

Then I called Armand Treusch.

He sounded busy, harried, and irritable. "No, Jacovich, I didn't call you," he said. "Why would I? You're suppose to call *me*."

A frisson of uneasiness scampered up my spinal column. "Well, somebody from your company did."

"It wasn't me. I'm too damn busy. You have anything for me?"

"Not yet," I said, wondering who at TroyToy *had* tried to reach me. "But I'm working on it."

"All right, all right, get back to me when you've got something to tell me," he barked, and put the receiver down none too gently. I had the feeling he didn't do anything gently. Being a toy maker seemed a curious career choice for him—just as with the former professional wrestler who in 1998 had been elected governor of Minnesota.

Armand Treusch and I were never going to be best friends, but his check was warm and fuzzy enough for me. I reflected on the truism that if work was nothing but fun, I'd probably have to pay my clients instead of the other way around.

I booted up the computer and checked my various databases for Consumer Watchdog, but couldn't find them anywhere. That would probably not turn into a major problem; Ed Stahl knew every*thing* about every*one* in Cleveland.

He didn't disappoint me.

We met at five-thirty in the warm, dark bar of Johnny's Downtown on West Sixth Street, one of my favorite Cleveland eateries. The lounge was crowded at the cocktail hour, mostly with men in expensive suits, attorneys and judges and politicians and some of Cleveland's richest and most powerful. A few of them were waiting for tables for an early dinner, but the fine-dining crowd usually showed up a bit later in the evening. At five-thirty, most of

Johnny's patrons were just unwinding after a hard day moving city mountains and playing Monopoly with real city blocks and real money.

Ed was sucking on a Jim Beam at one end of the bar, isolating himself somewhat, presumably so his pipe smoke wouldn't bother the other patrons. But Johnny's is the kind of place where expensive cigars are routinely smoked at the bar, and I don't think anyone would have noticed.

Ed was in a greenish-hued tweed suit that would have looked at home on an itinerant drifter, and his thinning hair was in flyaway mode. He was making notations in the reporter's notebook he always carries, big sloppy scrawls that would probably be illegible to anyone but himself. I hiked up onto the stool next to him.

"Milan Jacovich," he said, still writing in his notebook. As a journalist, Ed considered himself on duty twenty-four and seven. "Friend, fellow sports fan, truth-seeker, and jovial compadre of my declining years." Ed was probably close to sixty, but hardly declining.

"So who's the big-shot city official you're meeting tonight?" I said, signaling to the bartender.

"You'll have to read about it in the newspaper."

"Be that way. Keep secrets."

"Ah, Milan." He smiled, smacking his lips over his pipe stem and sending a cloud of blue smoke toward the ceiling. "Secrets are my business. Yours, too."

I asked the bartender for an Irish whiskey. Johnny's Downtown isn't a Stroh's-beer kind of place.

"How's that gorgeous lady you've been taking advantage of?" he said. "Or have you screwed that one up already and she's dumped you for an investment banker?"

"No, it's just fine, Ed, and thanks for your concern." Ed was my severest critic, and never let me forget that I can't seem to sustain a relationship, despite the fact that he hadn't had one of his own in years—if ever.

The bartender set my Bushmill's in front of me. I lifted it and Ed raised his glass and touched it to mine before we both drank.

"May I gather," he said, wincing as the bourbon lit up his stomach, "that you're desirous of picking my fertile brain about something this evening?"

"What makes you think that?"

"Because it's not baseball or football season so you aren't looking for tickets."

I squirmed my butt around on the stool. "Am I *that* much of a user?"

He waved a dismissive hand at me. "Forget it. We're all users. That's what makes the world go around. We all use each other."

"Pretty cynical," I said.

"No, pretty truthful. Every relationship is symbiotic in some way, Milan, or it doesn't last. Whether you use someone for laughs, support, sex, influence, or just as a pleasant drinking companion, you're still using." He gave me a wry smile. "God knows I've used you and your adventures among the lower life-forms as a source for some of my more trenchant and pithy columns these last few years. And you use me when you're too damn lazy to go woodshedding for information. So what is it I can tell you that you don't already know?"

"Ever hear of an outfit called Consumer Watchdog?"

He frowned, contemplating the cloud of tobacco smoke that hung over his head like a toxic fog. "Hmmm, give me a second. In my dotage, I seem to be suffering from CRAFT."

"CRAFT?"

"An acronym for Can't Remember a Fucking Thing." Idly he jiggled his glass, and the ice cubes tinkled like sleigh bells. "Unless I have them mixed up with some other outfit, Consumer Watchdog is a local Ralph Nader–type group that tries to make sure the suckers like you and me don't get suckered."

"How come they aren't in the phone book?"

"Under what? Zealots? I'm talking *way* grass roots," he said. "They don't have an office. It's kind of a one-man show—one-*woman*, actually. I think she probably runs it out of her dining room."

"Then how is anyone supposed to reach her?"

"Since I've never wanted to," he said, "I haven't given much thought to that."

"How does she operate?"

He swirled his ice cubes around some more. The bartender looked over and Ed lifted his glass and pointed to it.

"She's more of a gadfly than anything," he said. "If she learns about some substandard business practice, especially one aimed at the little guy, the homeowner, the working stiff, or about some defective product or other, she makes a stink about it to the press."

"Is that all?"

"I can't remember, frankly. Come to think of it, there have been one or two class-action suits, but they would have the names of lawyers all over them, not hers. So you couldn't tell it by me."

"This woman isn't an attorney?"

"I don't think so. I've talked to her a few times, but I never figured there was anything in the way of a story there. She's been a little more successful with the electronic media." He pointed at the television set at the far end of the bar, where Vivian Truscott was holding forth with the afternoon news. "The folks over at Channel Twelve and Channel Five pay a lot more attention to her than I do."

"Why is that?"

"She's photogenic, from what I remember of her. And I don't run pictures with my column. As you know. Oh, she's made the *Plain Dealer* a couple of times, too, but not through me."

"You remember her name?"

Ed traded in his glass of half-melted ice cubes for a fresh drink. He puffed his pipe. Sipped. Puffed again. "Something like Moise, I believe. Albanian or Rumanian or something." He pronounced it Moy-ZAY. "Helen Moise." He nodded as it came to him. "Yes. I remember now."

"Is *she* in the phone book?"

"I don't know, I've never looked her up. She always calls *me*, never the other way around."

"How does she earn a living?"

"As I recall," Ed said, "she doesn't have to. She married well—big-time industrialist. And she divorced even better."

"Oh."

"Yes. So now she eases her conscience for having all that money without earning it by running around doing good works."

"Most people who marry for money wind up earning it, Ed."

"I suppose so. But it doesn't dampen her enthusiasm the slightest bit to get her lovely mug on television all the time."

He leaned back comfortably on his stool, his fertile memory going into overdrive. "A year or two ago, she got all exercised because there was a group going around on the near west side selling their services as re-roofers, mostly to retired people. Turned out they were a band of gypsies who just took the down payments and disappeared into the mist, never to be seen again. She set up such a hue and cry that it made the paper and the nightly news, but nobody ever got caught, and none of the suckers—excuse me, victims—got a nickel of their money back. Vivian Truscott actually did a one-on-one sit-down with Moise about it on the news."

He raised his freshened drink at the TV screen. "Good old Vivian," he said. "The shining jewel in Cleveland's journalistic crown. Long may she wave." His tone was sardonic, but it was nothing personal. He had the usual disdain print journalists reserve for on-air news anchors.

I glanced up at Truscott's image on the screen. The sound was low, but her words seemed to cut through the quiet rumble in the lounge.

"The body of an unidentified man was taken from the Cuyahoga River this morning by the Cleveland police near the Coast Guard station," she was saying, her pretty face set in the serious-yet-come-fuck-me mode she employs for reporting stories about death and disaster, and then the screen morphed into a shot of a body bag on a litter being carried up the dark riverbank, the TV lights lending a surrealism to the already gruesome scene.

"He carried no wallet, but police sources say he appears to be of Native American extraction, and between sixty and seventy years old," Truscott continued. "Anyone with information regarding this John Doe is requested to call the police department." She gave the number as it was superimposed across her chest. "A police spokesman said identification is pending."

My blood starting running colder and more sluggishly in my veins, and it had nothing to do with the ice in my drink.

Chapter Five

The next morning, bright and early—well, early anyway, the brightness of the previous morning having given way to cold and gray skies again as the sun decided it had done enough for us for one February—I presented myself at the Third District Police Headquarters on Payne Avenue and East 21st Street. I knew it well; I used to work there.

They've remodeled the old rock pile recently, sprucing up the interior, sandblasting the gray stone, and refreshing the green paint on the window frames. The fierce-looking eagles atop two soaring columns still flank the front entrance. But for all the face-lifting, it still looks unmistakably like a police station. The new-paint smell doesn't quite cover the stench of old sorrows and squeals and sins and uncleared cases that had accumulated from the time the place was built and permeated the very walls.

From my uniform days I knew the sergeant at the desk. He was Jimmy Dockerty, a grizzled, overweight old harness bull with a Brian Donlevy 'stache in the middle of his florid potato-face, and a hairline now best viewed from the rear. He'd recently been assigned desk duty so he could ride out the rest of his thirty to retirement without getting his ass shot off. I shook his outstretched hand and told him I wanted to see Lieutenant McHargue.

The light behind his pale blue eyes flattened at the sound of her name. "Whyn't ya go to confession instead, Milan? Get your sins off your chest. The priest'll go a lot easier on you than McHargue."

"Tell me about it," I said.

"A hard woman," he observed. "Glad I'm not married to her."

"How is your wife?"

He grinned. "Ah, still a devil. But after thirty-one years, she's *my* devil, you know what I mean?" He picked up the telephone on the counter, punched a few buttons, and mumbled something into it; I caught my name. Then he said, "Yes, ma'am," and put it back into its cradle.

"She says to send you up. She's in L'ten't Meglich's old office upstairs," he told me, and he dropped his eyes to the blotter on the desk. "You know the way."

I knew the way.

How many times before had I climbed those stairs? To visit Marko Meglich in his sanctum as head of the homicide division, to argue with him, to hear for the five hundredth time how betrayed he had felt when, after he'd mentored my career in the department, I'd ankled uniforms and spit shines and turned in my badge for a private investigator's license? Like career military enlisted personnel, most cops feel that if you aren't a police officer yourself, or never wanted to be one, that it is somehow a personal affront to them.

I'd never felt as though I were affronting Marko; it was my life, after all. But now that he was gone and I could never quite lose the idea that it had been because of me, the little weasel of guilt lived inside me and chewed my guts out on a daily basis. I was glad they'd remodeled the old Roaring Third, and glad that Marko's office no longer looked the way it did when he was alive. It was easier that way, somehow.

I went down the hall, stopped in front of the open door of the small office, and knocked on the doorjamb. Lieutenant Florence McHargue looked up from her paperwork and frowned, even though she'd been expecting me. Then she motioned for me to come in and sit down.

McHargue is a solidly constructed African-American woman somewhere in her forties, and had risen rapidly to her lieutenancy. Some unregenerate misogynists in the department resented her success, and when she had been appointed to replace Marko Meglich, many of her immediate subordinates were scared to death of her icicle sarcasm and ready temper. But she hadn't earned that gold shield because of any quotas, gimmes, or entitlements; she was one damn good, tough cop, and the worst blue-serge sexist had to accord her a grudging respect.

Unfortunately, I was not on Lieutenant McHargue's Christmas list of favorite people. So it hardly surprised me at all when she didn't say hello or shake hands, but greeted me with, "If you're here to use this department to help you out on one of your private cases the way you used to when Meglich was alive, you're shit out of luck, Jacovich. Do I make myself clear?"

"And a gracious good morning to you, too, Lieutenant."

She always wore blue-tinted glasses, whether she was inside or outside, but I could see her eyes narrowing behind the lenses. "I'm kind of busy for small talk right now," she said in a voice like the crackle of a wadded-up grocery sack, "so I hope you didn't come here because you were feeling lonely."

Her animosity toward me made me want a cigarette; I had puffed a thousand of them in this office, Marko and I turning the air blue with the smoke from our Winstons, the familiar red and white package being the vice of choice of most Slovenians. But since I knew that McHargue was a nonsmoker and fairly rabid about it, I fought down my urges. "As a matter of fact," I said, "I'm here to help this department out on one of *your* cases."

She sat up a little straighter in her chair, and I felt glad I had at least gotten her attention. "What case might that be?"

"The Indian you fished out of the river yesterday."

She nodded. "Little Running Doe."

"Was that his name?"

"We don't know his name, Jacovich. He's a John Doe, and since he's an Indian, the guys are calling him . . ."

"Oh, I see." Cop humor. Cop irreverence. People who deal with death and violence and degradation and brutality on a daily basis develop a callous indifference to it to keep from going home some night in the slough of despond and putting a bullet through the roof of their mouth.

"That was a bad business," she said. "He'd been knifed in the back and his throat was cut. Almost decapitated."

"Yeowch!" I said. "That wasn't on the news."

"No, we didn't give the media that information, and we don't expect you to, either. And that includes your buddy, Ed Stahl."

I nodded. Ed wasn't on the crime beat anymore, being a columnist, but he was always on the lookout for a good story. He wouldn't get this one from me, though.

"This Indian," McHargue went on. "What has he got to do with you?"

"Nothing personally, I never met him. But the day before yesterday a man answering his description sat right across the street from my apartment from the first thing in the morning until late at night."

She sighed. "The day before yesterday it snowed."

"I noticed. That's why I thought it was so strange."

She drummed her fingers impatiently on the top of her desk. "What do you mean, he sat across from your apartment?"

"You remember where I live, Lieutenant McHargue—just across the street from the Mad Greek Restaurant at Cedar and Fairmount." I made a triangle with both hands by way of illustration; my apartment building was on the point of that triangle. "There's a bench outside the Baskin-Robbins ice cream shop. He sat there all day."

She didn't say anything.

"At least he was there first thing in the morning and last thing at night. I can't vouch for in between."

"Did you talk to him?"

"No. I had nothing to say to him."

A smile played at one corner of her mouth, and she held up her right hand in a kind of open-palmed salute. "You might have started with 'How?' "

I chose to ignore that one. I suppose black people are entitled to offensive ethnic remarks just like everyone else. "I just thought you might be interested in his whereabouts the day before he died."

"I am," she said. "But all the facts point to robbery. The stab in the back, to disable; he was, after all, a big man. The missing wallet or any money or valuables he might have been carrying. And maybe to keep him from identifying the perp, the throat-cutting, the final *coup d'état*." I'm afraid she pronounced it *cooty-tah*.

"It all adds up to a robbery to me, Jacovich. Of course, we're looking into it. . . ."

"Well," I said, not entirely convinced that her hypothesis was correct, "I'm here just doing my civic duty."

"And you didn't know who he was? Never seen him before?"

"No," I said. "I only noticed him because you don't see many Indians with long pigtails on the east side."

"You're a real solid citizen, aren't you, Jacovich?" She opened her top drawer and pulled out a slim file. "Well, thanks for being so willing to do your civic duty, because I'm going to ask you to do some more."

"Oh?"

"Make sure it's the same guy, all right? Swing down to the morgue and take a look."

I winced. I don't like going to the morgue; it gives me chills just walking through the front door, and if I have to actually look at a cadaver, nightmares for months thereafter. "Do I have to?"

"No," McHargue said, showing me a crooked whisper of a smile I had seen before and knew to be the precursor to an explosion of, at the very least, biting sarcasm. "But you said you wanted to help us, so help. Just because you saw *some* Indian on a bench doesn't necessarily mean it was *our* Indian."

"How many Indians do you think there are running around Cleveland?"

Her hand moved toward the telephone, even though I had never said I'd do it. "I'll call the coroner's office and tell them you're coming."

"Right now?"

Her half-smile went away, scurrying back into the deep, dark cave where it usually lived, replaced by what threatened to be a fearsome glower. "No, not if you don't want to. Not if you have pressing business of your own. We've got an open homicide of an unidentified victim, Jacovich, but you just take your time. Next week is fine, next month . . ."

"All right, all right," I said, shaking my head and putting both hands in front of me as if to ward off a speeding bus, and with that much effect. "You know, Lieutenant, you're a rarity. The right person in absolutely the right job. I think you were *born* to wear that gold badge."

"I'll take that as a compliment," she said. Now that I'd knuckled under to her demand, she was feeling better about me. "But as a matter of fact, I spent several years teaching high school before I came on the force."

"You did?"

"Math."

"Too boring for you?"

"I'll say it was. And I figured, after having to deal with twenty hormonally charged adolescents every day, punks and perps and wise guys and murderers and rogue private dicks would be a piece of cake."

"And has it worked out that way?"

She tried not to look smug, but her eyes glittered. "Let me hear from you as soon as you've seen the Indian," she said.

I resisted the urge to say "Yes, ma'am." McHargue goes postal when I call her ma'am. "I will."

We sat there and looked across the cigarette-scarred, battered desk at one another for a while. Then she raised her eyebrows.

"Buh-*bye*," she said, and put her weight into it.

The Cuyahoga County Coroner's Office is in University Circle. The main floor of the building, where the reception area was located, could have been that of a medical complex, circa 1950. The woman at the desk had been notified of my coming, and directed me downstairs. I knew the way, I had been there before. It wasn't until I reached the basement, where the cadavers are kept, that the formaldehyde smell of institutional death hit me like a mailed fist. It got to me, and I shuddered, swallowing hard to fight down my gag reflex.

The attendant downstairs was expecting me, too. I followed him with dread, like Scrooge trailing reluctantly after the Spirit of Christmas Yet-to-Come, into a steel-and-concrete room. One entire wall was composed of large drawers, and most of them had tags hanging from their handles. I tried to shake off the creepy and many-legged creature that went scampering up my spine.

I stood with the muscles in my neck bunched and tight as if expecting a blow, as the attendant rolled the stainless steel drawer out of the wall, its wheels creaking in their metal runners. I took a deep breath and held it while he turned down the sheet so I could view the naked remains of what had once been a tall, striking man.

The night in the muddy, ice-choked river had not done the body any good, and the deep slash in his throat provided a second, horrifying, gaping mouth; whoever killed him had wanted to make sure the job was done. The long gray pigtails were arranged so that they hung down over his bare chest, matted and dirty from his sojourn in the water. His skin, a burnished copper color in life, had faded to a ghastly gray. It was almost like looking at a wax figure and not a real human being at all. I stared down at him just long enough to make sure, and then looked away, the taste of rust in my mouth.

It was my Indian, all right.

Well, he wasn't *my* Indian at all. I had nothing to do with him. Sure, that part of me that still was and always would be a cop was curious, was angry that he'd died that way. But there's lots more parts of me that *aren't* a cop anymore, and I know I couldn't go running around trying to chase down every homicide that turned up on the streets or in the waters of Cleveland. So I decided to heed Connie's advice and not go looking for trouble.

Still, I felt a tinge of sadness seeing this once-proud-looking man reduced to a slab of meat in a steel drawer. I guess John

Donne was right, that each man's death diminishes me, diminishes us all. But that tolling bell was not going to make me take stupid chances.

The morgue technician was a tall, amply girthed black man wearing steel-rimmed eyeglasses that were absurdly small on his large, broad face. His name tag identified him as B. Johnson. We had met before, the last time when I'd been down here with Marko Meglich, trying to ID a corpse that turned out not to be the fellow I was looking for.

"You want some time alone with him?" Johnson asked as if he didn't care one way or the other.

"No, I've seen all I need to see."

"Your call," he said, and replaced the sheet over the Indian's face. He rolled the sliding drawer back in until it clanged shut, flush with the wall. A removable label dangling from the handle of the drawer like a baggage tag identified its occupant as #3636328—JOHN DOE.

Not "Little Running Doe." The old Indian had at least been spared that final indignity.

"When will they do the post?"

Johnson looked at a sheet of paper encased in a flexible plastic folder also affixed to the drawer handle. "It's scheduled for to-morrow morning. Why? You want to watch?"

I suppressed another shiver. "No thanks. Been there, done that."

He grinned at me. "Civilians," he said.

I went upstairs, sucking icy air into my lungs the minute I walked outside. I knew I would smell that formaldehyde death-smell in my nostrils for days. I went back across the street to where I had garaged my car and dialed Florence McHargue's number on the cellular. Because I was still in the garage, the connection crackled disconcertingly.

"McHargue," she snapped. Even the way she said her name seemed like a stern rebuke.

"Milan Jacovich, Lieutenant. I just left the coroner's office. It's the same man, all right."

"You sure?"

"He was unique-looking. There's no doubt in my mind."

She didn't say anything for a while but I could hear her breathing through her nose into the receiver. "All right," she said. "I appreciate your help. Thanks."

"Would you let me know the results of the post when you get them?"

"Why?"

"Call it curiosity. I'd like to know whether or not he was dead before he went into the river."

"It's none of your business."

"It was none of my business when I came down here and ID'd him."

She let that one hang for about thirty seconds. Then she said, "You can obtain an autopsy report from the coroner's office for twenty bucks like any other citizen. It's a matter of public record."

"I figured after I trotted down here to ID a corpse for you, you might want to save me the money."

I heard an exasperated breath shoot through her nose.

"If I were you, I'd try to find out why he sat on that bench all day in a snowstorm," I said.

Her voice turned double-edged sharp. "You would, would you? Well, thank you for that wonderful input. Do you wanna pin a badge back on, Jacovich? Of course, that still wouldn't give you the right to tell me how to do my job."

"Don't get testy on me, Lieutenant, I didn't have to come to you at all about this. It was just a suggestion."

"Well you can have your suggestion back," she said. "With a detailed set of instructions."

I was smart enough to move the receiver away from my ear before she slammed hers down in its cradle. I know I'm not the easiest man in the world to get along with, but I've never met anyone whose angry-buttons I pushed the way I did Florence McHargue's. I was starting to worry that she didn't like me.

I drove back down to the Flats. The death of this anonymous Indian was somehow weighing heavily on me. Violent death, even a stranger's, always does. But I tried to shake it off and concentrate on the much less hazardous business for which I was getting paid.

Back in my office, I put a pot of coffee on, enjoying the hissing, bubbling sound it made as it brewed. Perking coffee is a comfort sound, like wind in the trees or soft susurrant rain on the pavement or birdsong at the first rosy light of morning. When it was finished, I poured some into my Marko Meglich mug, fired up the computer, and began searching my databases.

It took me about five minutes to find an H. Moise. She was listed as living in Beachwood, not far from my apartment in Cleveland Heights. I thought for a moment about what I was going to say, and jotted some notes on a sheet of yellow lined paper to make sure I kept my made-up story straight. Then I lifted the receiver and punched out the numbers. It rang three times before it was picked up.

"Consumer Watchdog." It was the same voice I'd heard when I called this number from the Winking Lizard. If Helen Moise indeed ran her consumer-advocate operation out of her own home, it was a peculiar way to answer the phone, seeing as how she probably got calls from relatives, from lovers, from friends, from telemarketers. Unless she had another, private number.

"Hi," I said, trying to sound chipper. "This is Leon Kobler, calling from the *Repository,* in Canton." Canton is a twin city with Akron, to the south, and the *Repository* is its daily newspaper. I don't know who Leon Kobler is—I made up the name on the spur of the moment. If I'd thought about it more thoroughly I would have chosen another name; I don't think I look like a Leon.

"Yes?"

"Is this Helen Moise?"

"That's right," she said, but her voice sounded suddenly guarded. "What can I do for you, Mr. Kobler?"

"Well," I said, "we're doing a story on consumer-advocate groups like yours, and I was hoping I could interview you."

"Oh?"

"Yes," I said. "If my editor decides to use the piece we'd send a photographer out, too. We'd like our readers to see you—where you operate."

"Well . . ."

I smiled. Ed had told me of Moise's appetite for publicity, and I'd baited my hook well. "We've heard good things about your work, Ms. Moise, and I think our readers would be very interested in your story. I won't take up too much of your valuable time, I promise."

"I guess that would be all right," she said, a lot less reticent than she was trying to sound. "When did you have in mind?"

My smile broadened as she swallowed it. "I was hoping for sometime tomorrow morning."

Chapter Six

Evening. A beautiful woman, a bottle of wine, a box of chocolates with only one or two missing. Time to put aside the stresses and concerns of the day. But I couldn't; I'm not made that way. More to my sorrow.

"Remember that Indian who was sitting across the street all day the other day?" I said to Connie.

"Sure. What about him?" She was curled up on the opposite end of my sofa, drinking the chenin blanc we hadn't opened two nights before. Which was okay, I figured, knowing virtually nothing about wine—it just gave it that much more time to age. Her shoes were off, as usual, and she had her legs tucked under her; she often sat that way.

"I hate to have to tell you this," I said.

"What?"

"The police found him floating in the river."

Her brows knit together—not a good sign. She put down her wineglass. I had always kept bargain-store goblets around the apartment; in the past I had served wine so infrequently that I would just as soon have drunk it out of jelly glasses. But since I started seeing Connie, the restaurateur and wine maven, I had purchased two fairly decent sets of crystal from Pier One Imports at Cedar Center; one for white wine, which we were drinking from now, and eight elegant wide-mouthed glasses for reds.

"When?" she said.

"Yesterday. I heard it on the news."

She rubbed her left upper arm with her right hand as if it were cold.

"Are you sure it was the same man?"

"Um—yeah, I am." I cleared my throat as if I were about to recite in school. "I went down to the morgue this morning and identified the body."

She stiffened a little, and her blue eyes went halfway to gray as her frown deepened. "Why?"

"I wanted to make sure it was the same Indian I saw."

She squirmed around on the cushion, taking her legs out from under her and setting her feet on the floor. "What's the difference if it was or not?"

"To me, no difference at all. But I thought maybe if the police knew he'd been sitting across the street the day before he died, it might be helpful to them."

Her voice got a little louder, a sign that her Irish temper was on the rise. "I thought we discussed that thoroughly the other night. I thought we said that it was none of your business."

"It wasn't," I said, "until somebody cut his throat and put him in the river."

The last of the Irish color left her cheeks. "Oh."

"Yeah."

"I still don't see where it was any of your concern."

I shrugged. "I figured that if it was the same man, the police would want to know that he'd spent more than twelve hours sitting in the cold in front of Baskin-Robbins the day before he died. It could mean something."

She was chewing on the inside of her cheek; another bad sign. "So you got yourself involved anyway. You promised me, Milan . . ."

"I'm not involved, Connie, I was just trying to help."

After a moment, she said, "It seems to me that you'd have enough to do just taking care of your industrial and security work without having to stick your nose in murders all the time."

"I do," I said. "I'm on an industrial espionage case right now. That's what I'm concentrating on. I just took an hour off this morning to help out the police. I used to *be* a cop, remember."

She took a deep breath. "Well, I'm glad you're not involved. I get very nervous when you poke around among people who kill other people."

"I hesitate to point out that if I didn't poke around murders, you and I would never have met."

She raised an eyebrow and smiled, her dimples deepening. "Don't you think we would have met anyway? That we were destined to meet?"

"We make our own destinies, Connie. I think. Every day we're presented with choices. The choice I made brought me into your restaurant."

"You probably would have come anyway, eventually—for dinner."

Now it was my turn to smile. "I don't go to expensive restaurants like the White Magnolia unless I have a date."

She waited a moment, and her smile lost a little of its luster. "Yes, but what you're supposed to say is that you would have taken one look at me and sent your date home in a cab."

"That would have been extremely unchivalrous of me. Besides, one of my problems is that I rarely say what I'm supposed to."

The dimples almost disappeared. "I didn't mean it like that."

"Sorry, I didn't mean what *I* said to sound that bad, either."

She nodded, unconvinced, and picked up her wineglass again. "You can get pretty snarky about your work sometimes."

"That's because it's what I do for a living, what I've chosen to do with my life. I could have been a lawyer or an insurance salesman or a dock worker, or I could have gone to work in the steel mills like my father. I didn't. I'm a security specialist and private investigator."

"But this Indian is none of your business." Her tone was almost plaintive and whining.

"If I saw some guy slapping the hell out of his wife on a street corner, or a little kid in the gutter whose bicycle had just been hit by a car, it wouldn't be any of my business either. But I doubt if I could just walk away."

"No," she said, and there was brine and gall in it, "you're not the type to walk away. More's the pity."

"Why?"

"Because the guy hitting his wife would start hitting you instead and you'd wind up getting hurt, and if you touched the kid before the paramedics got there his parents would probably sue your ass off."

"Those are chances I'd have to take, Connie. We take chances every time we walk across the street or drive our cars. If you're going to live in this world, you've got to be part of it, to participate."

"To contribute," she said, basting the word with irony.

"That's a high-minded way of putting it, but yes. It feels good to give something back sometimes."

"Even if you put yourself in danger?"

"Connie, I went down to police headquarters and talked to Lieutenant McHargue for five minutes, and that's only dangerous if she's in a bad mood, which I admit seems to be the case most of the time. Then I went to the coroner's and spent two more minutes looking at someone who is long past hurting me or anybody else. It wasn't pleasant, but it didn't come anywhere near being dangerous. I didn't think it was that much of a sacrifice."

She shook her head and looked at me more in sorrow than anger. "You won't leave it at that, though. I know you."

"I have no choice but to leave it at that," I said. "Even if I wanted to do something about it. Which I don't, by the way, because I don't have a client. And I wouldn't know where to start anyway. I don't even know the man's name."

She cocked her head inquisitively.

"There was no identification on the body."

"Then leave it alone, Milan."

"I'm leaving it alone, Connie."

She dipped her head for a sip of the wine; the level in the goblet was low, and I poured her some more. She looked at it a long time before she took another sip. "Why are we fighting about this?"

"I didn't know we were fighting."

"It feels like it."

"We're discussing," I said.

"Is that what it is?"

"I hope that's what it is," I said. "I don't like to fight."

"That's why you get beaten up so often."

I smiled to lighten it up. "If you think I get beaten up, Connie, you ought to see the other guys."

She put the glass down with a definitive clink. "That's a point of pride with you, isn't it, Milan? Being tough."

"Hardly," I said. "And I'm not tough, just big."

"Oh, you're tough, all right. And it damn near got you killed out in Lorain County last fall. How do you think that made me feel?"

"How do you think it made *me* feel?"

"You're missing the point."

"No, but I think you are. Your father and brothers are ex-Marines. Is being tough a point of pride with them, too?"

"Yes it is," she said quietly. "And I hate it."

"Connie . . ."

"In that house, I live in constant danger of testosterone poisoning."

I didn't reply. There's no point in trying to answer the unanswerable.

She shook herself. "I'm sorry, I'm just in a mood tonight. But it gives me the creeps, wondering whether the next time I see you, you might be in the drawer next to your Indian friend."

I was about to remind her that the Indian wasn't my friend, that I had nothing to do with him, that for every time I got involved in something dangerous there were twenty other times that my work put me in contact with no one more dangerous than, say, Armand Treusch. But I didn't.

Instead I said, "Connie, I don't like being on the defensive. It makes me uncomfortable."

She sighed deeply and put her feet down on the floor, preparing to rise. "Milan, I don't think we can salvage this evening, do you? Maybe it'd be better if I just headed home."

The skin on the back of my hands prickled. I wanted to tell her not to go, to stay and talk this out, whatever the hell *this* was. But I didn't. "Whatever you're comfortable with," I said. It came out colder than I had intended.

She looked at me levelly. Then she got up, went to the guest closet by the front door, and shrugged into her coat. I watched her do it from where I sat. When she put her hand on the knob, I got up and went over to her.

"I'm sorry you feel like you have to go," I said.

The corners of her mouth twitched, and the dimples hinted at a reappearance and then thought better of it. "I was kind of expecting you to beg me to stay."

"Begging isn't my thing, Connie."

She blinked once. Her eyes were really dark now, like a pond in late gray winter. She reached out and put a cool hand on the side of my warm face. "I know," she said.

And then she was gone.

I can't say I slept well. First of all, I hadn't expected to be the sole occupant of the bed, and that was enough to seriously disrupt my rest. And I was pretty upset at the way Connie and I had left things. It wouldn't be the first time that my work had gotten in the way of a relationship.

But men, they say, are defined by what they do for a living, and I suppose that is as true of me as of anyone else. I have a master's degree, and I could pretty much pick out the career I wanted; I chose this one. Because when all the shouting is over and done, I love my work.

I love ferreting out a wrong and making it right. It satisfies me, it fulfills me, it makes me feel good about myself when sometimes little else does.

But was it too much to expect Connie to understand that?

After all, it isn't as if I'd been a bus driver or a tool-and-die maker or a sales rep when I'd first started seeing her, and then switched to investigation and security. We'd met when I walked into her father's restaurant looking for a killer. She shouldn't have been surprised that I sometimes have to come in contact with some pretty hard people.

The hell of it was, of course, that I had nothing to *do* with the Indian. I just did what any good citizen would have done when they thought they had some information about a major crime. And what I was currently working on, the Armand Treusch–David Ream business, wasn't likely to get very dangerous.

So I wasn't armed or expecting trouble when I pulled into the driveway of Helen Moise's home in Beachwood, just east of the Shaker Heights border, at ten o'clock the next morning. It was an elegant, expensive house, big and modern and a little ostentatious. I didn't care for it. I'm a traditionalist, and the Tudors and Georgians and Cape Cods look more fitting in northeastern Ohio, which used to be part of the Western Reserve of Connecticut. However, the broad sloping lawn that rolled up to the doorstep, covered with now-grayish snow and dotted with three dogwoods and a lovely sugar maple, presented a homey approach to the square angles and sharp lines of the house itself.

When Helen Moise came to the door, I saw she fit the house perfectly, possessing a lot of square angles and sharp lines herself. She was about my age, with jet black hair, and olive skin that obviously had been burnished by multiple sessions in the tanning booth—most Caucasian Ohioans look a bit unnatural sporting deep tans in February. The black cardigan sweater and fawn-colored slacks she was wearing set off the summertime coloring, and small round eyeglasses with neon-green plastic rims magnified her big, dark eyes.

"Mr. Kobler?" she said, and I had to stop for a moment and remember that was supposed to be me. "Come on in."

I wiped my feet carefully on the raffia mat in the vestibule as she took my coat and hung it in a closet just off the airy entry. Then she led me into a large, two-story living room with a highly polished tile floor, a lot of furniture upholstered in hot pastels, and enough potted plants to dress the set of a Tarzan movie. The one wall not covered with indecipherable contemporary art held a large rectangular framed television screen, one of the new flat models, and it looked like it had been hung there for decorative purposes as much as for watching *60 Minutes*.

She indicated that I should sit down in a dangerously over-pillowed rattan chair. She chose the hot purple sofa for herself, and sank languidly down onto it in one motion, crossing one leg over the other. Her movements were very sensual, and for a moment I wondered whether David Ream's phone call to her from the Winking Lizard had not been personal. "So you're doing a story on consumer advocates?" she said. "It's about time somebody did."

"Why is that?" I said, getting out my notebook. I wanted to take notes on the interview anyway, but the little Spiral pad made me look, and feel, like an authentic reporter.

"Because for some reason, American consumers are very trusting, and as a result very easily bamboozled. Maybe it's because everybody is looking for a bargain. I don't know. There are literally millions of people out there running scams, manufacturing substandard or defective merchandise, not backing up their claims and their promises. Consumer advocates like me try our best to protect people, to let them know they're being screwed over."

I made a few meaningless notes. "Are you working on anything in particular right now?"

She smiled. "That would be telling."

"Isn't that why you're doing this interview? To tell? To get your message across?"

"Of course it is," she said, sounding annoyed, "but not until I have all the facts. I don't want a lawsuit."

"I'd imagine lawsuits came with the territory."

"You can't sue someone for telling the truth, Mr. Kobler. That's why I want to be sure before I say anything for publication. But you can write that what I'm working on right now is going to raise a *lot* of eyebrows!"

She took a cigarette from a glass box on the coffee table and lit it with a heavy silver table lighter right out of the fifties. She smoked dramatically, confidently, as if she were paid by the hour to do so.

"Okay," I said, and jotted "raise a lot of eyebrows" in my notebook. It was a dumb thing to write down, but I was trying to look authentic and reporterly; I knew I'd eventually tear this page out and throw it away. I figured maybe if I got her talking, she'd eventually open up and I could find out what her connection was to David Ream. "How did you get started being a consumer advocate?"

"Because of my mother." She made herself more comfortable on the sofa, the cigarette nestled in the V of her second and third fingers. "Five years ago I bought her an old house in the Ohio City area—that's where I grew up, where she's lived most of her life. Back then, the properties in that neighborhood were a lot cheaper than they are now. The idea was to rehab the house, turn it into something really classy and cute so she could sell it for twice what I'd paid for it and use the money for her old age. Well, one day these people came knocking on the door offering their services to redo the roof."

I nodded.

"And it needed doing, I have to admit that. So, without talking to me or anyone else, without checking them out first to make sure they were legitimate, she just handed over a down payment, and they told her they would come by and do the work the following Monday. This was on a Wednesday, I think . . ."

"A big down payment?"

"Seven thousand dollars," she said. "Of course they never showed up. My mother is sixty-eight years old—well, she was sixty-six then—and a recent widow, so she'd never done anything like that before on her own. She was so proud of herself, she was feeling really capable and independent. They gave her a business card and all that, and an official-looking contract, but she didn't bother checking up on them before giving them the money. And when they didn't show up and she called, the number was nonexistent and so was the address. I think, from her description, that they were gypsies or something . . ."

"That's too bad," I said, meaning it.

"So when she called me, hysterical, I did some checking of my own. I found out they had scammed several other elderly women in the neighborhood the exact same way. Some of them even lost more than my mom. I was frustrated. I didn't know what to do. I figured the money was gone, but it wasn't about the money anyway, it was about victimizing senior citizens . . ."

"A-huh."

"So I got on the phone, I started writing letters to the newspapers, to all the TV stations. I wanted to make sure everybody knew about them, that no one else would get taken that way. My mother was luckier than most—I have enough money to see that she'll never go without. But a lot of the older people they swindled, it was their nest egg, their life savings . . ."

She shook her head.

"And I guess you were successful?" I said. "In publicizing it? In warning people?"

"I suppose so," she said. "I got some ink in the *Plain Dealer* and some of the suburban papers. And I was on the Channel Twelve news. I have no idea how much good it did, but the scam *did* stop. I don't know whether it was because of me turning up the heat on them, or because they had milked the area dry already and were ready to move on to more fertile fields."

"So that's when you decided you wanted to make consumer advocacy you life's work?"

"No," she said. "It never really occurred to me then. But after I was on TV a few times, and in the neswpapers, people started calling me to help them. You know, with complaints about being swindled. Home repairs, auto mechanics, things like that. Some of them even offered to pay me."

"And so a career was born," I said, smiling.

"I wouldn't call it a career. Most of what I do is pro bono, anyway. Thank God, I don't need the money. . . ."

"Then why do you do it?"

"To right wrongs, I suppose." Her smile was twisted and ironic. "God, that sounds pretentious and self-aggrandizing, doesn't it? I guess I enjoy it. But I've got to do *something* with my life. I got married very young to a very wealthy man, and when we were divorced I didn't know how to do anything except give parties and arrange benefits. I'm virtually unemployable in the normal workforce. And I didn't want to open a gift shop or anything itsy-poo like that." She held up a cautionary hand. "Please don't print that, okay?"

"All right, I won't," I promised, and it certainly was not a lie. "So you spend your time getting reparations from car mechanics and roofers and carpenters?"

Helen Moise's smile was as hard as a crowbar, and just as appealing. "Hardly," she said. "I've expanded my base of operations."

"In what way?"

She leaned forward, warming to her subject. "Suppose," she said, "I find out that some big company is deliberately manufacturing some product that's defective? Or even dangerous."

"Okay."

"If I take it to an attorney, he can file a class action suit on behalf of all the people who have been cheated. Or hurt."

"Ah," I said, scribbling some more. "And that's how you make your money? On the class action lawsuits?"

She made her face a blank.

"You're in for a piece, aren't you?"

"Well." She took a deep breath, wanting it to sound right. "I get a certain percentage of the lawyer's fees, yes. But as I told you, I don't really need the money. It's not about money."

"I see," I nodded, but I didn't believe her for a second. Call me a hardened cynic, but in my experience I've found that it's always about money.

"Now, this project you're currently working on?" I said. "The one that's going to raise some eyebrows? Do you imagine that's going to turn into a big class action suit, too?"

She nodded. "One of the biggest."

"And is this a local firm?"

"Well, they're based locally, yes. But they're a national company. International, as a matter of fact."

"No hints?"

"I can't. Yet." She cocked her head to one side, quizzically, like a bird listening for the whir of the hawk's wings. "Do you have kids, Mr. Kobler?"

"Yes, two boys."

"I never had children of my own," she said with what might have been longing, "although I always wanted to."

I nodded, not following. Then she said, "Well, as a parent, you'll thank me when this is all over."

"I will?"

"Oh, yes!" she said, accenting the *oh*.

I didn't know, maybe I *would* thank her. "How do you go about verifying what you're working on, Ms. Moise?"

"Call me Helen, please." It was almost flirtatious. "Everyone does."

"Helen, then."

She beamed as if I'd granted her the greatest of favors. Then she frowned a little. "I'm not sure I completely understand the question. Verifying?"

"I'm just trying to figure out how this works. I mean, you just don't wake up one morning and decide you're going to check out IBM or Nabisco . . ."

"No, of course not. It usually stems from a complaint. Not always, but usually . . ."

"And how do you get your information?"

"I have my ways," she said mysteriously.

"Your ways?"

"My sources."

I cleared my throat. "Like someone on the inside?"

"Now, you know I can't tell you that." The smile warmed up a few degrees. "Not yet, anyway. I wouldn't want to cost anyone their job."

A thought winged its way across my brain like a cloud scudding past the moon—the thought about the regular checks deposited into David Ream's account all the time he was supposedly out of work. "And these sources of yours. Do you pay them?"

And then the smile disappeared altogether. "Sometimes I've been known to—cover expenses."

"You must have quite a lot of money in reserve, then. Your class action suits are profitable."

She shook out her hair, the way some women do when they're telling you they live in the most expensive neighborhood in town. "I don't like talking about money, Mr. Kobler. It takes away from what our real job is here."

"Which is?"

"To keep people from being victimized. To demand that companies—manufacturers and suppliers and service providers—take some responsibility for what they do. Otherwise, it's worse than stealing. It's . . ." She floundered, looking for just the proper word. "It's nothing short of criminal."

Then she put both her feet flat on the floor and stood up, and I guessed the interview was over.

Chapter Seven

Helen Moise hadn't been very helpful except in a general, background kind of way. As I thought back over the time I spent with her, I realized she'd actually been pretty cagey; she gave me no opening into which I could have driven a direct question about David Ream.

Maybe she was used to talking to the press, giving them enough for a story that would get her name or face into the media, but not letting them close enough to reveal anything at all meaningful.

Of course, I *wasn't* the press, but she didn't know that.

When I got back down to my office, the radiator was kicking out a lot of heat, but clanking and sputtering like bad rap music in the process. My downstairs tenant, Tony Radek, who runs the wrought-iron company, always complains about the noise, despite the fact that his enterprise makes more racket than any ten radiators. I don't know, maybe he was right. The cost of revamping the heating system in a building nearly a hundred years old made me more complacent about the musical pipes, though.

I had grabbed a couple of donuts from Presti's in Little Italy on my way downtown from Beachwood, and I ate them in lieu of lunch before I plunked myself in front of my computer to transcribe the notes I had made from my conversation with Helen Moise, eliminating the ones I'd scribbled on my pad just so I would look like I was writing a story; they were worthless. I was beginning to wonder if the whole interview had not been, as well.

Was David Ream really spying on his employer for her? I wondered. Perhaps, but that didn't explain the eight hundred dollars a week he had deposited into his checking account for the eight months he'd been out of work. He couldn't very well have been doing industrial espionage against TroyToy before he was even working there.

Maybe his dealings with her *were* personal. He wouldn't be the first, nor the millionth married man to have an affair, and Helen Moise was attractive and a little flirtatious. But I ascribed the way she had acted with me less as a come-on than as trying to make a good impression on a man she believed would write a favorable story about her. Canton was not Cleveland, but *The Repository* was widely read throughout northeastern Ohio, and to some people any kind of publicity is their drug of choice. According to Ed Stahl, Moise fit that profile beautifully.

Besides, from what little I'd seen of David Ream, he didn't seem like the philandering type.

Sure, there's a type! There are some men whose sexuality defines them. An observant eye can spot it on them across the room like a splash of vibrant color. Whether or not they act on it, their sensibilities are finely attuned to women. Their eyes devour a room the way a veteran NFL quarterback three points down with ninety seconds left to play looks downfield for a receiver, until lighting upon a female who strikes their fancy, and then they stand up a little straighter, their chests out and stomachs sucked in, holding their chins a little higher and breathing more deeply as if energized by the close proximity of an object of desire.

But David Ream had sat in a restaurant crowded with women of varying degrees of attractiveness for forty-five minutes without ever glancing around, not even raising his eyes from his food once it had been served to him.

Armand Treusch had his gut instincts, and I had mine, and mine made me willing to place a large wager that drab, mouse-gray David Ream was no player.

Thinking of Armand Treusch, I remembered the previous day's phone call from TroyToy. If it wasn't Treusch, who had called me?

I only knew one other person at TroyToy, and that was Catherine McTighe.

I had my reservations about calling her to ask, but in the end I decided that she might have forgotten some important crumb of information that might point me in the right direction. So I tapped out the number of the office in Solon and asked the operator, correctly this time, for the human resources department; I learn slowly, but eventually I get it.

I recognized the voice that answered as the woman at the desk, she of the clipboard and the suspicious nature.

"This is Mr. Jacovich," I said. "Remember, I was in the other day to see Ms. McTighe?"

I heard her suck in her breath. "Yes?"

"Would you connect me with her again, please?"

"I'll see if she's in," she said, and put me on hold. From my visit to the site I knew Catherine McTighe's office was only a few feet away from the receptionist's desk, so she knew damn well whether McTighe was in or not. The music that flooded out of the receiver was a lush orchestral version of a chirpy, syrupy Leroy Anderson tune from the 1950s. I moved it away from my ear and waited until Catherine McTighe came on the line.

"How nice to hear from you, Mr. Jacovich," she said. "What can I do to help you?"

"I think the question is, what can I do for *you*?"

"I don't understand."

"You did call me yesterday, didn't you?"

There was a moment's pause. "What makes you think that?"

"Welcome to the electronic age, Ms. McTighe. When my phone rings and I'm not in the office, my beeper goes off and there's a readout that tells what number is calling me." I took a deep breath and then fired off my little white lie. "You're the only person at TroyToy I know."

Another pause, and then she laughed. "Damn," she said, "hi-tech will get you every time."

"Why did you call?"

"I got to thinking about it after you left," she said. "About our conversation. So I took the liberty of doing a little checking up on you. You're not working for any insurance company."

"I'm not?"

"No," she said. "You're an industrial security specialist."

"Yes, I am. It says that on my business card, though."

"Yes, but the insurance company story was bullshit, wasn't it? You lied to me."

I didn't say anything.

"Are you spying for a competitor of ours?"

"No, not at all."

"That would make me very angry, Mr. Jacovich. I've been with TroyToy for a long time, and I'm loyal."

"I admire that," I said. "Believe me, I'm not trying to hurt TroyToy."

"It's a damn good thing, because I let you wheedle some confidential information out of me that I shouldn't have. So I was calling you up to tell you so."

"Well, sorry I made you mad."

"I think I deserve an explanation."

"I'm afraid that's not possible. Client confidentiality and all that."

"Oh, I get it," she said without rancor. "I spill my guts to you, but you don't tell me squat, is that the idea?"

"You hardly spilled your guts, Ms. McTighe, you just answered a few questions, that's all."

"I feel used."

"Again, I'm sorry."

She waited for a bit. "So no explanation, huh?"

"I'm afraid I can't right now."

She made a tiny throat-clearing sound. "Well, then, I think you owe me a dinner, at least."

That took me by surprise, and for a moment I exercised my Miranda right to remain silent.

"Speechless, are you?"

"No," I said finally. "That sounds very interesting, but I'm—uh—seeing someone."

"I'm not talking about posting the banns, just dinner."

"I know," I said.

"And maybe I can think of something else that'll be useful to you. To whatever it is you're 'investigating.' "

"Oh?"

"I always think better on a full stomach."

"That sounds a little like blackmail."

"It's harmless blackmail, though," she said gaily. "Your virtue is safe with me. Especially on the first date."

"Well," I said. "I'm going to have to ponder that."

"Up to you. When you think it over, you know where to find me."

"Yes," I said, "I do."

I hung up, bemused. Attractive women were flirting with me all over the place. I couldn't imagine why—with a mid-forties waistline and a Slovenian hairline fast heading north, I'm hardly the matinee-idol type. Still, it was a nice feeling to be wanted.

It was even more intriguing to think that perhaps she could cast some light on the David Ream situation for me. But I wasn't going to sleep with her to get her to talk about it. Not my style.

Since I seemed to be in my devastatingly sexy mode, though, I decided to call Connie Haley, make another date for this evening, perhaps for a lovely dinner someplace romantic and special, and try to make up whatever ground had been lost the night before.

It didn't work.

First of all her father, Leo, answered the phone. We ate up some time chatting about the Cavaliers; he's a big basketball fan, while I can take it or leave it. It took a while because Leo, a voluble Irishman, was never one to use three words when thirty would do. And when he finally put me on hold to transfer the call, Connie left me there listening to piped-in James Galway recordings for almost five minutes.

"Dinner? Um—I don't think so, Milan," she said when she finally got on the line. "Not tonight."

"You have another date?" I said teasingly, while a cold knot formed in my stomach in case the answer was yes.

"No. I just think I'd rather not go out tonight, that's all."

I swallowed. "You aren't still angry about last night, are you?"

"I never *was* angry," she said. "Just—I'm just trying to reorder my priorities, that's all."

The cold knot turned to hard suet beneath my rib cage. "And I'm the one getting reordered?"

She waited far too long before replying. "It's not that. I just want the night off, okay?"

"Connie," I said, "I think this needs to be talked about. In person, not over the phone."

She sighed. "There's nothing to talk about, Milan. My God, we've never been a twenty-four and seven couple."

"I know," I said, "but after the way we left things last night, I thought it would be kind of nice to make up."

"There's nothing to make up. I told you I'm not mad."

I lit a Winston and took a deep drag before I answered. When I finally did, it came out pretty flat. "Yes," I said.

"Look, I'll call you in a day or two, all right?"

"I'll count the minutes till then." It sounded nastier than I meant it. Or maybe I did mean it to be nasty, I'm not sure.

"*Now* who's mad?"

I already had the receiver away from my ear and on its way to the cradle. "Nobody *I* know," I said.

From long, sad experience, I have learned that when a woman tells a man she "needs some time" to think things over, to reorder her priorities, more likely than not there is an *hasta la vista* waiting in the wings.

The last time a woman said she needed "time," I'd told her she had exactly thirty seconds. That was Mary Soderberg, who had been the big post-divorce crash-and-burn love affair of my life, and before those thirty seconds had ticked by, she was gone.

Eventually Mary came back again, or attempted to, but that's when my Slovenian stubbornness and my sometimes misplaced sense of pride kicked in, and I managed to screw that up, too.

I don't pick the most appropriate women, that was my trouble. For six months I went with a woman named Jane who said she decided to date me because I was the first man she'd ever met who hadn't said "Me Tarzan, you Jane" right off the bat.

I was trying to be more careful with Connie Haley.

If it weren't for that damned Indian, I thought, none of this would have happened.

And then I was ashamed of myself.

It's not like me to blame others for my shortcomings, and I supposed I was as much at fault as anyone for what seemed to be happening between Connie and me. It sure wasn't the old Indian's fault.

I don't know why he'd spent an entire day sitting on a bench across Fairmount Boulevard in the snow, but he was a living, sentient being and someone had practically cut his head off and dumped him in the river like a dead cat, and, if only by virtue of his humanness, he deserved better from me, more compassion than to be posthumously blamed for my romantic troubles.

Well, I thought, I had done what I could about him. After the fact, admittedly, but I'd tried to do the right thing. I'm sure that if I'd walked across the street and asked if he needed help while he was alive, he would have turned me down. Why wouldn't he? I was a perfect stranger.

Was I falsely assuming that he'd needed help? I knew next to nothing about Native American customs; maybe it was his vision quest, or whatever—perhaps there was some religious or ritual significance? Or maybe he just *liked* sitting in the snow.

After all, Cleveland Heights is nowhere near the river where he was found. It was probably a simple robbery that had gone awry—an elderly man, alone, obviously out of his element, would seem an excellent target for the predators of the night. Things happen like that all the time.

Cleveland is not a violent town, as big cities go. We've had our share of high-profile murders—the gruesome Kingsbury Run torso killings earlier in the century that had cost our then–safety director Elliot Ness a political career, the still-controversial Sam Sheppard case that fueled a television series and a movie and a brave quest by Sheppard's son to clear his father's name, the more recent murders of a Shaker Heights teenager and a southside housewife. And I had been involved in a couple of others, too, that hadn't made the newspapers.

Thank goodness for that.

But still, Greater Cleveland is a good place to live. Our crime rate falls far below those of glitzier cities like Miami and Los Angeles. The death of one anonymous man is no reason to rush to judgment.

Yet the Indian had not only shouldered his way into my consciousness, but in death he had kicked off a conflict that was threatening my relationship with Connie Haley.

I sat at my desk, my fingers playing paradiddles on the manila folder containing the David Ream files, allowing my annoyance to bloom into anger. Damn it, I had not done anything wrong! Connie was out of line on this one.

I flipped open the folder to take my mind off myself. I hadn't made much headway with Armand Treusch's inquiry. Maybe a new bit of information would open the floodgates.

Bringing the phone to my ear, I punched out a set of numbers.

"Ms. McTighe, this is Milan Jacovich," I said. "You're on for dinner tonight—if you're free."

Chapter Eight

It wasn't a date, okay?

As far as I was concerned, I was still seeing Connie, although I had to admit a certain confusion as to whether or not she was still seeing me.

But this dinner meeting with Catherine McTighe didn't feel like a date; I wasn't going through agonies deciding what to wear, I didn't even care particularly that I was a bit overdue for a haircut, and I didn't feel that unmistakable fillip of excitement in my gut at the anticipation of seeing her.

I was getting paid to turn over several medium-sized rocks to see if anything pertaining to David Ream lived under them. And Catherine McTighe was the head of personnel—oops, human resources—at the company where he worked and had interviewed him in depth at the time of his hiring. Maybe she knew something that would help me.

So it wasn't a date; it was business, and would be charged off to my client along with mileage and telephone and other meals eaten away from the office.

I fool other people sometimes, but rarely myself, and I had to admit that if I hadn't had the fight with Connie—or whatever it was I had with Connie—I probably wouldn't have been having dinner with Catherine McTighe, David Ream or no David Ream.

But it wasn't a date. I generally pick up my dates at home; we arranged to meet that evening at Giovanni's, the elegant Italian and continental restaurant on Chagrin Boulevard in Beachwood. It was probably a little pricey for a business meeting, but the food is marvelous and the ambiance sumptuous. Catherine McTighe lived in Solon, near TroyToy, and Giovanni's was about midway between us. Besides, Armand Treusch was paying for it.

Reservations were a must on the weekends, and even now, in midweek, I had begged prettily on the phone to secure a table.

I got there before she did and was installed in a booth against one wall by a hostess who looked like she should be on a fashion runway in Paris modeling the latest creation of Isaac Mizrachi.

I ordered a Bushmill's on the rocks to while away the time before Catherine McTighe got there. I hate waiting for people in restaurants because I never know what to do until they get there. I don't want to look anxious or ultimately irritated if they are late, but it's hard to appear cool and unflustered when you are the only single diner in a restaurant full of couples.

She arrived only about five minutes past the appointed time, making her way through the tables like the Queen of England. She wasn't so stunning looking that every eye turned to watch her progress, but a couple of men did manage a surreptitious glance they hoped their female companions wouldn't notice.

I slid out of the booth and stood up as she approached. Her smile was dazzling, the hand she extended to me still cold from the weather outside.

"I feel like I dragged you to this dinner kicking and screaming," she said as she wriggled her way into the booth. "I hope you don't hate me for it."

"I'm not kicking and screaming at all, Ms. McTighe," I said. "I appreciate your taking your free time to talk to me." I sat down again.

She regarded me with amusement and shook her head. "*Mzzzzzz* McTighe. Are you always this formal, *Mister* Jacovich?"

"Sorry, I was a business major at Kent State, and they told us to always keep it businesslike."

"Is this what this is?" she said, mock-pouting. "Business?"

"As I explained to you, I'm involved right now."

"But you aren't *involved*-involved, are you? Or else you wouldn't be here." She missed her calling; she should have been a prosecuting attorney.

"Well," I admitted, "we are going through kind of a rocky patch right now."

"I figured as much." Her eyes were laughing at me, at my discomfiture.

"But we're still . . ." Embarrassed, I ducked my head, feeling a little silly, a little high school.

"Okay," she said. "I read your lips. But I still think it would be a little more friendly if we used first names. You're not going to make me have to say Mr. Jacovich all night, are you?"

"I could never do a thing like that to you," I said, laughing. "So Catherine and Milan it is."

"I'm relieved," she said. "But no one has ever called me Catherine except for my Aunt Maureen, and she's dead. Most people who know me call me Cat."

" 'They call me Cat, who speak of me at all,' " I quoted, grinning, hoping it didn't go over her head.

It didn't. "*The Taming of the Shrew,*" she said. "A literate private detective."

I gave a self-deprecating little shrug. "Shakespeare was a required course for the master's degree."

She ordered a martini, and I was pleased to note that it wasn't a chocolate one, or a blue one, or one with cranberry juice. It wasn't even vodka; just a good old-fashioned Tanqueray gin martini, straight up with an olive, the way martinis were meant to be drunk before they became a trendy novelty at cigar bars.

When it arrived, she tasted it like a connoisseur and gave a small nod of satisfaction. Then she set it down on the table. "Nice," she said.

"Martinis aren't one of my vices."

"I'd like to hear what your vices are, then."

"I don't have many. Damn it."

"Cigarettes," she said.

"How did you know that?"

"You're not the only one good at detecting." She pointed at my hand. "Telltale nicotine stain on the right index finger."

"How do you know that's not a birthmark?"

She tapped her forefinger against her temple. "And you're not usually a bourbon drinker, either."

"I'm drinking bourbon right now."

"Yes, but you're sipping at it carefully, like it was medicine. My guess is that you're a beer guy at heart."

I inclined my head. "Not a bad guess. *Mzzzz* McTighe."

"Why aren't you drinking beer, then?"

I didn't want to tell her I was class-conscious enough to feel funny drinking Stroh's in an elegant place like Giovanni's. "It fills me up before dinner. Speaking of which . . ." And I looked around for the waiter.

"So what's the deal with David Ream?" she said. "Are you ever going to level with me about him?"

"Sure I am," I said. "Just not now."

"Oh?"

"I'm like you. I think better on a full stomach myself." And I bent my head to the menu as the waiter approached.

An excellent dinner was consumed with small talk as a side dish, two people who have just met compressing their life histories into brief conversational snippets. I found out that Cat McTighe was from a small town in Pennsylvania and had worked in the human resources department of the University of Pittsburgh before Armand Treusch had recruited her to the Cleveland area. Thirty-four years old, engaged once, never married. Ethnic roots were Irish, of course, and Catholic.

And I told her of my life, very briefly; high school football, which won me a partial scholarship to Kent State, combat military police unit in Cam Ranh Bay, came back and was dragooned onto the police force by my best friend. Left after a few years to open my own business. Divorced, two boys, one of whom, my elder, Milan Junior, was following in my athletic and scholastic footsteps at Kent.

That was one of the biggest reasons I hated the whole idea of dating; I get tired of talking about myself. I've heard it all before.

I figured that an after-dinner drink would be the lubricant to get Cat McTighe to open up a little more about David Ream. I had a Rémy Martin and she opted for a Drambuie, which is a Scotch-based liqueur sweet enough to make your teeth ache for a month.

Cat saw through it. "Well, this was a terrific meal, but I suppose now is when I have to sing for my supper, hmm?"

"You don't have to. But it would be helpful."

"I'm still not comfortable with spilling confidential information about one of our employees, you know."

"I'm sure not," I said. "But I hesitate to point out that you were the one who called me."

"Yes, I did."

"Why?"

"You want the real reason?"

"Sure."

She turned the wattage up on those beautiful brown eyes. "Because I think you're very attractive, I noticed you don't wear a wedding ring, and attractive single men over forty are at a premium in old, married Cleveland."

"That's very flattering, Cat," I admitted, "but as I told you . . ."

She waved a dismissive hand in front of my face. "You're involved. Yeah, yeah . . ."

I laughed.

"Besides, you seem like a very honest, sincere guy. Even though you lied to me about being with an insurance company. There's something about you. Your sincerity just *leaks* out."

"Hmm, I'm going to have to work on that."

"Don't even think about it," she warned. "Don't change a hair for me. Stay funny, valentine . . ."

"My MO, Cat, is that if I ever *do* change a hair, it's going to be for me and not anyone else."

"Yes, I figured that about you, too. Stubborn."

"I've been called that a few times," I said. "But I've always discovered that when someone knows exactly who they are and is relatively happy with it, they're perceived by others as being stubborn."

"Are you saying you're not stubborn?"

"I'm stubborn as hell. Look, could we not talk about me for a while? I really need to know some things about David Ream."

She nodded grimly. "Oh, you're stubborn all right." She sighed. "Okay. David Ream. Ask."

"Anything you can tell me that isn't in his personnel file."

Her eyebrows shot up and the big brown eyes got even bigger. "You have his personnel file?"

The back of my neck tingled, like it had when I was a kid and got caught doing something naughty. I could have kicked myself for mentioning the personnel file; I wasn't usually that careless. "I mean, I just want your unofficial impressions of him," I said, trying not to stammer, trying to save the moment. "Anything he might have said casually."

She failed to notice that I hadn't answered her question. "I didn't know I was supposed to be paying attention to the casual stuff."

"You weren't. I'm just trying to jog your memory. What was your overall impression of him?"

She lifted her glass to her lips and tossed back a mouthful of the sweet liqueur, then licked her lips in enjoyment. She was a hearty drinker, unlike Connie, who always kind of dips her head to the glass and sips like a graceful, long-necked heron drinking from a pond. "Well," she said, putting the glass down on the table, "he's a fairly bland guy. Have you met him?"

"No, I haven't."

"He's quiet. A little wimpy, I guess. Intense. Maybe a little sad."

"Sad?"

She shrugged. "I don't know what made me say that. Maybe because I like my men with a little joy and mischief in their eyes." Her gaze bored a hole into the middle of my forehead, white-hot. "Like your eyes."

It wasn't a date, I told myself, and brushed off the personal reference. "So David Ream looked lifeless?"

"Not lifeless, exactly. Just kind of—defeated. Is that a good word?"

"It's a perfectly good word if it's accurate."

"I don't know how accurate it is; I'm no psychologist. But that's the way he seemed to me. I kind of figured the boss would have him for breakfast and spit him out before a month was out. Army can be a very mean man when he spots weakness in anybody."

"Army?"

"Armand Treusch. He's the honcho at TroyToy."

Army, I thought. For a flickering moment I wondered whether the diminutive was used out of any sort of particular affection. Then I dismissed it. Cat McTighe had worked for Treusch a long time; it was only natural she'd call him by his first name. And I was sure there were very few people in the world who were referred to by their friends and associates as "Armand."

"Was it this family medical problem that was making David Ream sad, do you think?"

She bobbed her head. "It might have been. I don't know."

"Can you tell me anything else about that?"

She looked at me.

"I mean, the exact nature of the problem?"

"The exact nature." She shook her head good-naturedly. "Boy, you're some piece of work, Milan."

"Why?"

"You are so goddamn formal! 'The exact nature . . .' I'll bet you say 'penis' and 'vagina' when you're in the throes of passion, too, don't you?"

I could feel the hot flush creeping up my neck, over my face, inflaming my ears, and hoped that the understated lighting in Giovanni's dining room would somehow conceal it.

No such luck.

She noticed, all right. And it seemed to amuse her. "Gotcha, didn't I?"

"Not at all. You took me by surprise," I said, and hated how stuffy it sounded.

"I do that sometimes."

I laughed to cover the blush. "And you call *me* stubborn."

"You are."

"Maybe so, but you're so single-minded they ought to *frame* you."

Now it was her turn to laugh. "Listen, Milan, this is quid pro quo. You get to snoop about David Ream, and I get to flirt."

"So far the flirting seems to be winning."

"Yes, well, I don't lose often."

"Are you a bad loser?"

"There's only two kinds of people in this world," she said seriously. "Bad losers—and liars."

I thought about that for a minute, and had to agree with her. "Maybe, but I'm still on the wrong end of a shutout here so far."

"We can't have that. But I'm sorry, I forgot the question."

I shook my head. Cat McTighe was the *most* exasperating woman. "I was asking if you knew what Ream's family medical problem was."

"Oh, yes," she said. "The exact nature." She took another belt of Drambuie, leaving her glass almost empty.

"You want another one?"

"I wouldn't say no," she said, and I reflected that there were probably few things Cat McTighe ever said no to.

I waved down the waiter and ordered another round. It wasn't until she tasted hers that she began talking again.

"Well, I lied to you, too," she said.

"Oh?"

"You asked me at the office if I knew what medical problems had kept David Ream out of work, and I said I didn't recall."

"I remember."

"Well, I did. I just didn't want to tell you."

"How come?"

"I thought it was none of your business."

"How come it's my business now?"

She nodded thoughtfully. "Because, as I told you before, I trust you. You're sincere."

I was beginning to wonder if she was even capable of saying

anything without attaching a compliment or a personal remark to it. So I just waited.

"David Ream's little girl had been very sick. Still is sick, as far as I know. And he took several months off to care for her. She's only four years old, and he and his wife were afraid they were going to lose her."

"I'm really sorry to hear that," I said, meaning it.

"As it is, they think there was some permanent brain damage."

Sadness draped itself over me like a cloak. I hate hearing things like that about children. I shook it off.

"What was it, meningitis or something?" I said, dipping into my not-so-vast storehouse of medical knowledge.

"No," Cat McTighe said. "She was poisoned."

We ransomed our coats from the checkroom and went out to brave the bracing cold of the sprawling parking lot. Giovanni's is located on the ground floor of an office complex, so at night there were plenty of parking spaces. I walked her to her car; it was a new Toyota Camry.

"Well," she said, "thank you for a delightful evening. Good dinner, good company."

"Thank *you*."

She dug a little remote from her purse and pointed it at the car, which beeped a couple of times as the lock clicked open and the dome light flashed on inside. "You're a pretty good guy when someone can get you to loosen up a little."

"Let's be careful with those compliments, Cat; they might go to my head."

She shook hers. "I don't think so. Are you ready to tell me what this investigation of David Ream is all about?"

"No," I said. "I have to respect my client's confidentiality."

"If there ever comes a time when you don't have to, will you tell me then?"

"You'll be the first."

"You have any idea how long it's been since a man said that to me?" She laughed. Opening the door of the Camry, she turned to look at me, keeping the door as a barrier between us. "I know this was strictly business for you, Milan, so I don't expect you to try to kiss me good night, even though you know damn well you want to. That we both want you to."

I started to say something.

"Right, you're involved," she said. "But keep me in mind if that situation happens to change."

"I'll do that," I said.

"I really hope you do." She cocked her head to one side. "Did you get what you wanted from me?"

"I think so. I'll have to put it all together to see if it fits, but you were very helpful."

"That pleases me."

"Did *you* get what you wanted from *me*?"

The grin she gave me as she slid into the car beneath the steering wheel was positively lascivious. "Not yet," she said.

CHAPTER NINE

The next morning I got to my office at about ten o'clock. There was no real reason to arrive early. It was funny—although I'd run my business out of my apartment for many years, now that I had an office it seemed a lot easier to think about work there than at home.

I took a pack of three-by-five index cards from my drawer and began labeling them. DAVID REAM. ARMAND TREUSCH. HELEN MOISE. CAT MCTIGHE. CAITYLNN REAM. I jotted down notes about each of them on their respective cards, and then I laid them out across the top of the desk and began shuffling them around to see if they would make any sense. I guess I'm a visual thinker, but often the ploy of the index cards helps me put things in perspective much more than does a computer monitor.

This time it didn't.

I couldn't figure out Ream's phone call to Helen Moise, but even if I'd been able to make a connection to her consumer advocacy and her class-action suits, it certainly wouldn't point to industrial espionage.

I understood now the eight-month employment gap; any father with a gravely ill child who could afford to would have certainly done the same. I still didn't comprehend the weekly deposits Ream made during his work hiatus, but I figured they couldn't be salary checks. Employers are required by law to take out taxes and social security and the like, and the chances are slim that the figure would have come out to eight hundred dollars, even.

Of course if he were not on salary, but consulting, no deductions would be made from a fee. Maybe he had been freelancing.

I let my fingertips rest on Cat McTighe's card. I didn't think she had anything to do with David Ream other than checking out his employment application, but how could I be sure? Maybe she was playing with my head; maybe she planned to feed me information in spoonfuls over the course of several dinners out. I shook off the thought; I wasn't going to play that game.

I pondered for quite a while, made a couple of phone calls that were dead ends, and was ready to go to lunch when I heard footsteps coming up the old wooden stairs to the second floor. They stopped in front of my door, and whoever it was knocked almost timidly.

"It's open," I called.

The man who came in was little more than twenty, slight of build and dark complexioned. He wore a heavy blue and yellow University of Michigan parka over jeans and work boots. His hair was very black and his skin a kind of golden beige, and for a moment I thought he might be either Latino or Middle Eastern.

"Are you Mr. Jacovich?" he said. He pronounced it correctly, but very carefully, the way he might a foreign word he had just learned.

"That's right."

"I wonder if I could talk to you for a couple of minutes."

He didn't look as though he was going to try and sell me anything. Door-to-door salesmen have that too-bright, too-eager smile of desperation I can usually spot a mile away, and this kid had a sad, almost hangdog look. Besides, his hands, encased in brown wool gloves, were empty—no sales kit, no samples, no order pads or four-color brochures. His manner of speech was as halting and tentative as his knock, and his large, gentle brown eyes reflected depths of sorrows yet unknown. He brushed a stray cowlick out of his face and took a few tentative steps into the room.

"I guess that all depends on what you want to talk about, doesn't it?"

"My name is Edgar Ettawageshik," he said, and he pulled off his right glove but made no effort to shake hands. "The man the police found murdered in the river—the Indian man you identified at the coroner's office—was my granddad."

My neck hairs gave that caught-in-the-cookie-jar prickle again. I stood up and reached across the desk for a handshake. "I'm very sorry for your loss," I said. "Maybe you'd better sit down."

His shoulders seemed to slump with relief; until that moment I hadn't realized how tense he was.

"Why don't you take your coat off?" I said. "Would you like some coffee?"

He shook his head and peeled off the parka, hung it on the back of one of the client chairs, and sat down in the other one. He had on a red and white flannel work shirt, and the belt around his waist was thick, braided leather that looked like deerskin, with a large and ornate silver buckle.

"I thought your grandfather had no identification when they found him."

"He didn't," Edgar Ettawageshik said, and the pain he must have been feeling inside thickened his vocal chords and made his voice raspy. "But apparently the story was picked up by the wire services and a friend saw it and knew my grandfather had come to Cleveland, so he called us."

Other people's sorrows upset me; maybe I chose the wrong career path at that. I wanted a cigarette badly, but didn't do anything about it.

"Then I called the Cleveland police and got a description," Ettawageshik continued, "and I just knew it was Granddad. So I drove all night to get here. I just came back from the . . ." He swallowed hard. "From seeing him."

I'd been there, I knew what he'd had to look at. "I'm sorry," I said again.

He nodded mute thanks.

"I guess Lieutenant McHargue told you I had seen your grandfather sitting across the street the day before he died."

"Yes," he said. "It was kind of you to go to them—the police. Kind of you to want to help. Not many people would take the trouble."

"I used to be a police officer," I said.

"Yes, that lieutenant told me so, too."

He clasped his hands between his knees, and we both let the moment hang there a while.

"What brings you to me, Mr . . . Ettawageshik?" I hesitated and stumbled over the name; I'd finally found one more difficult to pronounce than my own.

He smiled the faintest of smiles in acknowledgement of my good try. "Well, I wanted to thank you. But the thing is—I need your help, too" he said, choking it out as though it was lodged in his throat like an errant piece of prime rib. "Your professional help."

"Private investigators aren't allowed anywhere near an open homicide," I said. "I'd lose my license."

"I understand that, sir."

I only like to be called "sir" by waiters. I shifted uneasily. "Then how can I help you?"

He looked lost, adrift. "I don't know where to start."

I did, but to tell him so seemed obvious.

"Um," he said.

I just waited.

"I guess I should tell you why my granddad was in Cleveland."

"Yes," I said, and centered a yellow legal pad under my right hand, trying to think of the last time I'd heard anyone use the expression "granddad." It seemed quaintly archaic and sweet, and considering the way Edgar's granddad had ended up, there was wormwood in the sweetness, too.

It took him a minute to compose his story, but when he finally started it, his voice was stronger and more confident than it had been since he'd walked in. "We're Odawas, Mr. Jacovich," he began. "Our tribe is scattered all over western Michigan, but our family lives in Cross Village; that's about thirty minutes south of the bridge to the Upper Peninsula."

I nodded; I'd once made a happy round-trip across that bridge, on my way to a long, romantic weekend on Mackinac Island with Mary Soderberg. A long time ago.

"I'm living in Ann Arbor right now because I'm a junior at Michigan. Civil engineering major." He ducked his head modestly. "I got a full scholarship."

"You must be a smart guy."

Shaking his head sadly, he said, "I used to think so. Now, I'm not so sure. Anyway, I have a sister. Her name is Wanda. Got married a year and a half ago to a guy named Frank Takalo. Frank's a construction worker, but there hasn't been a lot of work in the last few months. Michigan's having a hard winter, and when that happens the building trades always take the hit."

"Same is true in Ohio."

"My granddad—*Joseph* Ettawageshik is his name . . ." He dropped his eyes. "Was."

"Yes."

"He retired two years ago; he was a construction worker, too. He never finished school, not even grade school, but he was self-educated. He was the family historian. He loved to do research on the Odawas, and pass the stories down to us. He only read on like a fifth-grade level, but he used to go in to Petoskey to the library all the time and look up things about the tribe, even about the family. He never made a lot of money, but he was honest and worked hard all his life . . ." His voice faltered a little.

"Go on," I said.

"Well, Wanda and Frank had a baby two months ago. A little boy. They named him Andrew."

I nodded. I knew little about the Odawa culture, but I remembered vaguely from my various trips through Michigan that in the nineteenth century there had been a great chief of the Odawas, Andrew Blackbird, and that many male children were named in his honor.

Edgar Ettawageshik fumbled in his back pocket and drew out an inexpensive cloth wallet. He flipped it open to the photo section and extended it across the desk so I could see the snapshot of a healthily chubby, perennially baffled-looking infant with a healthy shock of straight black hair.

"He's very cute," I murmured politely the way one does when shown baby pictures.

He snapped the wallet shut and squeezed it back into his pocket, leaning forward. "A week ago, little Andrew disappeared."

"Disappeared?"

He nodded. "One morning Wanda went to wake him and feed him and he wasn't in his crib. Someone had taken him away during the night."

I'm not a crier, but this time I came pretty close. With two sons of my own, I could easily imagine the terror, the pain little Andrew's family must have been feeling. "Ah, God, I'm sorry." I said. "Was there any sign of forced entry?"

He nodded. "The window in the baby's room had been jimmied. Probably a crowbar, from the looks of it."

"And you're sure it was nobody in town?"

He shook his head resolutely. "Those people are our friends, Mr. Jacovich, the ones who aren't actually related to us. Besides, in Cross Village nobody could keep a secret like that for more than ten minutes."

"Was there a ransom demand?"

"That's what's so scary—no. Wanda and Frank don't have anything anyway. Their little house is rented, they have a ten-year-old Ford pickup. And less than two thousand dollars in the bank."

I nodded; it would take a very stupid kidnapper to make a ransom demand from an impoverished family. "Does Frank have enemies?"

"No, he's too nice of a guy. I mean, sure, everybody has someone that doesn't like them very much, but to steal their baby . . ." He cleared his throat. "No. Couldn't be."

I felt the corners of my mouth being pulled down as if weights were attached. Baby kidnappings happened sometimes, and the best-case scenario was that the culprit would turn out to be a deranged woman who had just lost her own child and whose grief and paranoia had led her to steal somebody else's.

The other possibilities were too gruesome to think of. Weird cults who practiced human sacrifice or the drinking of human blood. Insane people who just liked killing. Worse . . .

"You've been to the police, of course."

"Oh, yes," he said. "But as you can imagine, the Cross Village police force isn't exactly—sophisticated. And our tribal cops—well, they're even more inept. Something like this is beyond their comprehension."

"What about the state police?" I pressed. "Or the FBI?" I almost didn't say that; my experience with Federal cops of any stripe had been very negative over the last few years. But a child's life hung in the balance, and I couldn't afford to let my personal prejudices get in the way of his safe return to his family.

"They've all been notified," Edgar Ettawageshik said. "We did all the things we were supposed to. But we're Indians, Mr. Jacovich. We've all learned from experience that law enforcement or anybody else doesn't give a good goddamn about us except to make sure we don't get all liquored up and kill somebody with our trucks." There was a sardonic twist to his lips I was certain was genuine.

"What did Lieutenant McHargue say?"

"All she's interested in is who killed Granddad. She says the kidnapping is outside her jurisdiction."

I nodded, feeling lousy, but understanding. I'd run into similar situations with Marko; law enforcement officers have enough to do on their own turf without trying to solve crimes that have taken place elsewhere. Marko only forgot that rule once; it cost him his life.

"I can imagine what you're going through, Mr. Ettawageshik . . ."

"Call me Eddie, please," he said, and his smile was crooked, affecting only the right side of his mouth. "It's easier. And after all, I'm just a kid."

"Eddie, then. But I still don't understand why you came to me."

He put his hands flat on his thighs, but that didn't conceal their slight trembling. "Before this, Granddad never went outside the state of Michigan in his life. He came to Cleveland because he found out something about Andrew, about what might have happened to him." He leaned forward, and I could almost smell the fear on him. "Mr. Jacovich," he said. "Please. Help me find my nephew."

Well, he couldn't pay me, although he offered to. He proposed to send me fifty dollars a month until my fee was paid off, but I refused it; I'm not that hard up. I was being paid well enough by Armand Treusch that I could afford to help Edgar Ettawageshik pro bono. I took a dollar bill from him as a retainer, gave him a receipt, and had him sign a contract anyway, just to make it legal.

Then I gave him the dollar back. "It'll just put me into another tax bracket," I told him.

At first he didn't want to let me work for nothing; his Native American heritage is a proud one. But I convinced him to give in by reminding him that I had dealt myself a hand in his family's troubles by going to the police about his granddad in the first place. He finally agreed, and although I could tell he wasn't at all comfortable about accepting what he perceived as charity, he was also pretty relieved. I felt better, too; the kidnapping of a small baby was not something I could just walk away from. And a kid from a poor Indian family going to school on a scholarship would have no resources with which to hire a private investigator, not even a cut-rate one. God knows there are plenty of those around.

I talked to him for almost an hour in my office, taking notes despite the fact that a little remote-control button under the desk allows me to record everything. He perched on the edge of the chair as if he was about to take flight like a frightened sparrow.

Two days after baby Andrew had been taken from his crib, Joseph Ettawageshik had disappeared as well, leaving a note scrawled in pencil on a scrap of grocery sack, saying "Gone to Cleveland to find Andrew." Nothing more.

"What made your granddad think the baby was in Cleveland?"

"I don't know," he said.

"There must be something, Eddie. He didn't pick Cleveland out of a hat."

He shook his head in mute sorrow. "I just don't know."

There seemed to be only one way to find out, I thought, and

that was to trace Joseph Ettawageshik from his home to that bench. It promised to be a long trek.

After Eddie left my office, I called Armand Treusch at his office, but he wasn't in. I asked the operator for his voice mail.

"I'll be out of town for the next two days on another matter," I told the tape after the beep. "I'll be back on the investigation after that. Just wanted to let you know you won't be charged. Leave a message for me if there's a problem."

I hung up, went to my file drawer, and dug out a map of Michigan.

"You're going *where*?" Connie said. Through the receiver her voice was sharp, harsh.

"I'm going to Michigan. Just for a day or two."

She didn't say anything for a while. Then, "It's something about that Indian, isn't it?"

"In a way."

"In what way? What does that mean?"

"I'm not getting involved in finding out who killed him," I said. "It has to do with a kidnapping."

"How does that connect with the Indian, then?"

I took a deep breath and told her. After I finished, all I heard was the sound of her breathing through her nose.

Then she said, "That's pretty serious stuff."

"It is," I agreed.

"It might be dangerous."

"So is driving down Cedar Hill when it's icy, and I do that a lot."

She laughed. There wasn't much mirth in it, but it was definitely a laugh, and that, at least, was a good sign.

"Will you be careful?"

"I'm always careful, Connie."

"You are not!"

"Sure I am. I have proof."

"What proof?"

"I'm still walking around," I said.

Chapter Ten

I thought about booking myself on an early-morning flight to Grand Rapids. It wasn't all that close to Cross Village, but it seemed the most logical place for me to rent a car. Eventually I decided against it. I'm not fond of puddle-jumper flights, especially in bad weather, and besides, I'm the most comfortable when I'm in control and not at the whim of airlines and snowstorms. So on my way home I dropped in to the nearest AAA office for some maps. I'd gotten detailed directions from Eddie Ettawageshik, so the maps were just a backup.

I drove up Cedar Hill through falling snow. It wasn't a "My Favorite Things" kind of snowfall with big six-pointed flakes that stay on your nose and eyelashes, but it was a long way from a blizzard, too. It was just nasty, cold, wet stuff that dusted the tips of the slumbering winter grass and melted on the pavements and everywhere else, the kind of snow that always makes February in the Midwest seem as though it's six months long.

I parked in my assigned space beside my apartment building, and then made a quick detour across the street to what used to be Russo's Stop & Shop and is now Russo's Giant Eagle market, where I picked up an onion, a head of romaine, a six-pack of Stroh's, mushrooms, and a big plastic jug of Tide. Then, braving the elements, I put my head down and crossed Fairmount Boulevard to hearth and home on foot.

I clawed my mail out of the too-small box in the vestibule, and when I got upstairs to my apartment, transferred it directly to the wastebasket without reading it, saving out only the bill from my son Stephen's orthodontist. With the advent of email and fax machines, no one ever writes real letters anymore.

From the freezer I extracted a link of klobasa I'd purchased several weeks ago from Dohar's in the West Side Market, and put it in the microwave to thaw. Klobasa, for the uninitiated, is delicious, garlicky sausage, virtually identical to kolbasi, kolbasz, keilbase, or any of the other myriad spellings favored by the Poles, Hungarians, Czechs, Serbs, and Slovaks. Klobasa is the Slovenian spelling, the one I grew up with.

When it was thawed I boiled it while I cut up the onion and sautéed it in a big frying pan, then put the sausage into the butter and onions to brown. I tore chunks of romaine into a colander, washed them, wrapped them in paper towels to dry, and took a handful of mushrooms from the package for a salad. I ate the klobasa and onions with horseradish, in a sandwich made of our local Orlando Bakery Ciabatta bread, sliced lengthwise. I like Slovenian sausage on Italian bread; I'm eclectic, if nothing else.

Washing the whole thing down with a Stroh's, I thought about Baby Andrew Takalo, and why, when he'd gone missing, his great-grandfather Joseph thought he might find a clue to his whereabouts in Cleveland. I was hoping that he had shared the reason with the baby's parents, even if they hadn't realized it at the time. It would be my job to see if I could shake loose some memory they didn't even realize they had.

It wasn't going to be easy, I knew, even though Eddie was going to smooth the way for me and convince them to talk to me. After all, Frank and Wanda Takalo lived a pretty insular life in their chilly little town near Lake Michigan; I had no doubt their idea of a big city was probably Grand Rapids. And I was an outsider, a white man at that, and from long and bitter experience with the white establishment, they had no good reason to believe they could trust me.

I felt vaguely guilty about leaving Armand Treusch high and dry; he was paying me, after all, and Eddie Ettawageshik was not.

But a missing child took precedence over some vaguely imagined industrial espionage, even though the case would put no more in my pocket than the token dollar I'd already accepted from Eddie and then returned.

Still, I *was* running a business . . .

I washed my dinner dishes, such as they were—salad bowl, frying pan, and stockpot, plus the utensils, thankful I didn't have a whole sinkful to deal with. The last three significant women in my life had all been fond of fine food, and had introduced me to the joys of gourmet dining and good wine. Still, when I am all alone, it's too much of a fuss to cook fancy. I'm usually just as happy fixing a sandwich for dinner and eating it at the kitchen table, or if I'm really rushed, standing up over the sink.

Then I went into my den, sat down in my big leather chair, and switched on the television. It was set on a cable channel, and came up in the middle of a silly movie with Tim Allen and Kirstie Alley playing socialites hiding out on an Amish farm, for what reason I didn't know, since I'd missed the first half of the picture. It was the typical Hollywood fish-out-of-water formula, and seemed only sporadically amusing.

I hit the mute button on my remote, thumbed through my Rolodex for a minute, and found the number for Suzanne Davis, an acquaintance of mine who's a private investigator working out of Lake County. The Greater Cleveland community is small enough that all the PIs know each other, just as, I suppose, all the actors and cardiac surgeons and advertising executives do, too, and I had spent some pleasant afternoons over coffee or drinks with Suzanne Davis.

She was surprised to hear from me; we hadn't seen each other in over a year.

"I've got some scut work I need taken care of," I said after we'd gotten past all the long-time-no-see and how-are-you amenities, "and I have to leave town for a couple of days. Have some time?"

"For you, sure," she said.

"At your usual rates."

She paused. "Is this coming out of your pocket?"

"What's the difference?"

"Professional courtesy is the difference," she said. "I'm not going to get rich off you, Milan. You'd do the same for me."

"Why don't you wait and see how long it takes you?"

"Do I have to surveil anybody? I hate long stakeouts. Women can't pee in a coffee can sitting in the car like you guys can."

I laughed. "Nothing like that," I said. "I want to get hold of some medical records."

"From where?"

"That's the problem, I don't know. But they're for a little girl named Caitlynn Ream. Starting—oh, I don't know, let's say a year ago."

"Hmm," Suzanne Davis said. "Tough, but not impossible. I have a few sources at a couple of the local hospitals. If your gal was treated in one of them, we're in luck. Otherwise it might be a long haul."

"Tell you what," I said. "Check out your sources first. If we get lucky, we get lucky. Otherwise, I'll take care of it myself when I get back."

"And I won't send you a bill, either."

"Then I'll have to owe you one, Suzanne."

"Good enough," she said. "I like being owed. I'll get on it in the morning. Where's your trip to, anyway?"

"Michigan. Up near the Straits of Mackinac."

I heard her chuckle. "Central Michigan in the middle of February. Milan, I am positively *green* with envy."

The next day's weather was more of the same as I headed west on I-90 before the sun was even up. I was glad I didn't have to talk to anyone, or even think; I don't exactly shine first thing in the morning.

It took me about four and a half hours to get to Grand Rapids. The Ohio Turnpike was well plowed but slick; the good news was that the winter weather had sent into hibernation the ubiquitous orange barrels that denote highway construction and slow down traffic during the spring and summer.

Following the map AAA had provided, I found myself heading north on US 131.

It was a divided highway, two lanes going in either direction, and there wasn't much to see on either side of me except trees and farmland. For a state boasting a big, smoky, industrial giant like Detroit, much of the rest of Michigan is very rural indeed, not unlike the Ohio landscape between its large population centers of Cleveland, Columbus, and Cincinnati. I had to shake my head to keep from woolgathering as I drove, and I switched on the radio for a while to keep myself alert, but I couldn't get much of anything out there in the boondocks except country music, which, to my jazz-and-classical urban ear, was much less desirable than silence.

The road was dotted with snowmobiles, and I cursed every time I had to pull around to pass one. They were irritatingly noisy, buzzing like mosquitoes shattering the tranquility of the white landscape. There were not nearly as many snowmobiles in Ohio.

The slumbering farm acreage droned by, its visual neutrality giving me time to think. Why did Joseph Ettawageshik think baby Andrew Takalo was in Cleveland? Usually when a child is kidnapped and no ransom demand is made, the family thinks the worst; sadly, they are often right. But great-granddad had headed straight for Cleveland and, ultimately, to a violent end. I wanted to find out why, and coincidentally whether the kidnapping had anything to do with him now taking up drawer space at the county morgue.

I know, I know—Joseph's death was none of my business, as Connie had made abundantly clear.

US 131 slices right through the business district of the city of Cadillac, complete with a lot of traffic lights. It was sort of hard to slow down after cruising along at highway speed, but I didn't want to get nailed for exceeding the limit. The states of Ohio, Kentucky, Indiana, Pennsylvania, and Michigan are very competitive with each other, and their respective law enforcement agencies dearly love citing errant motorists from other jurisdictions.

North of Cadillac, the road becomes two lane, and several times

I got stuck going thirty-five or less behind a semi or a car pulling a trailer, although why the senior citizens with their homes on wheels would be cruising the northern highways in the dead of winter was a mystery to me. And there were a lot of small towns to creep through as well. The drive made the usual construction woes of the Ohio Turnpike look like a Sunday drive.

I stopped for lunch in Petoskey, a pretty lakeside community with a resort atmosphere that seemed somber under the blanket of dull-gray winter. Few of the restaurant customers had taken off their outerwear to eat, and there was a profusion of ugly parkas and checkered woolen work coats; in cold country they dress for warmth rather than fashion. The waitress didn't seem particularly pleased to see me. Folks up here usually refer to the tourists as "fudgies," because the perception is that they are all going up to lovely Mackinac Island to buy the famous fudge. I didn't have fudge, opting instead for an open-faced roast beef sandwich and a scoop of mashed potatoes with a lake of brown gravy in the middle.

From Petoskey north, US 131 ends, inexplicably losing a hundred points in the process, and becomes US 31, and when the highway curved around to hug the shore of Lake Michigan, I pulled off for a moment to watch the icy wind-driven waves crashing against the breakwater. The sun was struggling to peek out through the dark sky cover; it made diamonds on the snow, whose purity was crisscrossed and made ugly by the tracks of many snowmobiles.

From there, it was less than a half hour's drive to the home of the Ettawageshiks, Cross Village, in Emmett County.

The Indians had originally dubbed the village *Waganakisi,* or Crooked Tree. Sometime during the eighteenth century the Jesuits erected a large cross on the bluff, and after that the place was simply called La Croix until 1870, when the name was changed to Cross Village. A cross still stands there, replaced every few years when the weather rots the wood; I guess the village fathers figure if you've got the name, play the game.

The town's main street looked a little forlorn draped in the leftover dirty gray of a recent snowfall. There wasn't much there; a couple of churches, a gas station, a tourist-curio store that bore a sign saying "CLOSED FOR THE SEASON," some abandoned buildings, and of course a bar. What would a rural American town be without its neighborhood saloon? This particular one was made of wood and stone, and outside two colorful totem poles stood proud against the snow and wind.

I consulted the directions Eddie had written out for me in a cramped, almost illegible hand; he'd make a good engineer, all right. Not five minutes from the center of town, I found the house of Frank and Wanda Takalo.

As in many other parts of the country, some Native American tribes in Michigan had grown fat and prosperous from the fruits of bingo parlors and casino gambling on their lands. The bounty had evidently bypassed the Odawas of Cross Village.

The house was a postwar stucco badly in need of a paint job, with a wooden front porch that sagged in the middle. Small, cheerless windows were masked with gauzy white curtains. The whole house seemed to be listing the tiniest bit to one side. Frank Takalo's elderly Ford pickup was parked in the weedy driveway, right in front of a similar but slightly newer one I assumed belonged to Eddie. There wasn't exactly a curb, just a swath of snow-covered grass that simply ended where the paved, potholed roadway began. I parked the Sunbird there, got out, and walked toward the house, the crusty snow crunching under my feet and accepting my footprints.

They'd seen me coming; Eddie opened the door before I could knock, greeted me gravely and without a handshake, and led me inside to the small living room to meet the Takalos.

Frank was not a large man, perhaps only five feet ten, but he gave the impression of bigness. His hands were hard and callused, his shoulders broad, his neck corded with muscle, his forearms thick and substantial beneath the long sleeves of the green-plaid flannel work shirt he wore with a pair of jeans faded from many washings, the material thin and puckered at the knees. Except for a prominent nose that looked as if it had been broken a time or two, his features were small, especially his little dark eyes, which seemed like two irregular chips of obsidian almost embedded in the sharp slabs and ridges of brows and cheekbones. His leathery, weathered skin made him appear to be forty-five, although I imagined he was younger by at least ten years.

His wife, Wanda, was smaller, chubby, long ink black hair braided into a helmet around her head, her loose-fitting flowered print dress only partially disguising a belly not yet returned to normal after her recent childbirth. I immediately saw the familial resemblance between Wanda and her brother Eddie; her skin was the same light, warm brown, and her facial features were softer and more Caucasian than the Mongolian cast of her husband's. Brown smudges of fear and exhaustion under dark swollen eyes made her look older than her years, as well.

I gave Eddie my coat and looked around at the unadorned living room as I sat down, opposite the vintage console TV, in an orange discount-store easy chair, its fat arms worn and nubby under my hands, and declined Wanda's offer of coffee and pound cake. I don't know why. I normally *never* refuse coffee. But coffee in the company of others is a sociable thing, and as grief-stricken as the Takalos must have been, this was not a sociable occasion.

"Eddie told us about you, Mr. Jacovich. He says you maybe can help us." Frank spoke slowly, pronouncing my difficult Slavic name with a careful accuracy. His vowels were slightly nasalized, perhaps a trace of the French influence in the region centuries before. "I don't see how, but he says you can."

"I don't know if I can," I said. "I'm going to try, though."

"We want to pay you."

I shook my head. "Eddie and I have already discussed that, Mr. Takalo. It isn't necessary."

"We don't take charity," Frank said.

"This isn't charity. I'm a father myself—I have two sons. This is something I want to do, all right?"

"I want my baby back!" Wanda cried suddenly. They were the first words out of her mouth since a murmured hello, and they sounded as if they were being torn from her throat. Her eyes puffed up and got red, and tears began coursing down her round cheeks. "We'll give you whatever you want, I don't care what it costs. Please find him, find my little Andrew. Oh Jesus, God, please help us!" She buried her face in her hands, muffling her sobs.

Frank looked at her and then at me. "It was a hard delivery," he explained, licking dry lips. "We won't be able to have any more."

He moved slowly and awkwardly to his wife's side, his big hand almost obscuring her shoulder. It was a touching gesture from a hard-looking man. "Wanda, Mr. Jacovich will help us," he soothed.

It didn't soothe me, however. I suddenly became acutely aware of what I was attempting to tackle, and how important it was. In the case of a kidnapping such as this one, without a ransom demand, the prognosis was not good at all. Was I ready to face these sad, frightened people and tell them I'd discovered their baby was dead?

I was not.

But even though everything in me was saying I would be embarking on a fool's errand, I wasn't ready to walk away, either.

"Well, let's see what we can do here, then," I said, having trouble getting the words past the lump that had grown quickly and painfully in my throat. I took out my pen and notebook.

I had to ease them into it; they were both too upset to think or speak rationally. First we went over the ground Eddie and I had already covered—the jimmied window the night the baby was taken, the disappearance of Joseph Ettawageshik, the cryptic note. They offered little more insight.

"And you have no idea what made your grandfather think Andrew was somehow in Cleveland?"

Wanda shook her head miserably.

"All right then. Did you notice any strangers around here a day or two before Andrew disappeared? Anyone who didn't belong?"

Frank said, "There are always strangers around here. Tourists. On their way to Mackinac Island for the weekend."

"In February?"

He nodded gravely. "Even in February. People can be crazy. Mackinac—it's very romantic. Guys go up there with their ladies—some married guys with their girlfriends, you know . . ."

So there was more to the tourist business than fudge. "But Andrew was missing on a Monday morning, not a weekend."

His massive shoulders rose and fell helplessly. "I don't know. I didn't see anybody. Did you see anybody, Wanda?"

She was gnawing the skin next to her thumbnail raw. She didn't answer; instead, she just closed her eyes tight, as if in the darkness behind her eyelids there was no worry and no pain.

"Why Cleveland?" I said. "Once we know that, the rest will be easier."

Eddie Ettawageshik cleared his throat. "Granddad must have seen something or someone here from Cleveland."

"Someone who made him suspicious," I agreed. "But why was he sitting on a bench across from my apartment building?"

Eddie just shook his head. I could tell I was going to have to start from ground zero.

"May I see the baby's room?"

Frank nodded, and led me down a small cramped hallway. The master bedroom was at the end of the hall, to one side. There was a small bathroom next to it, and across from that, the second bedroom. He opened the door and I stepped inside.

It was a tiny room, not much larger than my own bathroom at home. The walls were unadorned except for a sadly merry Mickey and Goofy poster affixed to the plaster with Scotch tape. The crib looked as if it had nurtured more than only one baby in its time, and I figured the Takalos had either bought it used or borrowed it from some friends who no longer had a need for it. Over the crib dangled a cheap, plastic mobile of multicolored stars.

"I had to fix the window," Frank said. "To keep out the cold."

The window opening was small, large enough for a slim person to crawl through, though someone my size would have gotten stuck midway like a dog in a wrought-iron fence. The lower pane had been broken and was now covered with two thicknesses of hurriedly tacked-up plywood. I could see the jimmy marks plainly on the sill; the whole lower sash had been pried artlessly out of its moorings. Crowbar, I thought. Nothing fancy.

But the crib was directly under the window, against the wall. Little more would have been required than for a tall person to lean in and pluck the child from the mattress.

"Did they take the baby's blanket, too?"

"Yes. We were thankful for that; it was a cold night."

"Anything else? Bottles, pacifiers?"

His face colored slightly. "Andrew wasn't on a bottle."

I knelt down and looked under the crib. Someone had obviously cleaned the room up, but the light coming through the window caught infinitesimal slivers of glass sparkling where they were embedded into the yellow shag carpeting. You know how hard it is to clean up every smidge of broken glass.

"This had to have made a noise, Mr. Takalo," I said. "The wood breaking, the glass shattering. Didn't you hear anything?"

"There was a big windstorm that night," he said. "Howling off the lake like a coyote. This is an old house; it bangs and rattles all winter when the wind blows. Wanda could always hear the smallest sound the baby made at night and wake up, but otherwise she's sound sleeper. We both are."

Fortuitous circumstance for the kidnapper, I wondered, or foreknowledge? Meteorologists can predict rain and snow and temperature, but I wasn't that certain about the wind.

"Was the door to this room open?"

"It always is. And our bedroom door, too. So Wanda could hear if the baby cried." His flat, reedy voice caught on the word "baby."

We went back out into the living room. Wanda had curled up in the chair I'd formerly occupied, her knees drawn up under her, and was still working on the side of her thumb with her teeth. Eddie stood against the wall, half-leaning, his arms folded across his chest as if to ward off the cold that seeped through the walls and fissures despite the space heater that glowed orange-red in the corner.

"Do you have a picture of Andrew?" I said. "One I can take with me?"

"Ohhh," Wanda moaned. "We only have one!"

"I'll take good care of it, Mrs. Takalo. I'll have it copied and bring it back to you, I promise."

Frank's sigh came from somewhere in the vicinity of his shoes. He moved almost numbly into the back of the house, returning a moment later with a commercial baby portrait in a gold-colored frame, a larger version of the image Eddie carried in his wallet. The baby was chubby-faced, bright-eyed, smiling. Of course all babies tend to look like Churchill, but Andrew was beautiful nonetheless.

"Look," I said, "I'm going to stay around here tonight. Probably get a hotel room in Petoskey. I'll come back tomorrow. It would help if you all could set up some people for me to talk to."

"Like who?"

"Anyone who knew your grandfather."

"Everyone in town knew him," Eddie said. "He lived here all his life." He looked away as if he was embarrassed.

"What?" I said.

He glanced at Frank, then Wanda, then down at his work boots. "The people here, Mr. Jacovich, the Indian people—they aren't very comfortable with—well, you know, with strangers."

I hadn't even considered that. "Can you talk to them for me, then, Eddie? You and Frank?"

"What do you want us to say to them?" Frank said.

"Convince them to see me and cooperate. I need to find out if they'd talked to Joseph at all in the few days before he left. If he said anything—*anything* at all—about Cleveland."

"That'll take some time."

"Do it," I said. "It's all we've got."

I shook hands with both the Takalos, Wanda still so engulfed in grief that she couldn't meet my eyes. Eddie got my coat, threw on his parka, and walked me out into the stinging cold. The wind had begun to howl again, driving down the chill factor, and I could feel it knife through my clothes.

"Can I take a look at the outside of the house?" I said, hunching my shoulders deeper into my collar. "Under that window?"

"Sure," he said, and led me around to the back of the house, the snow soaking my trouser cuffs and seeping uncomfortably into my shoes.

Except for marks the crowbar had left on the outside of the sill, there wasn't much to see. Snow covered the ground and any tracks that might have been left.

"When the police investigated that next morning," I said, "did they find any footprints back here? Was it muddy?"

"It hadn't rained or snowed for a while, so the ground was probably dry." He looked away. "I don't know if they even looked around back here. I was in Ann Arbor when it happened . . ."

I wasn't a bit surprised. Not for the first time, it occurred to me that if I ever decided to give up my business for a life in crime, I would probably do well to practice it in a very small town, where police departments were generally underfunded and undermanned, and lacking in the sophisticated investigative techniques their big-city counterparts utilized.

"Who is the local top cop around here?"

"His name is Corley Goggins," Eddie said, and laughed.

"What's funny?"

"Top cop." He sniffled. "There are only three full-time police officers in the village. I guess if there is a top cop, it's Corley."

It was too cold for me to pull off my gloves to write the name down in my notebook, so I committed it to memory. "You think he'll talk to me?"

"It's not like he has anything else to do."

I looked around under baby Andrew's bedroom window a little more, yielding no results, and then Eddie guided me around to the front again and down the walk to my car.

"I'll do some more work around here," I said, "and then find myself a hotel room. I'll call you to let you know where I am. When you talk to your grandfather's friends, if you find out anything—anything at all—give me a ring."

He nodded glumly. "Granddad . . ." he began.

I waited.

"Granddad wasn't much of a talker. I mean, he was full of

stories about the old days. The old ways, you know." He flicked a look at me to make sure I understood what he meant, and I nodded back at him. "But other than that, he wasn't much on telling people what he was thinking. Even his own family. He was a quiet man, kept his own counsel . . ."

"Something this important, though, he must have told somebody."

He shrugged. "Could be. Some of the elders, maybe. But . . ." He shoved his fists into the pockets of his parka. "I don't know, Mr. Jacovich, maybe I should never have asked you. This is going to be hard."

"It's always hard, Eddie," I said. "If it was easy, you'd do it yourself."

The wind hit the car door as I opened it and almost tore it out of my hand. The engine coughed before it turned over, and the tailpipe left a plume of white smoke in my wake as I drove away from the solitary figure who stood forlornly in the cold.

Chapter Eleven

The police station was a lot like everything else in Cross Village. Built right after the war, it was showing its age; the bitter ravages of fifty winters had pitted and discolored the undistinguished gray cinder blocks.

Police Chief Corley Goggins had been around about as long, and bore some of the same marks of time. A buggy whip-thin man with pockmarked skin and a mouth like the torn pocket of an old raincoat, he had the permanent look of someone who'd just bitten into an unexpectedly tart apple.

To his credit, Goggins displayed none of the hostility toward me that I had found in other small-town police departments in the past. I almost wished he would; supreme indifference stings even worse than antagonism.

"Of course we investigated the kidnapping," he said, his almost nonexistent butt resting against the edge of a battle-scarred old desk in an office no different from that of a low-level civil servant anywhere. At one corner of the desk was a color photograph of a plain-looking woman forcing a smile and two preteen boys with military brush cuts and cold blue eyes like their daddy's; judging from the vaguely sky-like blue background and the stiff, formal poses, I figured it had been taken at the portrait gallery in the Sears store in nearby Petoskey.

"We did what we were expected to do," Goggins went on, "and we did it as thoroughly as we could. But we're just a little bit lacking in manpower and resources here, as you can see." And he waved his hand to indicate his meager headquarters.

"You could have notified the state police."

"I could have and I did. They came out, too. Went over all the same ground we did, asked all the same questions." He fished a crumpled pack of Camels from the shirt pocket of his khaki uniform and shook out a cigarette, not offering me one. It was just as well; I don't like Camels. "They got the same results."

"What about the FBI?" I said. "Kidnapping is a federal crime."

"I know that," he said sharply. "I'm a small-town cop, but I'm not stupid."

"I never thought you were, Chief. What did the FBI have to say?"

"They said they'll send someone up here when they can get a man—or woman—free and available."

"You told them about old Joseph going to Cleveland to look for the baby?"

"I did."

"That means the crossing of a state line."

He nodded. "I told them everything I knew," he said. "But it didn't seem to hurry them up any. I guess the disappearance of an Indian baby is not exactly high-priority with them."

"Jesus," I said.

"No need to blaspheme." He frowned as he lit the Camel, and spit the smoke out as he appraised me more carefully. I don't exactly look as though I've just stepped off the pages of *GQ*, but I suppose to his eye I seemed pretty citified with my cold-weather system and pressed khaki slacks, now dirty and wet at the cuffs from slogging around in the Michigan snow. "So what's your end of this? The Takalos paying you? I didn't think they had a pot to piss in, much less to hire a private star."

"They don't. I'm doing this as a friend of the family."

"Jacovich." He rolled the name around on his tongue like a sour-cherry hard candy. "What is that, a Jew name?" He asked it without rancor, as if it wouldn't have made any difference to him one way or the other.

"Slovenian," I said.

He looked blank.

"Slovenia used to be part of Yugoslavia."

"Oh," he said, still at sea. I didn't feel like explaining to him where Slovenia is. "So, uh, how does a—Slovenian private detective from Cleveland get to be friends with an Odawa family in a little nowhere town in Michigan?"

"I have friends all over, Chief."

He squinted at me. "Is that deliberately meant to be misleading?"

"I don't see what difference it makes how I know the Takalos."

"Well, I don't either," he said. "Yet. But I want you to know that your license doesn't mean rat scat in this state, and I take a dim view of civilians poking around in police business."

"If the people who were supposed to be poking around in it were doing their job, I wouldn't have to."

"I am doing my job, Jacovich, to the best of my ability. But a man's a fool if he don't recognize his limitations."

"Would you be quite so limited if the baby who's missing was white?"

Now his ass came up off the edge of the desk. He didn't want to get right in my face, I'm sure, because I was much bigger than he. But he pointed his chin at me, and his lower jaw seemed to be hewn from granite the way Coach Bill Cowher's does when an official's call goes against his Steelers. "I resent that. Don't give me any of that racism business, because I grew up in this town. I've known these Indians all my life. They're my neighbors and my friends."

"And that's why now you throw them back there into a cell when they get drunk, huh?"

"I do my job," he said, giving all four words equal emphasis. "They get publicly drunk, they sleep it off in the back—that's the law. I can't have them driving their old cars and trucks into people and hurting or killing them."

"Don't you ever get drunk, Chief Goggins?"

"Sure I do. In the privacy of my own home, where I can't harm anyone."

I glanced at the photo of Goggins's cheerless-looking family on the desk and couldn't help wondering how harmless his in-home drinking bouts actually were.

"I don't have a lot of history with the Takalos," I said. "But I'm a parent, too, and I can imagine how they must be feeling right now. Frightened, lost, grief-stricken. So I want to do anything I can to help them."

"Well," he said, "us small-town rubes are honored to have your big-city expertise."

"It can't hurt, can it? I used to *be* a cop."

"Ah, yeah," he said, and turned his back on me to walk stiffly around behind his desk to his chair. "*Used* to."

So I was on my own, with no help from the Cross Village constabulary. I wasn't surprised. Police departments everywhere react to private investigators with either mild irritation or high dudgeon, and I supposed with Goggins I'd come off on the better end.

But the long drive and the tragic faces of Frank and Wanda Takalo had knotted the muscles in my shoulders, and I decided to stop and have a beer before heading south to Petoskey, a warm motel room, and with any luck at all, a good steak.

The wind mourned a loud dirge, and tiny snowdrops peppered my face as I walked into the rustic saloon on Cross Village's main street. The grinning faces on the totem poles outside seemed to be gritting their teeth against the elements.

The moment I opened the door, all conversation ceased, and more than a dozen heads turned to observe my entrance.

This was not some fancy tourist cocktail lounge with piped-in music and pretty servers, but a bucket-of-blood local tavern that reeked of beer, cigarette smoke, sweat, and the echoes of long- and recent-past fistfights and knife brawls. It was well patronized even in the late-afternoon doldrums. The customers were all male, mostly middle-aged and up, and from what I could tell, all Native Americans. I was pretty sure any stranger would have caused a ripple, but I was still discomfited by having every eye on me.

I walked to the bar in that self-conscious way people affect when they know they are being watched, and sat down on a stool just opposite the door. The bartender, who had long black pigtails and a physique like a fire hydrant, took his time meandering over to me, and instead of asking me what I wanted, folded his arms across his chest and leaned against the back bar. He might have been thirty or sixty; I couldn't tell because he was missing quite a few of his front teeth, and his face looked as if it had been deboned like a chicken breast, leaving a prominent nose and lips like those of a rubber mask.

"I'd like a Stroh's," I said. "No glass." In the unnatural quiet my voice sounded in my own head like the blare of the public address announcer in Gund Arena.

The bartender glared at me. Since he didn't know that straight-from-the-bottle was my wont, he probably assumed that I didn't trust the cleanliness of his glassware, and was highly offended. He spun on his heel without a word and fished a Stroh's from the cooler, setting it in front of me with a resounding thump. He didn't bother removing the cap. I had to twist it off myself.

"Thanks," I said.

He didn't move, didn't blink, and didn't tell me how much the beer cost. I took a fiver from my pocket and put it on the bar; he took it, rang up a "No Sale" on the vintage cash register, and put it in the drawer.

No change. Five dollars was a pretty high ticket for a Stroh's.

Behind and around me, talk had begun again, albeit in whispers and droning murmurs. I did manage to overhear a "What the fuck's he doing *here*?" but chose to ignore it.

I took a long pull on the beer, and even though it was icy cold, it generated a warmth down in the pit of my stomach, where I needed it most.

After I'd been sitting there awhile, I dared a glance around the room. Even though the customers had resumed their own private conversations, almost everyone was still looking at me. I returned my eyes to the top of the bar in front of me. I wasn't intimidated, but I wasn't looking for trouble, either.

Nevertheless, it managed to find me.

About five minutes later, the front door flew open, the wicked Lake Michigan wind banging it hard against the wall. It stayed open.

I flicked my eyes toward the mirror behind the bar, which revealed three twenty something Indian men standing in the doorway in that aggressive posture of young hotheads spoiling for a fight. And they were looking directly at me, their eyes burning holes in the back of my neck. They didn't move for a long while.

None of them had dressed quite warmly enough for the occasion. One wore a denim jacket over a flannel shirt, one wore a short red and black checkered wool outer shirt, and the youngest and shortest of the three wore a Detroit Lions Starter jacket that, like the Lions themselves, had seen better days. A billed, checkered cap with earflaps sat at a cockeyed angle on his head. He stood a few steps in front of the others, who flanked him like Roman janissaries protectively surrounding a centurion. Just in case there was doubt in anyone's mind as to who was the Alpha Wolf.

"Hey, close the fucking door!" the bartender hollered. "You're letting all the cold air in."

The one in denim kicked the door shut. It cut off the shriek of the wind, but I can't say it made the atmosphere in there any more comfortable.

The young guy came forward to stand right next to me. The top of his head was several inches lower than mine—and I was sitting down. He was looking straight at my profile, while I regarded his in the mirror.

"Whose car is that outside?" he said, loudly enough for everyone to hear, but it was plain he was speaking to me. "With the Ohio plates on it?"

I turned my head to look at him; he was standing too close to me, taking up some of my personal space. His skin was dry and lifeless looking, the way skin gets when it's toasted by constant cigarette smoke and basted from within by fast food and bad wine.

I leaned forward from the waist as if I were going to kiss him, and it got the desired result, because it backed him up a step or two. "That would be mine."

He stopped backpedaling and set up a beachhead at his position of retreat, widening his stance a little and stretching his neck high. "What's Cuyahoga mean? On the license plate?"

"That's the county where I live," I answered. I thought about telling him that Cuyahoga was an Indian word meaning "crooked river," but it probably wasn't derived from the language of his particular tribe, and I didn't want to get into a cultural pissing contest with him, so I let it go.

"What's that? Cleveland?"

"That's right," I said.

"You from Cleveland?" he demanded.

"What was your first clue?"

He didn't like that. He glanced to his right, and I heard feet shuffling uncertainly behind me, watching the reflection of his two buddies as they began moving a few steps toward me.

"Yeah? Well, what are you doing here?"

"I'm *trying* to drink my beer," I said.

He squared his shoulders so he'd look a little bigger. It didn't work, and unfortunately there was no apple box within reach for him to stand on. "I mean Cross Village. What are you doing in Cross Village?"

"Minding my own business," I said. "Which is always a good idea."

His hands hung at his sides, and I watched as his fists doubled. The two men behind me stirred again, too.

"Take it easy, Ben," the bartender said.

The kid, Ben, didn't even look at him. "Fuck you, Yank," he said. He kept glaring at me. "That's your answer?"

"I came up here to get some fudge."

"The fudge store is closed in the wintertime."

"Ooops. My bad."

"I think you better tell me who you are, man," Ben said, moving within kissing range again in this aggressive and relentless flirtation.

"I think you better get out of my face."

Whatever response that might have triggered died a-borning as the bartender, Yank, stepped up onto some sort of shelf behind the bar and leaned his big head and shoulders between us to form a barrier, a DMZ. "Whatever this is, Ben, take it outside. Hear me?"

The kid was uncertain for a moment. Our confrontation had once again riveted everyone's attention, and there wasn't a sound in the room besides the dysfunctional buzzing of the neon COORS sign. He knew these people, and I suppose he had some face to save. Finally he shoved his balled fists into the pockets of the Lions jacket. "Yeah. Outside. Good idea, Yank."

Despite that, the boy didn't move for a few seconds longer. He stood nose to nose with me, and I tried not to find it ludicrous. I was much bigger than he, and he must have known that without his two buddies riding shotgun, I could have squashed him like a cockroach. And even factoring them into the equation, I wasn't very alarmed; they were all twenty years younger than I, or more, but they looked soft, only partway formed and used up at the same time. I doubted if I'd even work up a sweat.

But I just didn't *feel* like getting into a brawl for no good reason. Not today.

I finally made the kid called Ben blink, but if that bothered him, he shook it off and moved casually to the door as if it were his own idea. "I'll see *you* later, Cleveland," he said, and the three of them went outside.

Somewhere in the room a chair scraped against the floor. Otherwise, my audience remained silent, watching, waiting for the next act, and I realized it was my turn again. I said to the bartender, "What was that all about?"

His shoulders moved a fraction of an inch; I translated it as a shrug.

"Who's the kid?"

He didn't answer.

An old man sitting with three companions at a table against the wall called out, "That's Ben Crawfoot. And his brothers." His voice crackled with phlegm, as if he hadn't spoken in weeks.

"Safety in numbers, is that the idea?" I kept looking at Yank. "They're going to wait for me outside?"

He considered it as he might one of life's great, puzzling philosophical mysteries. Then he nodded.

"It's cold out there."

His head bobbed again, and it struck me that if anyone was keeping conversational score between Yank and me, I was ahead thirty–love.

"Why?"

Another hike of the shoulders, this time pronounced enough that I could identify it for what it was.

"I don't suppose I could talk you into calling the cops before this gets really ugly, could I, Yank?"

He regarded me impassively. "No phone." But his eyes involuntarily flickered to the deep hallway at one end of the room, which led to the rest rooms and, undoubtedly, a pay phone.

"Could you bring me another Stroh's, then?"

The rubbery lips flapped. "We're all out," he said. This time the shrug was broader, more pronounced.

My fingernail picked at the label on the bottle in front of me. I'd hoped that, the windchill factor outside being what it was, if I kept them waiting out there long enough they'd get cold and go home. But there was a limit to the amount of time I could nurse an almost empty bottle of Stroh's.

I lit a cigarette, not because I wanted one, particularly; just to give me something to do with my hands. Yank watched the process, then moved off to the other end of the room to serve someone else.

Talk in the bar had resumed, but lower in tone and more intense, like the hum inside a hive of hornets. Similar in feeling to the emotional electricity that crackles through the stands at Jacobs Field before a playoff game. My skin prickled from it.

I couldn't figure out why the Crawfoot brothers wanted to pick a fight with me. Surely it wasn't simply because I was white; even a small town off the main highway like Cross Village got its share of in-season tourists that kept the economy afloat, and I didn't think the locals were in the habit of confronting and threatening them. There had to be something else, but I didn't know what it could be.

I imagined I'd find out soon enough.

I smoked the Winston slowly, and when it had burned down to within half an inch of the filter, I stubbed it out in the plastic bowl-shaped ashtray in front of me. With a nod at Yank, I swung off the barstool, zipped up my jacket, and slipped on my leather gloves. I flexed my fingers, hearing them pop a little, and sighed. Then, to the rapt attention of my audience, I turned and walked out the door into a blast of icy wind.

They were at my car, waiting for me. Ben sat insolently on the fender, Bogarting a cigarette. His brothers just leaned. When they caught sight of me they both looked at him to make the first move.

"Get off my car, Ben," I said.

Ben took one last puff and flipped the cigarette toward me; it might have hit me if the wind hadn't caught it and spun it away into the middle of the street. He hopped down, his legs apart, his feet flat on the ground.

"Before somebody gets hurt," I continued, "why don't you tell me what this is all about?"

"You know what it's all about, man," Ben said.

"If I knew, I wouldn't be asking."

"What are you doing here, anyway?"

"I'm visiting friends."

"What friends?" he scoffed.

"I don't think that's any of your business."

"We're making it our business." he said. "We don't want you here. We're gonna make sure you never come back."

They tried to form a ring around me, but I moved sideways, crab fashion, so that my back was to my own car; that way, none of them could get behind me and pin my arms.

"I don't know what your problem is with me, Ben," I said, "but I can guarantee you that if you guys don't back off, someone's going to go to the hospital."

"It's gonna be you, man."

"Don't be too sure."

For a moment nobody moved; we made what certainly must have been a ridiculous tableau there in the blustery cold with the silent totem poles as our audience. The Crawfoot brother in the denim jacket had long, shoulder-length hair, and it was blowing around his face like that of a model in an arty shampoo commercial.

Tired of waiting, I finally said, "I've got things to do, Ben, so make your move if you're going to." The wind took my words and carried them away down the street.

As I had figured, Ben made the first advance, taking a few steps toward me. His fists were about chest-high, spread wide—not the ideal posture for a fistfight. I snaked out a fast left jab at his unprotected face, connecting sharply with his nose. It wasn't that hard a blow, but it snapped his head back and buckled his knees a little.

He blinked, completely startled, and a thin ribbon of blood trickled out of his nostril. He shook his head and wiped it away, looking at the smear on his hand with a kind of wonder.

"Fucker," he said breathlessly.

His brothers started closing in. I turned to face the bigger of the two, vowing that my next punch was going to be harder and do a lot more damage.

And then there was a squeal of rubber as an ancient Ford pickup truck roared around the corner and came to a screeching stop in the middle of the street.

Eddie Ettawageshik jumped from the driver's seat, leaving the door open.

"What in the hell is going on here?" he said.

Chapter Twelve

Forty-five minutes later we were back at Frank and Wanda Takalo's house again, Eddie Ettawageshik and I. This time I had accepted Wanda's hospitality and was sipping a cup of strong, bitter coffee; this time the three Crawfoot brothers were with us.

The small living room was overcrowded and claustrophobic, everyone forced to sit or stand too close to everyone else. The Crawfoots had all taken their jackets off and Ben had removed his cap. There was a wad of toilet paper jammed up into his right nostril, one of a series of them that had finally made his nose stop bleeding.

"I'm still a little confused, Ben," I said. I had heard a jumble of explanations on the street outside the bar, and quite a few more in the car on the way over here, but they were all so incredible, so unbelievable, I wanted to get them into my head with some sense of order and logic. "Why don't you just start at the beginning?"

"Already told you, man," he said.

"Tell me again."

He sighed, put-upon, and looked to the low plaster ceiling for succor. Then he leaned forward in the straight chair he was sitting on, putting his elbows on his knees. The Takalos and Eddie seemed eager to hear his story, too.

"Okay," Ben said. "About three weeks ago there were these two strange guys show up, hanging around town for two or three days, and nobody knows who they are or why they're here. Ohio license plates on their car, just like yours. 'Cuyahoga,' okay?"

"White or Indian?"

He looked almost disdainful, or as disdainful as he *could* look with bloody toilet paper hanging out of his nose. "White men."

"You remember what kind of car it was?"

"No, man, I didn't pay no attention."

"But you paid attention to the license plates?"

"I don't know why, just kind of stuck in my head, you know?"

"I don't suppose the license number stuck in your head, too?"

"Nah, why would it?" he said. "I didn't know who they were then."

"Was it an American car? Do you happen to remember what color?"

He fingered his sore nose gingerly. It wasn't broken, but I'd given him quite a pop, and it was already turning purple. I imagined he'd have two black eyes in the morning. "Dark. I think it was a minivan. Dodge or Ford, something like that."

It wasn't much, but I scribbled it down in my notebook, glad that we were in Michigan, where the automotive-powered economy tends to make people more aware of makes and models of cars than in any other state of the union.

"You didn't talk to them? You didn't approach them the way you did me?"

He looked abashed. "I didn't have no reason to—then. Hey, look, I didn't know you was helping out Frank and Wanda. I thought . . ."

"I know what you thought, Ben. It's okay," I said. "Sorry about your nose, too. How's it doing?"

He crinkled it and winced. "Shit," he said ruefully.

"So tell me some more about these guys from Ohio."

"They were here two, three days, and nobody seemed to know why. Until one day they show up at my cousin Marie's house. Her and her husband, Louie Fightmaster, like I told you before back at Yank's. They just had a baby, too. A girl, three months old, okay?"

"And . . . ?"

"And they offered her money," he said.

"Ten thousand dollars."

"Yeah."

"For what?"

He took a deep breath. "To sell them the baby."

Wanda moaned softly and shifted her position on one end of the sofa, bringing her knees up toward her chest. I gave her a sympathetic smile. I felt like moaning, too. It had hit me like a kick in the stomach.

It was medieval. Barbaric. Buying and selling children. Hard to believe it was actually happening here in modern, evolved America at the dawn of the twenty-first century.

Eddie said, "This is the first we knew about the Fightmasters, Mr. Jacovich. You think there might be a connection?"

"I'd bet the farm on it," I said. "Ben, when you heard about little Andrew going missing, why didn't you—or your cousin—come forward and tell someone what happened to your cousin Marie?"

He looked away, embarrassed. "I didn't know about Andrew till now."

"In a small town like this?"

He mumbled something, too softly for any of us to hear.

"Excuse me?" I said.

He raised his head along with his voice. "I *said* I been in jail all this past week, okay?"

He looked at his two older brothers. "All of us. We got drunk . . ."

"So you never heard about the kidnapping?"

He shook his head.

I turned to Eddie and the Takalos. "And you never heard about these Ohio guys trying to buy Marie's baby either?"

"Not a word," Eddie said.

"I think someone ought to tell the police about it. The Fightmasters should report it, especially since little Andrew was taken."

Eddie slumped against the wall. "We don't like going to the police in this town. Mr. Jacovich. We Indians don't get much of a hearing."

"Eddie, I understand prejudice, but the law is there for everybody."

"Tell that to Chief Goggins."

"You want me to? I will, you know."

"No," Eddie said, perhaps too emphatically. Then he softened the sharp edges of his tone. "Goggins has been kept in the loop. He's working on it."

Not very hard, I thought, but I decided not to push it for the moment. "These men who wanted to buy your cousin's baby, Ben—did they say why?"

Ben Crawfoot's face was blank, slack, confused. "You oughta ask Marie about that. She's the one who talked to them."

"I will," I said. "Can you set it up for me?"

With his finger he gingerly touched the tissue in his nostril, then pulled it out and examined it. The blood on it had dried. He put it in his pocket and sniffed. "I guess," he said.

"Good. I'll be back here first thing in the morning. I'll want to see her then. All right?"

He hesitated awhile. "I guess," he said again.

He wasn't giving me very much encouragement. Nor was anybody else. Wanda and Frank Takalo were more upset than before, if that was possible, and even Eddie was more glum than I'd ever seen him.

He walked me out to my car.

"Lucky for me you came along when you did to break up that fight, Eddie."

"From the looks of Ben Crawfoot's nose, I'd say lucky for *him*."

"Well, at least it's not broken. And what he told me about his cousins is probably really important, so it was all worth it." I shook my head as I opened the car door. "I just can't believe that in a community this small, no one heard about these baby buyers. And since it seems so obvious that the two things are related, it's not logical to me that the Fightmasters wouldn't have heard about Andrew's kidnapping and come forward."

"Well . . ." He cleared his throat. "They kind of keep to themselves, you know? Louie Fightmaster is a funny kind of guy."

"Funny how?"

He made a wry face. "You'll meet him tomorrow and see for yourself."

"I want you there with me, Eddie," I said. "He and his wife might feel easier about talking to me if you are."

His head bobbed. "Sure."

I turned sideways to him so the wind would blow against my back. "Okay, what's the deal with Goggins?"

"What do you mean?" he said, looking away.

"People come here trying to buy children, a baby is kidnapped, and nobody wants to talk to the police. Why?"

"The only time Goggins ever wants to see an Indian is on his way out of town for good, that's all. He's lived here all his life and he's been an Indian-hater all his life, too. He's seen too many John Wayne movies."

"You'd think," I said, "that if he hated Indians so much, he'd move somewhere else."

Eddie pulled the corners of his lips back in a rueful smile. "He wouldn't want to give us the satisfaction."

I shook my head; I didn't understand people at all sometimes.

"How do you read this, Mr. Jacovich?"

"What?"

"The baby. What happened to him."

"I'm not sure," I said. "But if Andrew was taken by the same people who tried to buy the Fightmasters' little girl, it gives me hope that he hasn't come to any harm."

He looked quizzical.

"We can rule out a psychopath, in other words. Insane murderers don't come around trying to buy babies."

"Who does?" he said.

"I don't know, Eddie. Maybe I'll find out tomorrow," I said. I got in, shut the door, and turned the key in the ignition, sending an icy gust out of the vents from the still-cold engine. I shivered; it was going to take a long while for the interior of the car to get warm again.

My interior, too.

* * *

There is a Days Inn along the highway south of Cross Village. There is a Days Inn almost everywhere you turn in the United States, just like there is an Applebee's and a Chili's and a T.G.I. Friday's in which to eat the same food they're serving in their other branches three thousand miles away, and a Red Roof Inn and a Wal-Mart and all those interchangeable hamburger joints that dull the palate and deaden the soul. Americans have become such a timid lot that when they venture far from home they want the assurance of exactly the same kind of food and service and hotel room and ambience they could get just down the street from their own houses. Thus the homogenization of America continues, and the rare small town that manages to retain its individuality usually does so because it's so economically inconsequential that none of the big chains want to bother with it.

So small-town life sputters and dies, and the "greater metro" areas reach out their concrete fingers of highways, bulldoze all the trees and in their place build suburbs and subdivisions that all look alike, and then name the resultant streets and lanes and ovals and runs and circles after the departed trees.

But I checked into the Days Inn anyway, for the same reason anyone else does; the rooms are clean and dependable and convenient and reasonably priced, and they generally serve pretty good free donuts and coffee in the lobby for breakfast.

The first thing I did when I got to my room, besides scoping out the view from the window and finding that, as all hotel rooms invariably do, it looked out on a vista of gravel roof, was to take a nice hot shower. It seemed as if I had been cold since lunchtime.

Toweling off, I realized that not much could be done here in Michigan by way of enlisting the local constabulary to help the Takalos. Chief Goggins was some piece of work, but I'd run into small-town cops like him before. While most of them are hard-working and honest, there are always a few who run their jurisdictions as their own personal dictatorships, and woe betide those ethnic minorities or socially marginal types whose well-being and interests fell outside the lines. I'd have to wait until I got home to Cleveland.

Which reminded me that in the real world, I did have an assignment from a paying client, and while viewed alongside the kidnapping of little Andrew Takalo, Armand Treusch's suspicions about David Ream didn't seem particularly riveting or vital, he was paying me good money—and I *was* running a business.

I dug my address book out of my overnight bag and, sitting on the side of the bed closest to the motel room's rather ineffective heating vent wearing clean shorts and a T-shirt that did little to help me stay warm, I called Suzanne Davis out in Lake County. When she answered, she sounded a little rushed, which she explained by telling me she was in the midst of cooking dinner; she had recently started dating a new Mr. Right and was going to impress him that evening with her culinary skills. A standing rib roast, she announced. The thought of it made me hungry.

"I don't want to interrupt you, Suzanne," I said. "I can call back later."

"Later," she said with a smile in her voice, "you might *really* be interrupting. With any luck. Wait, let me get my notes."

She put the phone down, and I stretched my feet out to put my toes directly into the trickle of warm air that blew weakly out of the vent. I was reminded of the sadly ineffective heaters in the old beloved Volkswagen Beetles. I flipped open my notebook beside me on the bedspread and clicked open my ballpoint, waiting.

After a moment, she came back.

"This took me a while," she said. "First I tried the big hospitals, naturally. The Cleveland Clinic, Rainbow Babies and Children's, MetroHealth. Came up empty. Then I started calling some of my closely guarded sources and finally wound up hitting pay dirt at this little private children's clinic out in Geauga County."

"Uh-huh."

"I didn't know a soul out there, so it was a damn good thing I could drop the name of my source. You know how hospitals are about giving out information to anyone who doesn't happen to be the patient's Siamese twin."

"Sure," I said. I looked around for a cigarette, and found I'd left my pack on the nightstand on the other side of the bed. I had to stretch to reach it, splaying my fingeres out to claw a book of matches into my hand as well; most of us are now so spoiled by having cordless units with which we can walk all over the house, we feel imprisoned when we have to talk on a phone that's actually connected to a wall.

"Well," she said, unaware of the contortions I was going through, "little Caitlynn Ream is one sick cookie."

I squeezed the receiver between my shoulder and my jawbone as I lit a Winston. "Oh?"

"She was two and a half years old when she was first admitted after going into convulsions one night."

"When was this?" I said.

"Last March. About eleven months ago. You want the exact date?"

"No, not right now. Go on."

"Well, they got her stabilized, and then in a few days they started some tests. After a while they found out she was suffering from a kind of toxicity that they think might have been traceable to some sort of plastic."

"Plastic?"

"Yes," she said, "like from a toy or something."

My skin rippled unpleasantly, and it wasn't from the chill in the motel room. "A toy?"

"That's as near as they could figure," Suzanne Davis said. "You know how little kids always like to put their toys in their mouths."

"But they aren't sure?"

"No way they really can be. But that's what they think."

"Uh-huh. So what happened?"

"They kept her in the hospital for about eighteen days, and then they let her go home, but they've been treating her once a week ever since."

"Treating her?"

"Speech therapy and things like that. There was some brain damage."

"Oh," I said, and all at once I wasn't hungry anymore.

"Might be permanent. They don't know yet."

Thinking of that tiny little doll growing up and spending the rest of her life impaired was twisting my guts into a hard, cold knot. "I see." The cigarette tasted harsh and bitter, and I stubbed it out barely half-smoked. "What's her doctor's name? And her therapist's?"

"The attending physician was a Dr. Rashed," she said, spelling it. "The speech therapist is a Lauren Vasek. But I doubt you could get anything out of either of them. This is confidential patient information."

"Who did *you* get it out of?"

"Somebody in records at that clinic," she said. "Somebody who owed my source a favor."

"You're not going to give me a name?"

"I can't. I promised, okay? Hey, Milan, for giving you what I already did, I think I deserve a parade. Don't push it."

I sighed. "You're right, Suzanne. Thanks."

"Like I told you, don't mention it."

"Well, good luck with your dinner tonight."

She laughed. "I don't know about luck. It'll probably be the exciting kickoff to what will eventually turn out to be just another in a long line of crappy, go-nowhere relationships."

"You sound pretty cynical."

"I'm forty-six years old and three times divorced, Milan. I've come by my cynicism honestly."

"It sounds like it," I said.

"Hey, you've been single for a long time. Don't tell me you aren't cynical, too."

"I'd hate like hell to think so," I said.

But after I hung up the phone, I took a while to ponder that. My three major relationships since my divorce had been difficult, to say the least. Two of them—with Mary Soderberg and Dr. Nicole Archer—had ended badly. And now Connie Haley seemed to be drifting away like an astronaut walking weightless in space, floating just out of my reach as if in some sort of bad dream.

I checked the digital readout on the room's clock radio. It was after six o'clock, and I was sure Connie would be home by now, her clerical chores at the restaurant ending before the customers arrived for dinner. I reached out my hand to call her.

But what was I going to tell her? That I was in Michigan, deeply involved in a death she had begged me to steer clear of, and a kidnapping that was really none of my business, and that three young men wearing redwood-sized chips on their shoulders that afternoon had come within a hair's breadth of seriously altering the bone structure of my face?

I thought not.

So I put it out of my head for the time being, or at least pushed it over into a corner so it wouldn't get in the way of more immediate concerns.

I'm very good at that, at compartmentalizing my feelings, the various segments of my life. I didn't like to talk about my work with my lovers, and Connie's reaction was a shining example of why not. I keep my romantic relationships apart from my sons; I keep my friends, like Rudy Dolsak and Ed Stahl, away from the other people in my life. It just seems easier to deal with all of it that way.

Instead of calling Connie, I dialed Eddie Ettawageshik, who told me that Ben Crawfoot had reluctantly set up an appointment with Louie and Marie Fightmaster for nine-thirty the next morning.

"He wasn't going to do it, Mr. Jacovich. I had to stand over him while he did. I hate to tell you this, but he's not so sure he trusts you yet, and neither are Louie and Marie."

"I don't know whether I trust them either, Eddie. But maybe the Fightmasters can remember something that can point me in the right direction. Otherwise, I'm afraid we're still in the starting blocks."

It was going to be a tough one, I could see that. If a client doesn't completely trust me, if they aren't honest and open about everything, I have to conduct my business almost as though someone had put a paper bag over my head. Maybe there was a hex—an Indian sign—on this particular investigation.

I had planned on roaming the streets of Petoskey in search of a decent place to have dinner; but learning about little Caitlynn Ream had taken away my appetite. Probably later in the evening I'd walk down the hall at the Days Inn and get a candy bar, a bag of chips, and a diet pop out of the vending machines, switch on HBO and watch whatever mindless movie they were showing, and call it a night.

Right at the moment I had two more immediate problems to chew on: the disappearance of Andrew Takalo and the death of his grandfather, and exactly what David Ream was doing with Helen Moise and Consumer Watchdog while he was ostensibly working for Armand Treusch and TroyToy.

There wasn't more I could hope to learn about the kidnapping until after I spoke with Ben Crawfoot's cousins in the morning—*if* they didn't change their minds about seeing me. And David Ream and his grievously ill little girl and Armand Treusch and his toys were in Cleveland, and not much could be done about them until I got back home except to conjecture. And I was doing plenty of that.

One thing struck me, though. Although they were totally unrelated problems, both, in vastly different ways, ultimately had to do with the victimization of children.

Chapter Thirteen

Sleep did not come easily. I never sleep well in hotel room beds, or maybe it was the Reese's Peanut Butter Cup and sour-cream-flavored potato chips marinating in Diet Pepsi in my stomach. More probably sleep was blocked by the twin cases that were gnawing away at the back of my skull, along with the very real worry that Connie Haley might never forgive me this trip to Michigan. Whatever the cause, I tossed and turned violently all night. When I finally rolled to my feet at seven A.M. the bedclothes looked as if the entire offensive line of the Cleveland Browns had had themselves an orgy.

After another shower and dressing in jeans and a plaid shirt in honor of the wintry climate, I started off the morning with coffee and donuts in the lobby of the Days Inn. The donuts were okay—I had a maple-covered one and a cream-filled—but they couldn't hold a candle to Presti's on Mayfield Road in Cleveland's Little Italy. I know that Krispy Kremes and Dunkin' Donuts have their ardent aficionados, but to them I say, "You've never tried Presti's." I worried a bit when Presti's moved down the street a block to newer and more elegant digs, afraid that the donuts would suffer, but I'm pleased to report it didn't happen.

I paid my bill, fully aware that this was on nobody's tab but my own, and comforted only that it was a tax write-off, and headed back north to Cross Village. Once again an anemic sun was struggling vainly to punch its way through the low gray clouds of morning; it had snowed again during the night, blowing wet and heavy across Lake Michigan, and the new drifts thrown up by the pre-dawn snowplows made hulking, surrealist lunarscapes on the landward shoulder of the highway.

My head was stuffed with too many ideas, too many problems. The information I'd gotten from Suzanne Davis about Caitlynn Ream's illness was burning a hole in me, I felt Connie Haley slipping away from between my outstretched finger, and I knew that with every tick of the clock it was going to be harder to find Andrew Takalo and discover what had really happened to his great-grandfather.

By the time I arrived in the village, I desperately wanted another cup of coffee before facing Louie and Marie Fightmaster, but I didn't think it was such a good idea going into Yank's Bar to get it. Instead I stopped at the gas station-cum-souvenir shop at the corner of the village's main street, topped my tank, and purchased some truly misbegotten coffee from the pretty Native American woman wearing a doeskin shirt. It was strong and acidic and hot enough to peel paint, and I sipped it from a cardboard cup whose taste overwhelmed it.

Not fortified enough but having little alternative, I checked Eddie's directions and headed for the home of Ben Crawfoot's cousins on the northern outskirts of Cross Village.

The Takalo house was modest, but compared to Louie and Marie Fightmasters' home it could have been the pleasure dome decreed by Kublai Khan at Xanadu. Constructed of the cheapest possible wood and siding, with a hardscrabble front yard that probably never saw grass during even the greenest of summers, the house seemed to perch precariously on the side of a hill dotted with denuded scrub oak trees, winter-dead thornbushes, and a dented maroon Ford Escort up on blocks like a huge and ugly lawn ornament. Plastic children's toys that might have been there since August were half-buried in the day-old snow. On the porch railing, the hide of a deer had been stretched, anachronistic in the same vista as the TV satellite dish on the roof.

Relieved to note that Eddie Ettawageshik's truck was parked in the driveway, I pulled up behind it and cut the motor, then trudged up the walkway through brown, slushy unshoveled snow to the front door. Inside I could hear small children laughing and yelling and crying over the low murmur of more mature voices and the tinny, artificial talking heads of the TV set. I wiped my feet as best I could on the rough raffia welcome mat, and knocked.

The woman who answered the door was built square and close to the ground, with a lined face and black hair shot through with gray; she looked as if she might be in her middle fifties. Dressed in a man's long-sleeved flannel shirt and faded denim pants, she sucked hungrily on a cigarette as if it were sustenance. It wasn't until she told me she was Marie Fightmaster that I realized she was at least twenty years younger than she appeared.

Two boys and a girl, all under the age of four, romped and tumbled underfoot in the tiny living room, squabbling over cheap toys and a few Oreo cookies whose package-mates were smeared all over their faces, they occasionally came dangerously and obliviously close to the glowing space heater near the baseboard. There was a battered infant seat, at the moment unoccupied, at one corner of the sofa. Big and broad as I am, I seemed too large for the space. Eddie Ettawageshik came out of one of a pair of kitchen chairs lined up against one wall and stepped forward to introduce my host.

Louie Fightmaster was tall and lean and hard, with prominent Mongolian cheekbones like apples dominating a long basset-hound face that looked as though it had been molded by a small child out of modeling clay, all lumps and whorls. I got the idea that smiling was not among its repertoire of expressions. He had the dry, grayish skin that often resulted from heavy drinking. His teeth were yellowed, and the deep crinkles at the corners of his eyes were further accentuated as he squinted against the pungent smoke that rose from the home-rolled cigarette in the side of his mouth. I estimated he was carrying only about eight percent of body fat. He didn't shake hands.

No offer of coffee or any other sort of hospitality was forthcoming. The Fightmasters were sullen (Marie) and hostile (Louie) and ear-splittingly noisy (the kids), and for a brief moment I questioned my good judgment in coming here; I questioned it for even getting involved with these people from another state, another culture, another world. But an old man was dead and a baby was missing, and despite what Connie might have believed, for me my presence was not optional.

There wasn't time for the usual get-acquainted niceties, because right after Eddie introduced him, Louie said accusingly, "So you're the one who broke Ben Crawfoot's nose."

"I didn't break it," I answered. "I bloodied it, though."

"He's just a kid."

"A kid who wanted to take me apart. I just made sure he didn't."

"You don't like Indians." It wasn't a question.

"If I didn't like Indians, I wouldn't be here."

Eddie shifted his feet uneasily and looked from Louie to me. "Come on, Louie, Mr. Jacovich is on our side. He came all the way from Cleveland to help."

"Cleveland." The word carried no judgment with it. "Well, what does he want with us?"

"Mr. Fightmaster," I said, "you know that little Andrew Takalo has been kidnapped, don't you?"

Marie Fightmaster cleared her throat. "We didn't know nothing about that until last night when Ben and Eddie told us."

Eddie nodded a discreet affirmation.

"I think that might have some connection to the people who tried to buy your baby."

"I threw them out," Louie said. "That was the end of it."

"Maybe not," I said. "If I could just ask you a couple of questions . . ."

"Shit," Louie said.

His wife took a step forward. "We wanna help. Ya know, the Takalos are kind of like our neighbors . . ."

"It's not our business," Louie said.

"Hey, Louie." Eddie took a tentative step forward. He was twenty years Louie Fightmaster's junior, but the older man could easily have broken him in two. His cause, however, must have emboldened him. "A little baby is missing here. And my granddad is dead."

Louie sat down on the other kitchen chair. He considered the matter for a long while before making his decision. "Then go ahead," he said, defeated and resigned, "ask your fucking questions."

Not the most auspicious of beginnings, I thought, but I had to play the hand the way it was dealt. I felt like an intruder, the elephant in the living room; no one had invited me to sit down yet, or to take off my coat. I didn't want to take notes; I thought that might intimidate them. So I simply turned to Marie, thinking she would probably be more forthcoming than her husband. "The best way, I think, would be to tell me from the beginning what happened. How did these men happen to come to see you?"

She shrugged. "I don't know. They just showed up here one day."

"In the morning," Louie put in.

"They said they were working for some people who couldn't have any children and wanted to adopt one."

"Did they give you their names?"

"Um . . . Yeah, but I don't remember. You know how when somebody says their name you don't remember it unless it's important? And I didn't think this was gonna be important. You know?"

I nodded. "How about a business card? Did they leave anything with you?"

"Nuh-uh," she said.

"They must have introduced themselves, though. You don't remember their names?"

She screwed up her mouth, thinking. "The redhead guy, I think his name was Bohunk or something."

I made a note of that, an eastern European name. "Okay," I said. "And then what?"

"And they said they knew times were tough, what with Louie not working and all . . ."

"How did they know that?"

"They didn' fucking say," Louie growled, bitterness twisting his features into something ugly and dangerous. "But they didn' have to. We're on the welfare. They coulda looked it up. *Anybody* coulda looked it up."

"And I don' know how they found out, but they knew we had a brand-new little baby . . ." With a jerk of her head she indicated the rear of the house. "She's asleep right now."

"Uh-huh."

"So anyways, they said they'd give us ten thousand dollars if we was willing to give them the baby to adopt."

Monstrous, I thought. Ten thousand dollars was a fortune to people like the Fightmasters.

"They said she'd be sure to go to a nice home, to people who'd love her." Marie's lip quivered.

"They said," her husband added, his eyes glittering with rage and humiliation, "that she'd be better off with rich people who could take care of her better." His mouth was a thin, hard line of mortification.

"And then what?"

"Then I threw them out of the fucking house," Louie said forcefully. "They seen too many fucking movies about poor dumb Indians, think they can come in here and buy an Indian baby like a sack of groceries! I grabbed them by their dirty necks and threw them out in the snow! Cocksucking, motherfucking bastards!"

Marie looked down at her wide-eyed children. "Louie, don't talk like that in front of the kids," she said, embarrassed.

"Yeah, an' fuck you too, Marie!" he flared.

Embarrassment turned to pugnaciousness as she put her fists on her hips and swiveled to face him. "Hey, asswipe!"

"Mrs. Fightmaster," I said, trying to cut through the tension.

"What!" she snapped. She was still looking at her husband, and he was standing spraddle-legged and combat-ready as if waiting for her to charge at him. The children had grown unusually quiet and had skittered across the floor on their little bottoms and were now pressed up against the wall, looking up at their parents with big, dark, heartbreaking eyes. I got the feeling this was not the first time similar scenarios had been played out in the Fightmasters' living room.

"Can you describe the two men for me?"

That seemed to relax Marie, at least for the moment. Her shoulders slumped, her hands dropping down to her sides. Louie still looked as if he was expecting a cavalry raid, but he stepped back a few steps, winding up next to Eddie, who flickered a nervous look at him, visibly uncomfortable with the proximity.

"Um," Marie Fightmaster said.

"Whatever you can remember."

She crossed her arms under her breasts. "They were both wearing suits and ties, I know that, cuz you hardly see anybody aroun' here wearing a tie. There was one of them I can't hardly remember at all, cuz he didn't talk so much. Like almost six feet tall, reddish hair, a real pale face." She looked at me and laughed nervously. "I didn' mean that as a joke," she explained.

"Okay," I said, and smiled back at her.

"The other one, the one who did most of the talkin', he was shorter." She held out one hand above her head, parallel to the ground, indicating someone who might have been around five foot eight. "A younger guy, maybe thirty or so, but he was awready losin' his hair a little. Dark hair." Her face brightened. "Oh yeah. And he had a cockeye, too."

"A what?"

"Ya know. One eye goes this way," she said, pointing right at me, "and one goes like this." This time she pointed off to her right at a ninety-degree angle. "A cockeye."

"And they were wearing suits?"

"Ya," she said. "Well, maybe they was suits and maybe just a jacket and slacks, ya know, I didn't notice that much, but both with ties. The redhead guy he was wearing a parka over his suit, which I thought looked sorta funny, an' the other guy had like a raincoat, ya know, the kind that has a belt." She laughed. "They was two real pussies, looked like to me."

"Two pussy white guys," her husband put in.

I turned to him now that he seemed marginally more amenable. "So you threw them out of the house?"

He nodded. "That's when I seen their car and seen they was from Ohio."

"From Cuyahoga County?"

He jerked his head down toward his chest once and then back up, which I interpreted as a nod. "That's an Indian word, I think. Cuyahoga. That's how come I remembered it."

"Did you tell the police about them, then?"

He snorted. That, I assumed, was a laugh.

"Did you tell anybody?"

He looked away, out the small living room window at the winter-blackened trees. "I dunno," he said. "I mighta. I was in Yank's that night later, talkin' to some people. I mighta. I got pretty drunk, so I don't remember it real good."

"What people?" I said.

"What people what?"

"What people were you talking to that night?"

"Shit." He wagged his large head from side to side. "There was a lotta different guys in there."

"You don't remember who?"

"The regulars," he said, annoyance creeping back into his tone. "Same guys that's ally's there. Yank. A couple a the Crawfoot boys. Jim Overshiner. And old Joseph Ettawageshik."

My stomach fluttered as I met Eddie Ettawageshik's glance. Some things were starting to come together.

I arranged to meet Eddie at the same gas station where I'd had the coffee earlier. We sat in my car with the motor running and the heater giving what comfort it could.

"So your grandfather knew about these two guys, and that they were from Cleveland, or at least from Cuyahoga County," I said.

"It looks that way."

"And two days later Andrew was taken."

He nodded.

"And he decided to take matters into his own hands and go to Cleveland to find him?"

"That's the way Granddad was. He was the head of the family, I guess he saw it as his responsibility."

"Did he feel the same way about the police that Louie does?"

"He would never go to the police, no matter what. Besides, I'm sure he figured the local police couldn't do anything."

"But kidnapping is federal. The FBI . . ."

Eddie shook his head. "Granddad wouldn't know anything about that. He never went past the seventh grade, Mr. Jacovich. He didn't read newspapers. He didn't look at television. My folks told me he used to listen to the radio back in the old days. Jack Benny, *The Green Hornet,* things like that. But he was a very simple man, very spiritual, who stayed in his village and lived among his own people. So when trouble came to his family, I guess his first instinct was to take care of it himself."

"But to just show up in Cleveland like that," I said. "It's a big city. How did he know where to go?"

He rubbed his face. "You've got me."

The car heater was pumping out warm air, and Eddie put his hands near the vent and rubbed them together. "What are you going to do now?" he said.

"Go back to Cleveland. That seems to be where the path is leading."

He sniffed. "I wish I could do something."

"You can," I said. "By asking more questions, talking to people. See if you can find out if any other families were solicited to sell their babies. Find some sort of connection, if you can. Anything, even the smallest thread. Get a notebook and take notes, or better still . . ."

I leaned across him, opened the glove compartment, and extracted a little microcassette recorder. "Here," I said. "This way you won't have to rely on your memory so much."

He smiled. "I can't think of too many of my people around here who would talk into something like that."

"Put it in your shirt pocket. That way they'll never know."

Uncertainty creased his forehead. "I wouldn't feel right about that. I'd feel like a sneak."

"How will you feel," I said, "if Frank and Wanda never get their baby back?"

A wave of pain swept over his face like clouds enveloping the moon. He reached out and took the recorder from my hand and put it in his jacket pocket.

"Good man," I said.

I said good-bye to Eddie and pulled out into the street, my tires slipping on the frozen slush; the snow removal in Cross Village was as might be expected. As I drove down the main street, past Yank's bar and the shuttered fudge shop, I wondered if I would ever see it again. Probably not, I thought, and for some reason I was saddened by the finality of that.

It wasn't long before I was on the highway heading home.

The asphalt was slick and treacherous on the way back east; cold and ice had broken down several potholes, and I had to drive carefully or else risk a flat tire or a broken rim. The tightness and tension were like a hot poker across my shoulders, and every so often I would rotate my head around and listen to the unpleasant popping sounds in my neck. What with side trips off the freeway for both lunch and dinner—since I refuse to eat at the chain restaurants or fast-food joints along the side of the road—I didn't get back to Cleveland until about nine-thirty that night.

As the downtown skyline rose up ahead of me, with the lighted tops of the Key Tower and Terminal Tower mystically hazy through a light, fluffy snowfall, I was struck by what a different world this was from the one I had just returned from, the milieu in which the Takalos and Fightmasters lived. They would be as alien and out-of-place here in a bustling urban landscape as I had been in Cross Village.

It must have been dizzying and threatening for old Joseph Ettawageshik, who'd never strayed more than hollering distance from the place where he had been born, to be sitting on that cold bench across from my apartment and watching more traffic pass by in a day than he probably saw at home in six months. And for him to die there, far from the friends and family he knew and loved, was the saddest thing of all.

In a strange way, I found myself *hoping* that his death had been somehow meaningful, at least connected with his quest to find and rescue his great grandson, and that he had not died for nothing more than to feed the temporary crack habit of one of the city's night creatures.

I had been doing a lot of thinking on my long drive, about both of the problems that were on my professional plate, and had eventually formulated a plan of action for each of them. I admit I'd given more thought to finding Andrew Takalo than to figuring out what kind of a game David Ream was running on TroyToy; side by side they hardly compared.

But Armand Treusch had hired me, and my professional ethics wouldn't allow me to let his problems fall between the cracks. I especially wanted to get all the information I could on Caitlynn Ream's condition, too.

But that was a given, beyond my abilities to fix. The Takalo baby's whereabouts and safety were not, so that was what nagged at me while I droned along Interstate 90, heading for home.

It was blowing cold when I parked my car behind my apartment building, but compared to the biting wind that sweeps up the bluff from Lake Mighigan and across the unprotected plain of Cross Village, it felt as if I'd relocated to a warmer climate. I picked up two days' worth of mail from my box in the vestibule and climbed the stairs. From behind Mr. Maltz's door I heard his television, blaring a Cavs game; he was a die-hard sports fan for all his ninety-odd years, and on the rare occasions when we met in the second-floor hallway he would offer his opinions on the Cavs, the Indians, the new Browns, often despairing of the overall greed of professional athletes and team owners alike.

I knew that some day, sadly, Mr. Maltz would not be there to bend my ear about sports, and as I put my key into the lock, I wondered whether old Joseph would have been that full of energy and brio had he been allowed to live out his natural life span.

Once inside and shed of my outer garments, I headed for the

refrigerator. I needed a nice, cold beer to smooth out the kinks of a long, hard journey, and to put into perspective the events of the last few days.

I jacked up the thermostat, threw on one of my several Kent State sweatshirts, and went into my den, put a CD of Cleveland-born saxophonist Ernie Krivda into the player, grabbed a pad of yellow legal paper and a pen from the top of my messy desk, and gulped down almost half the beer without taking a breath. Then I settled into my soft leather chair; that's where I do my best thinking.

Upon reflection, the trip to Michigan had turned out to be time well spent. The Fightmasters' experience with the baby buyers had shined a new light on everything, and I began making notes on some of the thoughts that had crossed my mind in the car.

Somebody in Cleveland was dealing in black market babies, that much seemed clear. Indian babies. If they couldn't buy one, they evidently had no qualms about stealing one.

But how did that work? I wondered.

You couldn't just sell someone a baby the way you might your snowblower. There had to be records, legal documents, adoption papers. If you can't sell a used car without registering it with the state Bureau of Motor Vehicles, surely there were strict rules about the transference of the custody of a human being.

Not that kidnappers lose a lot of sleep over rules.

The trouble was, Andrew Takalo had disappeared so recently, chances were great that there was no paper trail yet. I made a note to check adoption records anyway, but I held out little hope.

If there were to be papers filed, that meant the fine hand of a lawyer had to be in the mix somewhere. I levered myself up and went to the cupboard where I keep the Cleveland Metropolitan Area classified directory. When I brought it back to my chair to check it, I discovered the listings for "Attorneys" ran for seventy-eight pages.

At that rate, Andrew Takalo, or whatever his name would be then, was going to be in medical school before I found him.

Chapter Fourteen

I woke up with a scratchiness in my throat, the gift of February. I fumbled around in the medicine cabinet and found a couple of throat lozenges that had outlived their expiration date, and let them dissolve in my mouth. Before I even got dressed, I checked my telephone messages at the office. The only ones of any consequence were from Armand Treusch, three of them, escalating in unpleasantness from first to last, in which he bellowed like a warthog because I had disappeared for two days. His complaints were laced with profanity.

"When a man is taking my fucking money," he roared on the final message, "I expect a little action, a little loyalty. I don't know what the fuck is so important that you had to leave town, but in the meantime I've got a nigger in the woodpile here that you're supposed to be doing something about. Now you get on the fucking stick pronto or I'm going to ream you a new one, understand?"

I suppose as a paying client he was within his rights to be annoyed, but I didn't like it anyway, and I was developing an antipathy to Armand Treusch that bordered on contempt. I don't insist that everyone in the world like me, but if they are to deal with me it will be with respect, or not at all. And while I'm sure there must be *some* word that disgusts and enrages me more than "nigger," I am hard-pressed to think of it.

I called him at TroyToy, but he hadn't come in yet, and the operator asked if I wanted his voice mail.

I did.

"This is Milan Jacovich, Mr. Treusch," I said. "I have made some progress on my inquiry, even while I was out of town, and

I'll be following it up today. But I think you should know that there isn't enough money in the world for you to address me the way you did on your last call, and if you ever presume to do so again, I'm probably going to bounce you off a wall. With that in mind, sir, be patient and I'll be in touch with you later." I waited for two beats, added, "Have a nice day," and gently depressed the reset button.

There had been no messages from Connie in the two days I'd been gone, not at the office and not on my home telephone, either. I briefly considered calling her.

It was too early in the morning, and probably not the best idea, anyway. Too much going on. Too many things on my mind. Too many more pressing matters to worry about. A baby was missing, an old man was dead, a client was abusing me. I was startled to realize Connie was not that high on my priority list at the moment.

I had already made a pot of coffee, and I sliced a bagel in half and put it in the toaster. I don't buy the packaged ones; when I'm in the mood for bagels I get them fresh-baked at a shop called Bialy's in University Heights. These had been sitting in a paper bag on the counter for four days, long past their optimum freshness, but they were all I had in the house in the way of breakfast.

I cream-cheesed the bagel and put it on a napkin—I'll suffer any indignity to avoid washing dishes—and sat down with my coffee at the kitchen table, the yellow pad from the previous night in front of me. I hadn't retrieved the morning paper from the hallway yet, but I had other things to do first.

Before I had gone to bed, I had written down the names of all the attorneys who, according to their listings or ads in the phone directory, specialized in adoption. There were, to my dismay, nineteen of them. Too many to call, too many to visit in person. And even if I could have confronted each one, I hardly expected them to readily admit to kidnapping a child, anyway.

Then I thought of Joseph Ettawageshik on the bench across the street, and I went through the list again, circling the names of the attorneys in Cleveland Heights. There were five. But none of them had offices anywhere near the Cedar-Fairmount triangle. One was on Mayfield Road near the old Civic Auditorium, two were on Lee Road, one on Taylor and one at Cedar Center, a couple of miles east of where the old Indian had kept his snowy vigil. Not much help there.

With the napkin, I dabbed at some stray cream cheese at the corner of my mouth. Then I refreshed my coffee, reached for the kitchen phone, and speed-dialed Ed Stahl's direct line at the *Plain Dealer*. Ed knew a little bit about everything, and I figured he could help me.

"Twice in one week!" he said. "Business must be booming."

"Can I help it I'm so popular?"

"It's your ingratiating manner."

"Yeah, I work at it."

"You learned it from me."

"At the feet of the master."

"The master's feet hurt," he said. "Getting old."

"Not you. Not ever."

"What is it this time, Milan?"

I told him about Andrew Takalo.

When I finished, the only sound I heard was Ed lighting his pipe, smacking his lips to get the heat going. The *Plain Dealer* building was a no-smoking facility, and to drive by it on Superior Avenue during a workday was to see several wretched addicts huddled in the doorway, puffing desperately to finish their cigarettes before their coffee break was over. But Ed chose to believe that rules were for other people, and apparently he was right; the more militant newsroom contingent of the smoke police busted his chops about it sporadically, but management hardly ever.

Then he said, "I think about a year ago, one of our reporters did a story about that."

"About what?"

"As I remember, there seems to be a booming traffic in Native American black market babies."

"Why Native American?"

"There's always a paucity of white kids available for adoption," he said.

"Wait a minute, let me mark my calendar."

"Your calendar?"

"I want to make a note of the first time I ever heard anyone use the word 'paucity' in conversation."

"It's a good word," he said.

"An excellent word."

"And that's what they pay me for. To use good words."

"You use them well," I said. "Okay, there's a paucity of white adoptees. But why Native American kids?"

"Immersed as you are in seeing that American industry is not mortally wounded by employees swiping ballpoint pens, it might have escaped your notice that we live in a sadly racist society."

"I think I read something about that," I said.

"Therefore many white couples who are desperate to lavish their love and affection on a child of their own but are unable to do so via the more traditional, biological ways, prefer *not* to adopt black children."

"Indians aren't white, either."

"No, but they're *closer* to white," he said.

"That's an ugly reason for adopting a kid."

"Uh-huh."

"I need a favor, Ed."

"No kidding? A favor? Wowsers! Will wonders never cease?"

"Find out who wrote that story a year ago and have them call me? I'll be in the office some time after lunch."

"That's assuming they *want* to call you, of course."

"Who wouldn't want to?" I said. "What with my ingratiating manner and all."

I showered and dressed, camel hair sport jacket, blue shirt, red tie, and dark blue slacks, and went downstairs to my car.

It was probably not a good idea to stay away from the office so long; who knows what new clients I was missing. Sometimes I wished I had a secretary, the way Sam Spade had Effie Perrine, but then Sam Spade never had voice mail and pagers and beepers and remotes, either. Or a computer database.

I headed for Shaker Heights again.

This time Helen Moise wasn't expecting me; she was wearing a sporty little jogging outfit, but little or no makeup, and her hands fluttered to her face involuntarily when she opened the door and saw me standing there. Evidently she was not used to unexpected company.

"Good morning, Ms. Moise. I'm really sorry to barge in on you unannounced," I said, "but I happened to be in the neighborhood. I guess I should have called first."

"That's—all right," she said, making it painfully apparent that it was not.

"May I come in? For just a few minutes?"

She flicked a nervous glance over her shoulder, and I wondered whether a half-naked man was going to come padding out of the bedroom so we'd *all* be embarrassed. But when I got inside, I realized her uncertainty had been because the living room was in disarray, with manila folders and newspapers and magazines strewn around, a pair of fuzzy house slippers under the coffee table, and a half-drunk mug of coffee on a coaster. It seemed she was embarrassed to let anyone see her home looking as if someone actually lived there.

"I hope you didn't bring a photographer with you. Did you, Mr. Kobler?" Her hands went to fluff her hair. "I look a wreck."

I was glad she reminded me; I'd forgotten who I was supposed to be. "No, I didn't, Ms. Moise. And you look just fine."

She glowed at the compliment. "Please sit down." She hurriedly moved the morning paper off the end of the sofa. "You have some more questions?"

I unbuttoned my coat and slipped it off, putting it over the arm of the sofa, and then sat down. "A few more. Harder ones, this time."

She frowned. "Oh dear," she said in a forced, stilted way that made me think she probably *never* said "Oh, dear."

"You don't have a staff working for you, do you? You're sort of a one-woman operation?"

That relaxed her a little bit. It wasn't such a hard question after all. "Yes, it's easier that way." She gave me a chilly smile. "I like to be in control of things."

"Do you ever hire outside consultants?"

"Consultants?"

"You know. People not on the payroll but those you pay on an as-needed basis for whatever expertise they might possess in a given field."

"Well, yes. I have brought in outside people whenever I thought it was necessary. Sometimes as experts and sometimes as field investigators."

"When you do your—investigating. Of these companies that don't play fair with the consumers?"

"Yes?"

"Do you ever send one of your 'consultants' in as a spy, to function as an employee of the company?"

Her tanning-bed bronze complexion went a few shades paler. "I don't understand."

"It's simple. You want to catch a company in the act of violating its trust, but you can only learn so much from the outside. Have you ever hired anyone to go undercover and get a legitimate job at one of these companies just so they could report back to you?"

The pained expression on her face might have indicated heartburn. "Don't you think 'spy' is a rather harsh word?"

"Call it whatever you like."

She wet her lips. "This is going to have to be off the record, Mr. Kobler. It's not the kind of thing I would want in the newspaper . . ." She put a hand to her face, and a sharp vertical line appeared between her brows as the light dawned behind her eyes. She drew herself away from me suddenly, as though she had learned I had been diagnosed with the black plague. "Oh. You're not from a newspaper at all, are you?"

"No, ma'am," I said. "And my name isn't Leon Kobler, either." I handed her one of my business cards.

"Milan Jacovich," she read aloud, pronouncing the *J* and accenting the long *o*. I corrected her pronunciation, but I don't think she was paying attention to me. She was studying my card as though there would be a pop quiz on it on Friday.

"You're a private detective."

"That's what the card says. I can show you my license . . ."

"I don't want to see your goddamned license," she said, her voice sharp and angry now. "Can you give me one good reason why I shouldn't throw you the hell out of my house?"

"No, I can't."

"Or call the police?"

"Well, I can give you a few reasons why you shouldn't do that, mainly because I haven't broken any laws."

"You lied to me. You misrepresented yourself."

"If lying was a crime, there would be no personal ads in the paper and the singles bars would go out of business."

"You entered my home under false pretenses."

I didn't say anything; she had me there.

She pressed her lips together. "I need you to go. Right now."

I pretended I hadn't heard her. "Do you have an operative working undercover at TroyToy?"

Her eyelids fluttered as if I'd thrown sand at them. "TroyToy, what's that?"

"I'm sure you know, Ms. Moise."

She turned away from me, fumbling with the bottom button of her jogging suit. "Look, I don't have to talk to you."

"I know it," I said. "But I've been hired to do a job, and while that is rightly no concern of yours, I've got to tell you that if I find myself working for the bad guys, I'm going to be very unhappy. So you can really help me out here, and if you do, I'd appreciate it."

She didn't answer.

"All right, then. Do you know a David Ream?"

She jerked involuntarily, an unseen puppeteer was yanking her strings.

"Who?" She tried to make it sound offhand and airy; she failed.

"Let's not play games. I know he's been in contact with you. Now do you want to tell me why?"

She squared her shoulders. "No," she said. "I *don't* want to tell you why. It's none of your business."

"On the contrary, that's what my business is."

"Please leave," she said almost desperately.

"How about if I tell *you*, then?"

She was clenching her lips together so tightly they almost disappeared. She didn't answer me, but a look of resignation passed over her face like a cloud.

"Somehow," I said, "and I'm sure you have your sources, you found out that David Ream's little girl had been injured from ingesting the plastic on some sort of toy, and that he had quit his job to care for her full-time. You figured he was an ideal candidate to help you in your crusade against companies that took advantage of consumers, so you brought him on board here as a 'consultant' for the last eight months, paying him eight hundred dollars a week to do whatever, until you were able to get him into the chief accountant's job at TroyToy. You must have had some idea that TroyToy was up to something no good, and you wanted to be the one who brought them down. So David Ream *is* in his job as a spy—only not for a rival toy maker, but for you."

While I was talking, her back had grown militarily rigid and her face, usually attractive in repose, had almost imploded upon itself. By the time I finished, it looked like one of those little wrinkled doll's heads made out of dried apples.

"Did I get anything wrong?"

Suddenly weary, she plopped down on the other end of the sofa, right on top of the *Wall Street Journal* she had been reading, and put her head back against the cushion, listlessly parting her knees, "A few minor details," she said.

I waited.

"Just who is it you're working for, Mr. Jacovich? TroyToy?"

I nodded. "Armand Treusch had a gut feeling about David Ream, that he wasn't quite who he said he was. He hired me to find out. He figured Ream was spying for a competition."

When she spoke, her voice sounded as if she'd been up all night. "And now your little investigation is compromised."

"Yes, it is. But I told you, I don't like working for the bad guys."

"Well, you are," she said.

"So it seems. Do you want to tell me the whole story now?"

She sat up a little straighter. "I suppose I really should, so you don't screw up the details." She chewed at her lower lip, her eyes lowered as though she were trying to see what she was nibbling on.

I didn't say anything; I didn't want to break her mood.

"Do you have children of your own, Mr. Jacovich?"

"Two boys, yes. One's in college."

"Well then, you may remember that kids—little kids—chew on things. It's what they do."

"Yes."

"David Ream's daughter Caitlynn got toxic poisoning from chewing on the rails of a plastic playpen," she said.

"Seems to me as though he'd have a pretty good lawsuit there."

She nodded. "Ordinarily, yes. But the manufacturer is Taiwanese; the chances of getting any judgment against them in an American court that will stick are practically nil."

"So TroyToy had nothing to do with what happened to the Ream child?"

"No," she said.

"There's still the distributor to sue, though, and even the store where he bought the playpen."

"Sure," she said. "And the Reams are exploring that in terms of a lawsuit. It doesn't help their little girl, though."

"No," I said.

"I'd heard some things about TroyToy, things about some products they have in development, that scared me."

"Like what?"

"They're developing a little kid's tricycle—cheap crap, the kind of thing a low-income family might be tempted to buy. They're planning on calling it Troy Trike. It comes unassembled."

"Everything comes unassembled these days."

"Yes, but . . ." She pushed herself up off the sofa and walked across the room, then turned to look at me again. "There are a bunch of little tiny plastic parts. They disengage very easily."

"So if the child is going hell-bent for leather on the trike, it might fall into a million pieces and dump him on his head."

"That's one thing, yes," she said. "Or he might be tempted to put one of those little pieces in his mouth. And it's virtually the same kind of plastic that poisoned Caitlynn Ream."

"You'd think the product engineers at TroyToy would know that."

Her eyes flashed. "Of course they know it! But their market research people discovered that there was a dearth of cheap tricycles on the market right now, and they figured this one would be a big seller."

"So they went ahead?"

"They're going ahead," she said. "They're planning on putting it into the stores in time for Christmas."

"But if it's going to fall apart . . ."

"All Christmas toys fall apart, usually. What do you expect for $24.95? It's the joy of unwrapping them on Christmas morning that toy makers sell, not durability or utility." She shook her head, but it came out more like a shudder. "A Troy Trike under every tree."

"David Ream is an accountant, though. What made you hire him?"

She shrugged. "Number one, I knew he needed the money. And number two, if there was anyone who would be willing to go all the way on saving children from defective products, it would be someone whose own child had been damaged."

"Pretty cynical," I said.

"It's the toy makers that are cynical, Mr. Jacovich. Not me. What we do here is a public service!"

"How could you know there was going to be an opening for an accountant at TroyToy?"

"I didn't," she said. "Happy coincidence. I had David working on several other projects for me. Things he could do from his house, so he'd be there for Caitlynn. Remember, he'd quit his other job so he could be home to take care of her."

"And when the comptroller job came open at TroyToy?"

Nervously, she fingered the bottom button of her jogging suit top again. "It was like a sign."

"How did you happen to hear about the opening?"

She examined the toe of her tennis shoe. "One lucky break," she said grimly.

I left Helen Moise to her crusade shortly afterward, not completely convinced. I didn't believe in lucky breaks.

I didn't figure the damn toy was going to sell anyway. The name was too much of a Dr. Suess tongue twister. I kept mumbling "Troy Trike, Troy Trike" out loud in the car, over and over.

You try it. Three times. Fast.

I stopped off at Ruthie and Moe's Midtown Diner on Prospect Avenue for lunch on the way downtown. Other 1950s-style diners try too hard and create a phoney ambiance; at Ruthie and Moe's it's just *there*.

I sat at the counter working on my bacon and eggs and thought over the troubling meeting I had just concluded with Helen Moise. I was feeling very conflicted, very confused, hung up on some ethical barbed wire and struggling to get loose. A full belly made me feel better; it didn't bring me any closer to solving my problem, but food has always meant comfort to me, and Moe's coffee warmed and soothed me. It felt good on my raspy throat, too.

I got to the office a little past noon. I had a cleaning crew come in every night, so the place didn't feel as if I hadn't been there for almost three days, but the winter sun streaming through the tall windows illuminated every dust mote, and I ran a cursory feather duster over a few of the surfaces anyway, trying to create the illusion of *some* sort of order in my life.

I was just getting around to opening three days' worth of mail—bills, catalogs for electronic monitoring devices, catalogs for vitamins that would lower my cholesterol count and increase my sex drive, a few pleas for funds from some worthy cause or other ads for software, and wonder of wonders, a check from a late-paying client—when the phone chirped.

"Is this Milan Jacovich?" The voice was female and crisply all-business, and it pronounced my name right the first time.

"That's right," I said.

"This is Holly Butcher from the *Plain Dealer*. Ed Stahl said you wanted to talk with me?"

"I do if you're the reporter who wrote the article about Indian children being put up for adoption."

"Right," she said. "That was about a year ago."

"I could go look up the article in the library, but maybe you could give me the condensed version."

"What do you want to know?"

"A couple of things," I said. "First of all, why the big interest in Indian babies, specifically?"

"Well." She took a breath to martial her thoughts. "As you may or may not realize, adoption is not an easy process. Rightly or wrongly, the government is pretty sticky about who they allow to adopt children these days, so you're running uphill from the beginning."

"Okay."

"The availability of white children to adopt is very low. Babies, that is—there are plenty of older ones. But I'm sure you realize most people want the infants."

"Yes."

"Prospective parents' incomes, their health, their ages, their reputations—all those things are factored in. It isn't like calling up to order a pizza."

"I'm glad to hear that."

"Now, not only do most white parents hesitate to adopt a black child, but interracial adoption is becoming more and more difficult. The black community is usually pretty adamant about that."

"I understand that," I said. "Kind of. I can't see letting a kid rot in a public facility or a foster home when he or she could be raised by a loving family, but I know that everybody has their agendas, and I suppose you've got to respect them."

"So. The idea of a white family adopting a Native American baby becomes more appealing. And more accessible."

"That's what's hanging me up," I said. "It's still interracial, isn't it?"

"It is. But you're thinking of strictly legitimate adoptions."

"I was, yes."

"But there's a ton of money to be made in illegal adoptions. You're an ex-cop, Ed Stahl tells me. So you know who always shows up when there's a lot of money to be made, don't you?"

"Crooks," I said. "Hustlers. Bottom-feeders."

"Exactly."

"And you're saying that there are Indian babies being kidnapped to supply the adoption mills?"

"Happens all the time," Holly Butcher said. "More so out west than here, but it happens."

"You can't just steal a child like boosting a candy bar from a 7-Eleven."

"Well, the quick-buck guys use that as a last resort. They're more apt to go into an Indian community and try to *buy* a child first."

"How the hell could anyone sell their child?"

"Wake up and smell the coffee, pal. It happens in the Third World all the time. A poor family, subsisting on pennies, suddenly saddled with another mouth to feed that they can't afford, and then someone waltzes in and not only offers to take the kid off their hands, but they're willing to pay big bucks—at least it seems like big bucks to people in a family living below the poverty level. In squalor, even. And unlike in Asia and Africa, where children are routinely and openly sold into slavery and prostitution, the family is pretty well assured that here in America the kid will grow up in a good home, and have more advantages than it ever would have if it stayed put with its biological parents."

"What about the kidnapping?"

She snorted into the phone. "That's what happens sometimes when the baby brokers can't find a kid to buy. Lots of times they're on a tight schedule, working on direct orders from the adoptive parents."

"How do they get away with it?"

"Not that hard. Most Native Americans live fairly isolated from mainstream America. They have their tribal police, but they're sure not fond of the white establishment. And vice versa, frankly. And even if they do get the authorities interested in their case, these baby brokers are good. They're organized, they have a network all over the country, and they make pretty damn sure the child is almost untraceable."

"I see that up to a point," I said. "But the couples who do the adopting—they have to know that buying babies is illegal."

"The things that are illegal that people get away with every day would knock your socks off, up to and including kidnapping. You know that. And there are lawyers who specialize in those kinds of adoptions, so in the long run, everything at least *looks* legal."

I pulled a notepad across the desk toward me. "Who are the lawyers in Cleveland who routinely specialize in adoption of Indian babies?"

She hesitated for just a moment. "Now we're getting into the sticky part, aren't we?"

"Sticky how?"

"I'm smelling a story here, Milan."

"There isn't one yet," I said.

"When there is one, I want it. That's how it works. You want something from me and I want something from you. It's a circle jerk."

"Well," I said, and didn't continue.

"Look, I know you and Ed Stahl are very tight. But first off, he isn't a reporter anymore, he's Cleveland's wise old sage. And while I'm perfectly happy to let him get a column out of this later, I want the scoop first. It would make my bones at the paper. You know what I mean?"

"I know what you mean," I said.

"Do we have a deal?"

"What *is* the deal?"

"I give you a lawyer, you give me a story."

"If there is one."

"Oh, there'll be one, all right. I can feel it." There was a smile in her voice as well as what sounded like almost breathless excitement. "My toes are tingling, and that only happens to me either when a very sexy guy has just kissed me till I'm cross-eyed, or I sense a big story in the making, front-page stuff. I've got the killer instinct about stories, Milan, it's how I got my job. What do you say?"

I sighed. "You'll get your story."

"Great! Pleasure doing business with you."

"And now," I said, "I get my lawyer."

CHAPTER FIFTEEN

Tower City is a marvel of urban planning and renewal. It ties together the venerable Terminal Tower, once Cleveland's main railroad station, with the Renaissance and Ritz-Carlton Hotels, the Avenue shopping center and its movie theaters and restaurants, the Rapid Station, a medical center, and a department store. The law offices of Shanklin and Schach occupied only about one-third of a floor in another office building in the megacomplex, and their windows looked southward over the city rather than at the more prestigious view of the lake, but they seemed to have the standard trappings of a successful law firm anyway—the oversized reception room with a lot of wasted space, the hunting prints on the walls, the ugly modern furniture, and the dark green wallpaper. I had called for an appointment, explained what I wanted to talk about, and had been granted an end-of-the-day audience, so I only had to wait fifteen minutes before Claudya Shanklin summoned me into her office.

Shanklin was in her forties, short and dark and thin, and she spoke the same way she moved, in rapid-fire staccato bursts, while she stirred a spoon around in a Styrofoam cup of noodle soup. Her office was smaller than mine, unadorned except for her framed diplomas hanging on the wall, an exquisite crystal carousel horse on the edge of the desk, and a small microwave oven on a mahogany credenza. There was no photo of a husband, but she wore no wedding ring, so I suppose I shouldn't have expected one.

"Forgive me if I eat while we talk, Mr. Jacovich," she said. "I'm seeing you on my dinner hour."

She was skinny enough that I believed all she was going to have for dinner was a cup of microwave-heated soup. "I appreciate that, Counselor."

"Let me cut to the chase here, maybe save us both a little time." She slurped some noodles out of the spoon and I watched in fascination as they disappeared between her lips like worms into the beak of an early-morning robin. "This firm has never been involved in an adoption that wasn't strictly one hundred percent legal and aboveboard. We don't buy babies, and we don't kidnap them, all right? We have antennae out to the various agencies around the country so that we know when a suitable child is put up for adoption, and that is the *only* way we do it. Do I make myself clear?"

As clear as possible through a mouthful of noodles, I thought but did not say. Instead, I said, "Suitable?"

"Come on, we understand each other here. A couple comes to us looking to adopt, they have a very specific wish list. Age, sex, coloring, even family background."

"Family background?"

Her head bobbed in what I took to be a nod of affirmation. "No one wants to adopt the issue resulting from incest. Or for that matter, the child of a serial killer or one who might be carrying the seeds of a genetic disease. Could you blame them?"

"So you don't get the babies and then try to match them to the parents. It's the other way around."

"Right."

"Is that the usual way of arranging adoptions?"

"It's not common, but it's not uncommon, either. It's simply how we choose to do it."

"Sort of like a personal shopper."

She put the cup down for a moment. "Don't be hostile, okay? This isn't Baby Wal-Mart." She waited until I looked suitably contrite before continuing. "Some families aren't lucky enough to be able to have children and they're miserable. We make them happy. Some children are born without a chance in hell of having a good life, and we make *them* happy. Why the hostility?"

"Sorry," I said, which seemed to please her. I think she enjoyed deflating those who disapproved of her chosen field. "I didn't mean to be antagonistic. This is all kind of new to me and I'm trying to get it squared away in my mind."

"The only thing you need to get straight is that we are completely legal, and I might add, completely ethical in our practice of adoption law."

Through the big window behind her, I could see that it had begun snowing again. Another Alberta Clipper, the weather forecasters had warned, a big storm originating in western Canada and roaring across the Great Lakes to dump its snow on Cleveland. "But you are aware of some law firms that aren't quite so fussy, aren't you?"

"There are bad apples in every profession," she said, nodding agreement. "Bad doctors, bad lawyers, and I'm sure bad private detectives. But I can't concern myself with them. I'm too busy servicing my clients and seeing that some innocent kids who might have been born unlucky get a fair shake."

"You don't concern yourself with them, but you know who they are."

The spoon hovered between cup and mouth as she stared at me; I wondered how long she could hold it there before the noodles slid off and onto the desktop. "You actually expect me to implicate some other law firm? It doesn't work that way. First of all, we'd be looking at a lawsuit of our own. And secondly, if I knew for a fact that an attorney was hiring kidnappers, as an officer of the court I'd be obliged to report that. So you're wasting your time."

"If you knew for a fact," I said. "What if you just suspected?"

The suspense mercifully ended as the noodles disappeared into her mouth. "I can't afford to act on suspicions, even if I had any. And I sure as hell can't afford to share them with you."

"All right," I said. "Then let me ask you this. Does your firm facilitate *only* Native American adoptions?"

"And foreign adoptions, too. From China, Russia, Rumania.

Come on, you watch *60 Minutes* and those shows, you know the score."

"But it's fair to say that a large portion of the Indian adoptions in Cuyahoga County come through this office?"

"Come through *me*," she said. "It's kind of my specialty."

"Ever do any business with the Indian tribes in Michigan? The Odawas?"

"No," she said.

"A little Odawa infant was stolen. I have reason to believe he wound up here in the Cleveland area."

"Why come to me?"

I tilted my head at her. "Because Indian babies are your specialty."

"I'm very sad to hear about the child, but I can assure you I had nothing to do with it."

"I wasn't suggesting you had."

"That's good," she said in that way some lawyers have of threatening you while they're stroking you. "I want us to stay friends."

"The babies that you *do* place . . ."

"Yes?" She was eating rapidly now, the soup almost gone, and she was tipping the cup to get every last bit of it.

"How do you know they are really children who've been put up for adoption? How can you be sure they weren't either bought or stolen?"

"Simple," she said. "The tribes call me."

"You have an arrangement, then?"

She glared at me. "Put any name to it you want. But I work through the social service agencies of whatever state the birth parents happen to live in. Everything is carefully monitored, by the home state and by the State of Ohio." She gouged the last few noodles from the bottom of the cup and shoveled them into her mouth. "And by me. Personally."

"So you aren't even going to give me a hint as to where I should look for this baby?"

"A hint?" She laughed, but her dark eyes stayed cold and flat. "What is this, a kids' game? You're getting colder, you're getting warmer, hot, hot, hot? No hints. I don't know any hints to give you."

"Does it concern you that there is an Odawa family in Michigan grief-stricken, a mother nearly hysterical with worry over what's happened to her child?"

She leaned forward, wiping her mouth with a tissue from a dispenser she kept out of sight in her bottom drawer. "Of course it concerns me. I chose this legal specialty because I care about people, because I didn't want to spend my life adding up billable hours to sock some big megacorporation who pays me for screwing little guys. My heart goes out to the family in Michigan, but there's not a damn thing I can do about it, ethically or legally or any other way. I can't give you any names and I can't give you any hints. Sorry, but that's the way it has to be."

"I'm sorry too," I said, and stood up. "Thanks for seeing me, Ms. Shanklin."

"I can tell you one thing," she said. "For some reason, most of the couples who want a Native American child live out of the city. Like in the suburbs."

"Thanks for that," I said. "One more question?"

"Shoot. No guarantee I'll answer it, but shoot anyway."

"About how much does it cost, an adoption like that?"

She rocked back in her chair. "Taking all the costs and fees into consideration? Anywhere from forty to sixty thousand dollars."

"Those must be pretty tony suburbs," I said.

"Hey." She shrugged. "You get what you pay for."

There are twenty-eight communities in Cuyahoga County alone, and scores more in the contiguous counties of Lorain, Medina, Lake, Geauga, and Summit, and at least half of them might be considered not only exurban but upscale, so my job was simple. All I had to do was go knocking door-to-door and ask the occupants whether or not they had just adopted a Native American male baby. Sure.

When I got home, I checked the refrigerator for something that would approximate a dinner. The head of lettuce I'd bought several days before at Russo's across the street was drooping badly, so I tossed it into the trash and nuked a link of Italian sausage in the microwave and then set it to frying slowly while I tore open a box of macaroni and cheese and boiled the pasta. Draining it but not adding the milk the directions on the package called for, I mixed in the packet of "cheese food," sliced up the sausage in small chunks and dotted them over the macaroni, and put the whole thing in the oven for about five minutes. I watched the snow swirling outside the window as I ate it at the kitchen table and washed it down with a Stroh's, a Sinatra CD playing in the living room just loud enough for me to hear it but not so loud that it would annoy old Mr. Maltz across the hall.

It wasn't the healthiest meal in the world, I suppose, but my mother had been such a tyrant when it came to my finishing my childhood vegetables that since I've grown up I rarely eat them on my own unless I absolutely have to. Not eating vegetables is one of the few perks of being an adult.

After I had washed my dishes and the frying pan and set the baking dish in the sink to soak, I went into my den, took a deep breath to muster my courage, and dialed Connie's number.

I tried to ignore the tight feeling in my chest as I waited through six rings and then realized she was either not at home or not going to answer. My guess was the latter; the Haleys had an answering machine that would have kicked in after the fourth ring had it been turned on. They probably had Caller ID too, so she could have seen who was calling and chosen not to talk to me; I frankly didn't want to think about that.

I punched the off-button on the receiver, keeping it in my hand, and looked at my watch. Ten past seven. I knew I had much to sort out in my mind before I slept; some of it was personal, of course. I sensed that I was losing Connie, and that was a sorry and bitter thing, since it had less to do with anything I had done and everything to do with who I was.

My more pressing problems were professional, and a baby's life teetered in the balance.

And some of my problems were ethical. Those were the ones for which I needed help.

I activated the phone again, tapping out a number with a 440 area code.

"Suzanne," I said. "It's Milan Jacovich."

"Hi, there." Suzanne Davis sounded cheery; she also sounded as if she were chewing.

"Hey, I wanted to thank you again for the Caitlynn Ream stuff. It really helped bring a lot of things together."

"I'm glad, Milan."

"So I owe you."

"Come on, we already talked about that."

"A gentleman always pays his debts," I said. "At least let me buy you a drink."

"When?"

"Now. I can be out in your neck of the woods in about an hour."

She hesitated. "That's a hell of a drive in the snow."

"Yep."

"What's up?"

"I need to talk," I said.

There was a chuckle in her voice. "And you picked *me*?"

"It's something only a colleague can help me with."

"*That* sounds heavy. Well, I was planning on doing the laundry."

"What fun is that? Start now, and then when it's ready for the dryer you can throw it in and come out to meet me."

"Very efficient."

"Always."

"I'm not exactly dressed for nightlife," she said. "A very chic sweatshirt—from the Fraternal Order of Police."

"Perfect," I told her.

But by the time I met her an hour later in a little bar on Chillicothe Road in Mentor, she had changed to a short skirt and sweater. She was quite an astonishing-looking woman—not beautiful in any traditional sense, but tall and slim with wonderful, shapely legs, a Mediterranean olive complexion, a mane of long curly black hair that she ran her fingers through and tossed out of her face a lot, and the biggest, most astonishing blue eyes, which always met mine directly and with an unstated challenge. I hadn't seen her in over a year.

"I thought you were going to wear your FOP sweatshirt."

"Hey, you never know if Mr. Right is going to be sitting on the next stool." She grinned. "I believe in being prepared."

"I thought you were already seeing Mr. Right. What happened, did you burn the dinner?"

"The dinner was superb," she said, "and so was the dessert, if you know what I mean. But if you look in the phone book, you'll see pages and pages of guys named Mr. Right. This one isn't the right Mr. Right, that's all."

We took a small table in the corner and both ordered beer. The jukebox was playing Garth Brooks. Her eyes, huge and animated almost like a cartoon character's, moved about the room. Whether she was scoping out a potential future lover or just being the observant, canny PI I knew her to be, I wasn't sure.

"So what is this collegial problem you want to talk about?" she said. Suzanne had a way of saying virtually everything in a manner that made you feel she was letting you in on a secret.

"It's an ethical problem."

"Ah."

"Let me give you a hypothetical here . . ."

"Hypothetical," she said, nodding. "Naturally."

"Okay. Suppose you're hired to do a job. To investigate an employee for your corporate client. You do it, and you find out what the client wanted to know, which is that the employee is not what he seemed. But along the way you also find out that your client is completely corrupt, and might do a great deal of damage to innocent people if he isn't stooped."

"Ah-huh," she said.

"But you've taken the guy's money."

The corner of her mouth threatened a grin but didn't make good on it. "And spent it already."

"Well, not exactly . . ."

"There are a few variables here, Milan." She took a fistful of her hair and moved it behind her ear. It wasn't primping; it was a habit of hers, just getting her hair out of her face so she could function more efficiently. "Did this job come through the client's attorney?"

"Why?" I said. "Would that make a difference?"

"Legally, yes. An attorney, remember, is honor bound and legally bound to serve the interests of his client, no matter what the circumstances. That's why criminal lawyers can sleep at night. The thinking is—and the law as well—that everyone is entitled to the best legal advocacy they can get."

I nodded.

"And you function essentially as an arm of the attorney, so you're bound by the same strictures. If you happen to find out the client is screwing somebody else, and that somebody else is Mother Teresa, that's really none of your business. It's probably the reason his lawyer hired you in the first place."

"Okay."

"If you violate your trust and stick your nose in, the lawyer can make it really uncomfortable for you, maybe even get your license lifted. And then you'd have to get a real job." She shuddered. "I hate it when that happens."

"What if," I said, "it's a direct client-to-investigator situation? No lawyer involved?"

"Well, that's less black and white, sure. But you still have a moral obligation to your client. Even if he is a total sleazeball."

"Even if there might be lives at stake?"

She sipped her beer delicately. "You working for a serial killer, Milan?"

"Nothing that direct, no. But let's say he's doing something really harmful." I searched for the right metaphor. "Like illegally polluting a stream that could jeopardize the health of an entire community."

She thought about it for a moment. "Well, you're *still* morally obligated to him. But . . ."

She aimed a red-lacquered finger at me like a light saber. "If your client is doing something really bad, really low—well, I think that's something that has to be played on a case-by-case basis. If he's posing a danger to innocent people, then it becomes a matter between you and your conscience. And knowing you and your rather primitive definitions of right and wrong, I'd say you have to let your conscience be your guide." The grin erupted now, full-blown. "Didn't Jiminy Cricket say that?"

"He did at that. Jiminy Cricket. One of the great legal minds of the ages. My personal god."

She laughed. "Just remember, he said some other things, too."

"Like what?"

She was staring at a particularly hunky-looking guy in a leather jacket who had swung one blue-jeaned leg up onto a bar stool. " 'When you wish upon a star, your dreams come true,' " she sang in a husky, sexy voice.

"And your point?"

With her finger, she traced a line in the condensation on the outside of her glass. Then she pushed her hair out of her face with her fingers again and tossed her head. "That sometimes Jiminy Cricket is full of shit."

Poor Jiminy. Another childhood idol shot down, I thought as I drove back down I-90 through snow that seemed to come rushing at the windshield in sheets like in a bad 3-D movie. There weren't many cars on the freeway; while people in northeastern Ohio have learned to live with weather and drive around on the city streets in the worst of it, only the terminally insane go out on the freeways during a winter storm.

What was I going to do about Armand Treusch? Confronting and ringingly denouncing him seemed a little baroque in this day and age. Not only that, but it probably wouldn't stop him from putting his dangerous plastic tricycle into the toy stores of the world.

And that would mean that for the rest of my life I'd have to wonder whether because of my silence one of them had fallen apart and dumped a toddler on his head on the sidewalk, or whether one of the tiny plastic pieces had poisoned a little bloodstream.

So silence was not an option. But I wasn't sure if any of the other ones were viable.

What was normally a twenty-five-minute trip took almost an hour. When I finally got back to Cleveland Heights the snow had stopped, but the streets were white and slick. When I parked my car I zipped my cold-weather system all the way up to the top and put my chin down as I headed across the parking area, as if that would protect my sore throat from the onslaught of the cold.

In the apartment, the wall clock in the kitchen told me it was a little past eleven. As I pulled off my outerwear and hung it in the front closet, I thought about calling Connie again; I even started into the den to do it.

After eleven *was* pretty late to call someone, I had to admit, and she was a nine-to-five working person. I didn't want to wake her up; she might be cranky then, and things would just deteriorate more.

And then I stopped about halfway across the living room. Who in the hell was I kidding? I was afraid to call for fear she might not answer again, which might mean she was monitoring her calls and didn't want to talk to me, or might mean she was still out.

Late.

Perhaps with somebody else.

I went to the refrigerator and took out a beer, wrenching the top off almost savagely, feeling stupid, impotent, and an awkward, gawky fifteen years old. I rampaged back into the den and virtually hurled myself into my chair. It groaned; I'm too big to throw myself at the furniture.

I stared accusingly at the telephone. Wounded. Angry.

Thirsty. I practically drained the bottle in one long, upended draught, and then slammed it down onto the little table beside my chair.

That's when I noticed the yellow pad with the names of the adoption lawyers I'd culled from the phone book. I stared at it thoughtfully, then picked it up and stared some more, running my fingertips over the names I'd written there as if they were in Braille, half-memorizing them.

A hopeless morass of names, but an idea was forming in my head, and I sat there for a few minutes and let it set, all thoughts of lost love for the moment banished. I ripped the five sheets from the pad and folded them in half, then got up and carried them over to the window to look out at the Cedar-Fairmount triangle. At the bench on which Joseph Ettawageshik had spent his last day. I lit a cigarette, seeing the momentary reflection of the flaring match and of my frowning face in the pane. With only a brief thought of my raw throat, I waited until I had smoked it almost all the way down to the filter, then squashed it and went out into the living room to the closet so I could reclaim my parka. I stuffed the yellow sheets into the pocket, slipped on my gloves, and went out the door.

I braved the wind once more and crossed over to the bench in front of Baskin-Robbins. A few inches of snow covered it, so I couldn't sit down, but squatted low so that my head was at about the level the old Indian's had been.

I looked across the street.

There were four apartment buildings on the north side of Cedar Road, only two of which were clearly visible from the bench. But if one was to keep an all-day vigil watching them, this was the only place to sit for several blocks in either direction.

I straightened up and crossed both Fairmount and Cedar in mid-block to the first apartment building. All four of them were old-style brick eight-flats, probably built during the 1930s in that ornate, almost rococo style that was the fashion. I smiled thinking that we had to say the *nineteen*-thirties now, that it was a new century and new forms of expression were required.

I went into the first vestibule and checked the names on the mailboxes, but they yielded no information. Then I went out again and trotted eastward to the second building.

The mailboxes there told me that Apartment #3A was occupied by a W. T. Clemons, and many-legged excitement ran up my back as I realized the name was familiar. I dug into my pocket and fished out the folded yellow sheets, running a gloved finger down the entries.

There it was. At an office address on Prospect Avenue in the east forties.

Willetta T. Clemons, Attorney-at-Law.

Chapter Sixteen

There was a parking lot to one side of the four-story office building, only about two-thirds full of mostly economy cars and several-year-old compacts, dotted with treacherous patches of slick ice from the storm the day before. Snow had been plowed and piled up out of the way against the side of the building and was now in the process of turning disgustingly dirty.

This was a stretch of Prospect Avenue that hadn't yet experienced the facelift and resultant resurgence that its neighbors to the west, Playhouse Square and the Warehouse District, were currently enjoying, and the structures were squat, unlovely reminders of the dearth of architectural imagination that had stamped the postwar era. Closer to the lake in the east forties, the factories and warehouses of old industrial Cleveland had either been converted to trendy office spaces or left to crumble, but at least there was character there, a "feel," a few graciously ponderous remnants of a more felicitous time, some pizzazz. This midtown corridor neighborhood, however, was still nameless and faceless and completely lacking in personality.

I pulled the car into one of the parking spaces against the wall, cut the motor, and turned to Suzanne Davis in the seat beside me.

"You ready?" I said.

She shrugged. She had tamed her hair somewhat with a pair of barrettes, and was wearing a pantsuit today, an elegant brown one that she had accessorized with several expensive gold pins that made her look more like a well-to-do suburban matron than the three-times-divorced terror of the Lake County fern bars that she was. She had even donned one of her old wedding rings; I didn't think it prudent to ask from which marriage it had come.

I myself was not wearing a wedding ring; I had no idea where my old one was.

"I'm looking forward to this," she said. "It should be fun."

"Don't have too much fun. Remember, we're Leon and Suzanne Kobler from Willoughby Hills."

She shook her head. "You don't look like a Leon, for God's sake. Can't you pick another name?"

"Hey, I've been Leon Kobler before. Recently. I'm comfortable with it."

"I can't believe I'd marry a guy named Leon."

"You didn't, remember? We're just pretending to be married for an hour or two."

She shot me a grin that, on a male, would have been characterized as satyr-like. Her eyes twinkled. "This isn't the first time in my life I've pretended to be married for an hour or two. But never with a guy named Leon."

"Give it a rest," I said. I got out of the car and bustled around to her side to open the door for her, but she beat me to it.

"If you're going to pretend, pretend right," she warned me as she climbed out of the passenger seat without my assistance. "Married men never open car doors for their wives, okay? And the only reason single guys do it is so they can look up the woman's skirt while she's trying to get out gracefully."

"You aren't wearing a skirt."

"I know—I'm on to you."

We made our way carefully through the icy lot and went into the tiny lobby of the building. Next to the elevator was the directory, encased in glass, black foamy material with white plastic letters embedded in it. I saw that Willetta T. Clemons Co., LPA, was on the third floor. A low-rent office about ten minutes from her apartment at Cedar Fairmount.

"You want to walk up?"

"At these prices, hell no!" she said, and pushed the oversized black button to summon the elevator. We watched the overhead indicator as the car descended from the top floor to the lobby. Finally the door creaked open and we stepped inside. It smelled of bleach and deodorizer, which, upon reflection, wasn't nearly as bad as what it might have smelled like. It took about thirty seconds of fits and starts and stomach-flipping jerks for the car to rise some thirty feet.

When we got to the double doors, painted green to match the rest of the third floor hallway, Suzanne put her hand on the knob and turned her face up to me.

"What?"

"Before we go in, *Leon, darling,*" she said, "I think it's only fair to tell you—I've been having an affair." And she twisted the knob, threw open the door, and sailed into the domain of Willetta T. Clemons, Attorney-at-Law, leaving me red-faced and chuckling in the hallway.

When I finally got a look at the anteroom, I found it to be a strictly no-frills office, utilitarian furniture and a utilitarian receptionist in polyester slacks whose desk was flanked by two inner-office doors. There were no drapes or blinds on the windows, which looked south toward the rear facade of another building. This was a far cry from most law offices, and I had to wonder about an attorney who not only occupied such pedestrian digs but lived in a rented apartment on Cedar Hill. Maybe the adoption racket wasn't as lucrative as I'd been led to believe.

We introduced ourselves to the receptionist as Mr. and Mrs. Kobler, the ones with the four o'clock appointment, and she hung up our coats on a metal rack that might once have stood in the vestibule of a southwest side union hall, and bade us be seated on a hideous plaid sofa, giving us a clipboard with a form to be filled out. Suzanne looked at it for a moment and then handed it to me.

I dutifully filled in the blanks with the lies Suzanne and I had been preparing all morning. I was Leon Kobler. An insurance executive this time, figuring that a newspaper reporter might seem too threatening. I jotted down a phony address in the tony suburb of Willoughby Hills; it sounded right, and Suzanne lived close enough to it that no one would question her Lake County phone number. Under "Annual Income" I took my real one and quadrupled the figure before scribbling it in; anything less than that and we could not have *afforded* Willoughby Hills. Or an off-the-books adoption, for that matter. Suzanne was looking carefully over my shoulder, nodding in approval and re-memorizing the falsehoods.

I finally finished, and turned the clipboard so she could see it more easily. "There. How does that look?" I said under my breath so the receptionist couldn't hear me.

"Well, as fiction goes, it's not exactly *The Great Gatsby*, but it'll do," she whispered back.

"Everybody's a critic."

I returned the clipboard to the desk, the receptionist took it behind one of the inner doors and then came back without it, and we cooled our heels for a while. Whenever she thought the receptionist might be looking, Suzanne would even reach over occasionally and squeeze my hand in wifely fashion. She had a great sense of humor about the whole thing, and I had a suspicion that she was really getting into it, enjoying the charade for its own sake.

Finally after about twenty minutes we were ushered into Clemons's private office. It wasn't much more elegant than the waiting room. I took a quick look around, ignoring the usual law books and trappings. On the wall were two framed photographs, one of Willetta T. Clemons with several other people, including a former governor of Ohio, at what looked like a campaign victory celebration. The other was of the president of the United States, sans Willetta.

There were also two framed diplomas. One was her BA degree, from a small liberal arts college in Indiana; the other was her law degree, issued by a law school I had never heard of.

The lawyer was thirtyish, dough-faced, about fifteen pounds overweight, and she had no visible lips. She was in an ugly, dark gray business suit that could have been designed sometime before she was born, with a white blouse modestly buttoned to the neck, and she wore her brownish-blond hair long, down around her shoulders and curled at the ends. The effect seemed almost deliberately dowdy. She rose to greet us, taking our hands warmly in both of hers, and her smile was welcoming but a little sad, too, and I immediately pegged her for someone who was trying just a trifle to hard to ooze sincerity.

The introductions done, Suzanne and I settled on an old Naugahyde sofa against the wall and Clemons took a wooden chair with arms and pulled it up close to us, her knees nearly touching mine, creating an instant intimacy. "So," she said a little too easily, as if this was her standard opening line, "tell me all about the Koblers."

I was about to when Suzanne launched into an amazing recitation that she had apparently made up on the spur of the moment. I was not only stunned, but really impressed; I'd never really seen her in action before. As she spun out a sad tale of how her first husband had died before they could have any children and how she had married me in hopes of beginning a family even at her advanced age, only to find out she was incapable of conception, her words tore at my heartstrings even as I marveled at the ease and facility with which she boldly fibbed.

All the while Suzanne was speaking, Willetta Clemons took notes on a yellow legal pad, nodding sympathetically and occasionally motherly clucking her tongue, making as much eye contact with us as she possibly could. She had her character down pat.

It was a good deal like watching a scene played between Meryl Streep and Susan Sarandon; two fine actresses at the peak of their powers. It was hard to say which of them was the scariest, but I finally gave the nod to Clemons.

"And so," she said when Suzanne had finally run out of falsehoods, "now you want to adopt?"

"Very much," I said. It was the first time I'd opened my mouth since "hello."

"I assume that you've tried the regular channels. The state social service agencies."

"Of course we have. But we found out that's a problem," Suzanne told her almost tearfully. "Because I'm over forty. We both are, but I'm . . ." She looked quickly at me and then down at her lap. "I'm even a little older than Leon."

The lawyer nodded. "Have you thought about adopting a child who's a little bit older? Say five or six? That might be easier in the long run, because there are more of them than infants who are in need of good homes."

"We've talked about it," I said, "but Suzanne has her heart set on a little baby. No more than six months old."

Clemons scribbled more notes. "How did you happen to come to me, then? I mean, where did you get my name? Most of my clients are referrals from other attorneys."

"We've been kind of immersed in this adoption business for a long time now, Ms. Clemons. Talked to a lot of people. Your name came up. More than once."

"I see," she said, and for a moment I think she was trying to decide whether or not to believe that. "Well, Leon and Suzanne. May I call you by your first names?"

"Oh, yes," Suzanne said earnestly.

"Good. And you call me Willy. Please."

We both nodded acquiescence.

Willy shook a cautionary finger at us. "I'm not going to tell you this will be easy, because it won't be."

Suzanne looked at me unhappily, clutched my hand, and moaned deep down in the back of her throat.

"Now, now, Suzanne." I'd never really heard anyone say "Now, now," before. "It isn't impossible, either." Clemons raised her chin and delivered her next line with the evangelical fervor of a circuit-riding preacher. "*Nothing* is impossible."

I smiled back at her with all the radiance of a sinner who'd found redemption. "I hope you're right, Ms.—Willy."

"I *know* I am, Leon," she replied, seemingly pleased I'd called her by her first name. "There's more than one way to skin a cat." Her laugh was tinkling, merry. "Oh, I'm sorry if you two are cat lovers. No offense. That's just an old expression."

I waved a magnanimous hand to show her that on behalf of the cats of the world, I was not offended.

"Let me ask you this, Suzanne and Leon." She had learned the trick, probably in Client Relations 101, of using people's first names often when she spoke to them so they would think of her as a friend and ally. "Would you ever consider a trans-racial adoption? You know, adopting a child of another race?"

I made myself frown. "Well . . ."

"There is generally a much larger selection of minority children available for adoption, is why I mention it."

Selection, I thought. Like a used car lot. I worked hard not to let my feelings show on my face.

"As a matter of fact, for every healthy white infant available for adoption, there are at least forty families looking. And conversely, for every forty healthy minority babies, there is generally only one family. That's a sad fact."

Suzanne, a better actor than I am, saved me by jumping into the breach. "Oh Willy," she said with a trace of regret. "That wouldn't stop us at all. I mean, we aren't at all prejudiced. But I think it would be *so* difficult, a white family with an African-American child. So many extra problems . . ."

Willy Clemons nodded. "I'd have to agree with you on that, Suzanne. You'd be surprised how many of our prospective parents think the same way. And there would be problems with the African-American community as well. There shouldn't be, of course—several years ago Senator Metzenbaum sponsored adoption legislation that prohibits race from entering into it at all. But in practice, well, that's a different story." She voiced the rest of her thought carefully, delicately. "But how would you feel about a different minority. Say—Native American?"

"Indian?" I said.

"You know, many of them look almost white." She was selling her oblique racism for all she was worth, and I felt a warm glow of satisfaction inside my chest. This was going to be easier than I'd thought it would be. "It wouldn't be *quite* so much of a culture shock, you know?"

I nodded, wondering how much of a culture shock it would be if I punched Willetta T. Clemons in her nose. "Are there a lot of Native American children available?"

"Well, from time to time one *becomes* available," she said. "My staff would have to do some research."

Her staff, I thought, must work on a contract basis, because there wasn't much room for one in these little offices. I wondered if the staff included a tall, redheaded, pale-faced man and a short, dark-haired guy with a crooked eye, and if the research included kidnapping Native American babies from their cradles. "But what about the authorities?" I asked. "They've already told us that because of Suzanne's age, there would be difficulties."

Clemons gave me a dimply smile. "That's what you're going to pay me for, Leon. To take care of things like that."

"How much *am* I going to be paying you, Willy?"

She flushed. "I have to warn you up front. Since there are all sorts of expenses connected with an adoption like this, over and above my fee—you know, research, transportation, perhaps compensation for the birth family, things of that nature—that this will not be an inexpensive process."

"It doesn't matter," Suzanne assured her.

"Well now, wait a second," I said, playing the penurious husband to the hilt. "Let's define our terms here."

The lawyer smiled tolerantly at me. "I can understand your concern, Leon," she said. "Money doesn't grow on trees. For any of us."

"How big of a tree are we talking about?"

Suzanne shot me a dirty look. I guess she thought that's what a wife was supposed to do. I don't know, she's been married three times, maybe she *knows* what a wife is supposed to do.

"I would say offhand—and this isn't graven in stone, Suzanne and Leon, I'm just making a very rough estimate here—that we're probably talking somewhere in the neighborhood of sixty or seventy thousand dollars."

I gulped, even though it wasn't going to come out of my pocket. Involuntarily I said, "Wow! What do poor people do?"

"Now, Leon," Clemons chided me. "It's a simple fact of life that people who have money can do more things with it than people who have none."

"It's not that we can't afford it," I said defensively.

"Oh, I'm *sure* you can. There's no question in my mind about that. I didn't mean to imply otherwise."

Willetta T. Clemons was the most outrageous butt kisser I have ever met.

"Won't there have to be background checks?" Suzanne wanted to know. "I mean, you don't give a baby to just anyone, do you?"

"Naturally not. We always hire outside contractors to do a thorough investigation of our prospective parents."

I let my mind wander happily for just a moment, thinking about Milan Security or Suzanne Davis Associates being the outside contractors hired to vet the credentials of Leon and Suzanne Kobler.

Suzanne fidgeted nervously.

"That's not going to be a problem, is it?" Clemons said. "Let me know now, Suzanne. It will be a lot easier if there are no surprises."

"Well, I'm . . ." My pretend-wife looked imploringly at me, then back at the lawyer. "I'm a recovering alcoholic."

I had lost my grip somewhere along the way and found myself suddenly floundering around in an alternative universe, watching Suzanne and myself perform in a movie I'd never seen before. I don't suppose I was able to keep the shock off my face, so Suzanne came to my rescue once again. "I'm sorry, honey, I know you didn't want me to mention it, but Willy should know everything, don't you think? For the good of the baby?"

"I guess so," I mumbled.

"I've been sober for almost nine years now," she added.

Willy Clemons leaned forward and gave Suzanne's hand an attagirl pat. "I don't really foresee that as being much of a problem, Suzanne. And I'm proud of you. Good for you for staying sober! I personally think any little baby would be darned lucky to have a terrific mom like you."

"Oh, Leon," Suzanne said imploringly, turning to me and digging her nails into my arm, "let's just do it! Let's just write Willy a check right now."

"Well, wait a second," I harrumphed. "I think we need to talk this over a little bit first."

"What's to talk over?" she said. "We've been talking about adopting for years now."

"Well, yes, but I hadn't really given much thought to an Indian child. There are still going to be cultural differences . . ."

Suzanne's eyes welled up with tears and she put her hands in her lap, the better to wring them piteously.

Clemons turned a trifle cooler to me. "I can certainly understand that, Leon. Feeling as you do, you and Suzanne probably should have some long, serious talks about taking a Native American baby into your home."

Suzanne began to sniffle.

"I'm sorry. I don't mean to be obstructionist about this, but it's a brand-new concept, frankly." I leaned over to squeeze Suzanne's knee, probably a little harder than she had been expecting. "Come on, honey. Let's go home."

Suzanne gathered herself together slowly and painfully, all stops out for the Oscar, and we headed for the door.

"I'm sorry, Willy," I said over my shoulder. "I just have to think long and hard about a non-white child. I don't mean to sound like a racist, because I'm certainly not. But I wasn't expecting this. It's kind of a new idea, you know? And I didn't get where I am today by making snap decisions, especially about something this important."

"I understand perfectly, Leon," Clemons said, getting between us and linking arms so we looked like the three stars of a 1940s musical in the last corny scene, guiding us toward the door. "I'm not going to try and 'sell' you on anything, because that would only be destructive to everyone in the long run. There are plenty of childless couples who would jump at the chance, though. I can only tell you this. I've done several Native American placements in the past year, and they resulted only in joy and happiness and fulfillment for both the child and the adoptive parents."

I cocked my head slightly. I had my own ending to this meeting already planned, but Willetta Clemons had marched right into the hole I'd been digging for her with her eyes open. "I'm sure that's true, Willy. Maybe if . . ." I looked over at Suzanne. "Well, it might help us make up our minds if Suzanne and I could actually talk to someone who's recently adopted an Indian baby."

Suzanne clutched my arm as if it were all that was keeping her from falling off a high cliff. "Oh, Leon!" she said. "Yes! Could we? Could we, Willy? Oh, yes!"

"You're astonishing!" I said.

We hadn't really spoken until we had left the law office, gotten back into the car, and were heading down Euclid Avenue toward University Circle, almost as if we had to put some physical distance between ourselves and Willy Clemons so she couldn't hear us.

Suzanne grinned at me. "I thought that went real well, yes." She had pulled off the gold earrings and run her fingers through her tightly sprayed hair, and was almost looking like the Suzanne I knew.

"You're an amazing actress."

"So is Willy. We kind of fed off each other's energy."

"When you came up with that recovering alcoholic business I almost lost my teeth."

"I didn't mean to spring that on you unawares, but it was a spur-of-the-moment inspiration. I thought it added a note of pathos and verisimilitude." She shrugged. "I didn't want her thinking the Koblers were too perfect; she might have gotten spooked. Then again, I was afraid for a minute that it might have been too much, that she would have said that disqualified us as adoptive parents."

"Are you kidding? Clemons is so damn hungry to make a deal she would have agreed to give us a child if you'd told her you were hooking on Detroit Road and that I was an ax murderer."

"I can't believe it worked—that she's actually going to put us in touch with a couple who has bought a baby!"

"She smells Leon and Suzanne Kobler's money," I said. "It puts her into a feeding frenzy."

"She's something, all right."

I grinned over at her. "So are you. Really, I was very impressed. It's great working with you."

"Well, we're not finished yet," she said. "And now before our big meeting I have to go hunt up *another* Suzy Homemaker outfit like this one."

"For what it's worth, I think you make a great little homemaker. It's been a pleasure being married to you."

"About that, Milan . . ."

"Yes?"

"The next time you squeeze my thigh like that," she said, reaching out to give mine an enthusiastic grope, "you better be ready to come through."

CHAPTER SEVENTEEN

I arrived at the office fairly early the next morning, stopping at Presti's for another take-out donut breakfast. It was boding to be a busy day, and I wanted to get a good jump on it. Besides, the sky was cloudless blue, a rare enough occurrence in February, and the joyful sunlight streaming through my big windows and the flashes of brilliance off the ice-dotted surface of the Cuyahoga, the white-bellied gulls swooping and soaring, were all putting me into a lighthearted mood.

I made some coffee, and when it was done poured the first of it into my Marko Meglich mug. I booted up the computer and entered my recollections of our meeting with Willy Clemons the day before onto my hard drive. Adrenaline was beginning to shoot around inside me; I was getting close to little Andrew Takalo. I could sense it, almost taste it. And that might just mean that a grieving family in Cross Village, Michigan, would be smiling once more, very soon.

I caught up on some correspondence, replenished my coffee, and made my regular morning perusal of the *Plain Dealer*, which I'd brought with me from home. As usual, my first stop was Ed Stahl's column on page two. I barely skimmed the sports section; February in the sports world is a lot like summer in Antartica: not very significant. After I'd exhausted the paper, I wrote a check, which I carefully detached from the checkbook and put in the top middle drawer of my desk. Then I sat back to anticipate my ten o'clock appointment.

As usual, Armand Treusch was late, this time by twenty-five minutes. He was nothing if not a marvel of consistency. Being habitually tardy is a not-so-subtle way of telling the rest of the world they don't quite matter as much as the latecomer does.

When he walked in the door, I moved my foot to the button beneath my desk that activated a tape recorder concealed in a drawer. It was one of those gadgets I'd been talked into by Marko Meglich when I moved to this office several years ago. I'd thought it was frivolous and unnecessary, but it had held me in good stead several times since.

"All right," Treusch snarled without preamble as soon as he walked in the door, "First I don't hear from you for days on end and then I get this fucking summons to drop everything and come all the way downtown to meet with you." His pugnacious chin jutted out like the prow of a sailboat.

"I'd like to point out," I said, "that you were the one who told me never to come to your office—I thought you wanted this whole David Ream thing kept quiet."

"I did."

"I can understand why."

He frowned. "Exactly what do you mean by that?"

"Sit down, Mr. Treusch, and I'll tell you."

He took off his coat but didn't hang it up; instead he draped it over one of my client chairs as if he knew he wasn't going to be there too long. Then he sat down in the other. "This better be good."

"Oh, it's good, all right. I quit."

"Pardon me?"

"I'm quitting. Withdrawing from your case."

"I don't understand," he said at last.

"I'm leaving your employ. Severing our relationship. I'm not going to work for you anymore. Is there any way I can say it more clearly?" I opened the drawer, took out the check, and passed it across the desk to him. "This is a full refund of your retainer. Whatever work I've already done on your behalf, and whatever expenses I've incurred, it's all on the house."

He held the check almost delicately between two fingers, without looking at it. "Just like that?" His tone was softer and quieter now, almost deadly so, which made him seem as dangerous as a basking shark. Someone should tell him he was more effective that way than in his bulldog mode. But it wasn't going to be me.

"Just like that," I said.

"Do I get to know why?"

"Let's just say that I uncovered some things about you that make me not want to continue with the project."

"Uncovered some things about me," he repeated evenly.

"That's right."

"That wasn't what you were being paid to do, uncover some things about me."

"I know. It just happened."

"It just happened, huh? That's pretty unethical on your part, Jacovich. I could sue your ass off."

"You could, but you won't."

"No?"

"I think not."

"You seem awfully damn sure of yourself."

I shrugged. "It's a character flaw of mine."

"You've wasted a week of my time."

"I'm sorry about that. I can tell you that David Ream is *not* spying for a competitor of yours, which is what you wanted to know. That's just about all you get for nothing."

The bulldog reappeared, growling, intimidating. "What the hell is that supposed to mean? Don't give me double-talk."

"That was straight talk," I said.

"It was also pretty abstruse." He waved the check in front of his face like an antebellum Dixie flirt with a flowered fan. "What's this all about, Jacovich? Why are you bailing out on this? People don't just quit me, they never have. Hell, they die working for me."

"I'd just as soon pass on that one too, thank you."

"Uh huh." He pulled at his nose nervously. "So do I get to know what this is about?"

I leaned back in my chair. "TroyTrike."

I had to give him credit; he didn't miss a beat. There was a slight change in the color of his eyes, though—they went from brown to a kind of pea-soup green in the flicker of a second. "TroyTrike? Where'd you hear about that?"

"I heard."

"Where."

"I *heard*," I said.

He took only a moment to decide how he was going to handle it, then waded right in. "So? What's the big deal? That's no secret. We're going to be featuring TroyTrike at the Toy Expo in Chicago next month. That's when most of the retailers place their Christmas orders."

"Are you going to explain how it falls apart easily? Are you going to tell everyone about the little toxic plastic parts that kids can swallow?"

His ruddy face turned suddenly gray, and the eyes went from peasoup to the waters of Lake Erie on a partly-cloudy winter day. "You're nuts," he proclaimed, but there was a little uncertain quiver in his voice I'd never heard before.

"Okay," I said. "I'm nuts."

"You are. You're nuts."

We stared each other down for a while, and I took no pride in my childish satisfaction when he looked away first. "You don't understand," he said at last.

"Enlighten me."

"TroyTrike is a low-end item. By design. I mean, we wanted to come out with something inexpensive, accessible to really low-income families. If we manufactured it any differently we'd have to charge more for it, and there wouldn't be any use in that, we'd have just another tricycle and who would give a fuck? The whole point is to trump the competition, catch them with their pants down. To come out with something that nobody else is making."

"Maybe nobody else is making it because it's unsafe. And poisonous."

"It's *not* unsafe."

"No? Would you let your kid have one?"

He shifted his butt in the chair and cleared his throat nervously. "My kids are in their twenties," he said.

I smiled. "That's got to be the non sequitur of the month."

Understanding broke over his face like a sunrise. "Is that what David Ream is up to? Is this all about TroyTrike?"

I shook my head. "Sorry, Mr. Treusch, but I don't work for you anymore."

Neither of us spoke for almost a minute, but he had stopped trying to outstare me. Instead he was paying rapt attention to a spot on the wall about three feet above my head. For all his impetuous temper, Armand Treusch was a careful, judicious man, and he was thinking things over carefully.

Finally he leaned forward and gently laid the check on my desk. "I want you to take this back."

I didn't touch the check, or look at it. I kept my eyes fixed on his.

"And I'm going to write you one of my own to go with it," he went on.

I lifted an eyebrow—nothing more.

"For ten thousand dollars."

I didn't react.

"Okay, you're right, I'm being a piker." He grinned and ducked his head as if I'd caught him cheating at golf. "There's no reason you shouldn't have a nicer taste of the pie. You've earned it—in your own peculiar way. So let's say fifteen thousand instead. How does that sound?"

"It sounds impressive," I said. "For a bribe."

He wagged his head from side to side. "That's a label. Don't stick labels on things. Labels don't mean anything. You can think of it as kind of a retainer if you want to. Binding you to TroyToy in friendship and loyalty. And you don't have to do a fucking thing, that's the beauty of it."

"Fifteen thousand dollars is a lot of beauty."

"It is, isn't it?" he observed sunnily. He reached into his inside pocket and extracted an alligator-skin checkbook. "That's a literal thing, by the way. You don't do anything, and you don't say anything."

"You think money is going to make this go away?"

His smile was smarmy. "You hear about miracle drugs, but money is the best cure in the world, Jacovich. It can make anything go away." He flipped open the checkbook and took out a pen.

"You're a smart man," I said. "You don't really believe I'm the only one who knows about this."

"No, I never thought that for a minute," he said. He riffled the edges of the checks. "But you'll notice there are a lot of checks in here."

"You're something else, Mr. Treusch."

"Yes, I am," he said, his heavy brows knitting into a frown, "and you'd do well to remember that. What do you think, I'm some sort of little kid here? I've done my homework. My marketing people have projected we're gonna move at least seven hundred thousand units in the first year alone, with a profit margin of about nine dollars, maybe nine and a quarter per unit. You think I'm going to piss that all away because some jag-off like David Ream gets a wild hair up his ass?"

"There are more people involved than David Ream."

"And none of them like money, huh?" He scribbled away on the check. "None of them could use an extra couple of bucks for maybe a new car, a vacation in Florida? Whoever they are, I'll make sure they're well taken care of. David Ream, too."

"You think it's that easy?"

"Sure it is. What? Everybody is noble?"

"Everybody isn't noble," I said. "Some people are."

"Only in the talking about it, not when it comes down to pictures of presidents, and not for some abstract concept or cause. Let me explain it to you in simple terms. You do something to hurt me, hurt my family, the people I care about, then I'll go balls to the wall to stop you. But if it comes to strangers, people I don't know or care about, that's a different story. Because I—you, all of us—come first with ourselves."

He ripped the check from the pad. "I'll give you an example," he said. "You take something that's gonna hurt or kill you or your neighbors, then you're gonna dig in your heels and fight. That's a personal matter, and we Americans get into pretty high dudgeon about that. But let the government drop some bombs on Iraq or Belgrade, wiping out civilians, and nobody says boo-cat. It's an abstract, you get what I mean?"

"Oh, I see. And you're going to move seven hundred thousand TroyTrikes in Iraq."

"For Christ's sake! Grow up a little, okay?"

"Don't you worry about lawsuits, Mr. Treusch?"

"No, I pay lawyers to worry about them. Besides, I don't think that will be a problem. Poor people don't sue. They don't know how to go about it. Lawyers and judges and courtrooms scare them. And if anybody makes too much noise . . ." He smiled and waved the check at me. "The miracle cure." He put it down on the desk and slid it toward me. "Don't spend it all in one place."

I didn't touch it, didn't even look at it. "I'm not going to spend it at all."

"Noble, huh? Fine, be that way." Treusch stood up. "Look, you think you can hurt me? You or some little pissant like David Ream? Guess again, my friend. You could have helped me, but you can't hurt me. Because I'm rich and you're not. And in case nobody ever told you before, money talks and bullshit walks."

He took his coat from the other chair and began putting it on. "I haven't gotten to be one of the largest toy companies in the world by running scared from guys like you, so learn something from me. This is business, *big* business, capitalism in its purest form. Every parent in America, when they think of TroyToy, they get all warm and fuzzy. Like Disney, like Mattel, like Hershey chocolates. Family friendly. Christ, people in the ghetto, people living in some rat-hole shack in Appalachia without running water and fucking their sisters, they *all* have TroyToy products in their living rooms. We're a household name. And no wimpy number cruncher like David Ream, and no beat-up Cleveland keyhole peeper like you is gonna change that."

I still hadn't moved, which seemed to disappoint him. I think he was hoping for an answer, or at the very least another argument he could demolish. When he realized he wasn't going to get one, he just flapped his arms and walked across the room to the door. "So you don't like me. That's tough noogies. I'd rather you loved me, but believe me, I can deal with it this way." He buttoned his coat and then straightened it fussily, and pulled on his black leather gloves. "You deal with it, too."

He didn't slam the door as I expected him to, and I had to award him a few points for that. I listened to him clattering down the stairs. After a few minutes the engine of his car coughed and turned over in the parking lot; he burned a little rubber leaving.

I lit a cigarette and smoked half of it before I got up and went to the coffee pot for a refill. Then I took his check and mine to the copy machine and made five copies of each before I put the originals in a manila envelope, scrawled TREUSCH on the front of it, and locked all of them in the filing cabinet behind my desk, along with the audiotape of our conversation.

Maybe he was right. There are a hell of a lot of people who would think so, who think that when anything turns sour you simply throw money at it and it goes away. Treusch could afford fifteen thousand thousand to me, maybe twenty to Ream, even a payoff to Helen Moise. It would still hardly put a dent in his projected six-and-a-half-million-dollar profit the first year alone. And even if it did, he could cut a corner somewhere else and make it up in a week.

There might even be a few more people, a lot tougher than I am, who figure as Treusch did that for a payday that big, there are one or two expendable kids. Kids like Caitlynn Ream, even like Andrew Takalo, who are nothing more than fodder for the cash cows, the profit-makers. What's a little plastic lug nut lodged in the throat of a three-year-old, or a busted head or kneecap, when weighed against six million bucks?

The trouble was that Treusch knew what he was talking about; it could be possible to buy off just about anyone. Maybe Helen Moise, although I wasn't certain whether she was in it for the money or for getting her name in the paper. Maybe even David Ream, damaged daughter or no. I didn't want to consider that.

I pondered for a minute how high *my* price might be; it was certainly a hell of a lot more than fifteen thousand bucks. I would like to think I was incorruptible, that Armand Treusch didn't *have* enough money to purchase my integrity, but when it comes down to reality, you never can tell.

In any case, I had to figure out what I was going to do about it. One thing was as sure as the sun coming up in the morning: I wasn't going to cash his check.

What I was going to do with it I hadn't yet decided.

Shifting my mental gears to a more immediate concern, I reviewed my notes on the Takalo kidnapping, smoking too many cigarettes and drinking too much coffee in the process. It didn't seem to me to be a leap of logic that the men who had bargained with the Fightmasters to buy their child—the crossed-eyed man and the redhead with the eastern European name—were the same ones who had spirited little Andrew out of his crib.

But were they working for Willetta Clemons? Was the Indian child for whom she had so recently found a home, the one whose adoptive parents I was angling to meet, Andrew Takalo? Was it some other kidnapped or bartered baby? Or was the adoption strictly legitimate?

I didn't think the latter to be true. Clemons had hinted to Suzanne and me that the legalities should be left to her, which probably satisfied a lot of longing, childless couples who didn't even realize they were turning the other way so as not to see what might or might not be legal. It didn't sit well with me, but I hesitated jumping to any conclusions that might later prove false, either.

It wasn't easy juggling my two cases at the same time, especially since I now was not going to earn any money from either of them.

No matter what the outcomes, I was seriously mucking about in other people's lives.

It might be argued that that is normally what I do for a living. But I was going to cause some pain somewhere, and that was making me uneasy.

I didn't want to think about it on an empty stomach anymore. I locked up the office and drove up out of the Flats to East 55th Street and Sterle's Slovenian Country House. It was a longish drive, considering how many other restaurants there were between there and my office, but I figured a pork chop with potatoes and gravy, eaten in the same room with thirty other people who shared my ethnic heritage, even though I might not know them, would go a long way toward settling me down.

Midway through lunch, my beeper vibrated in my pocket. I checked the readout to find Suzanne Davis was calling me. I finished eating, ordered coffee, and made my way to the pay phone in the vestibule.

"Milan, you rat!" she said when I got her on the line. "You forgot our anniversary!"

"Anniversary?"

"Yes. We've been married one whole day."

"I was waiting to see if it was going to last."

"Well, it'll last at least until this evening. If you're not busy. I just got a call from Willy-girl. She's set up a meeting for tonight with the couple who just adopted an Indian baby."

"At their house?"

"Yes," she said. "Out in Hudson."

That fit the profile. Hudson is a far-flung suburb in Summit County, southeast of the city, where almost half the households make more than seventy-five thousand dollars a year.

"Is Willy going to be there?"

"I don't know," Suzanne said. "Does it matter?"

"Not really," I said.

I hung up to hurry back to my table and finish my coffee; a couple of people at the other tables smiled at me, and I realized that I was smiling, too. Whatever residue of cynicism and disgust Armand Treusch had left me with that morning had been replaced by a soft, rosy inner glow. I couldn't be sure, but I thought that I might be within a few hours of finding Andrew Takalo.

Chapter Eighteen

Before we made the drive to Hudson, Suzanne Davis and I met for dinner out in Mayfield Heights at the Gates Mills Grill. I had opted for the casual look for the evening, corduroy jacket worn over a dark blue sweater. Suzanne had found another matronly pantsuit, this time in gray with a gay paisley scarf at her throat, but I don't know where she dug it up; habitually she wears black. Always the consummate pro, she had remembered once more to slip on the wedding ring.

"I can't believe that if it's the Takalo baby these people have, we're just supposed to walk away and do nothing," she said over her veal piccata.

"We have no authority, remember? We don't do anything and we don't say anything. We just smile and thank them and get back in the car and go home so they won't suspect a thing. Don't worry, they aren't going to disappear into the night." I took a sip of coffee. "Unless we spook them."

"Well, I won't," she said. "I'm the great actress, remember?"

"How could I forget?"

"It's going to take all my towering talent to fuss and coo and make goo-goo eyes at the baby. The last time I was anywhere near a child under the age of twenty-five, I *was* one."

"Pretend it's a cat," I suggested, knowing she had four of them running around her house.

"*That* I can do," she said. "But you—you're another story altogether, Milan. You always wear your feelings on your face."

"I guess I do at that. I'm a lousy poker player, too."

"No wonder you haven't gotten married again."

I laughed. "Is that what marriage is? Hiding your feelings?"

"Sometimes you have to," she said, and she was dead serious. "Otherwise most marriages wouldn't last a week." Then she smiled ruefully. "I had one that didn't go much longer than that, myself."

I thought about that. I thought about Connie, too. Maybe Suzanne was right, maybe I should just shut up and go with the flow, not letting Connie know when I was hurt or upset. But it's not how I'm made, and I figured that if I was going to spend the rest of my life with someone, I couldn't do it by walking around with a put-on happy face all the time while inside my ulcer bloomed like a sunflower.

"Here's what I found out today," she said. "When someone wants to give their baby up for adoption, they basically sign away their parental rights."

"Like a quitclaim on a house?"

"Sort of. And once they sign, then the child is placed in the adoptive home."

"And that's it?" I said. "It's a done deal?"

"No. Not for six months. There's kind of a holding period."

"So who is the child's legal guardian at that time?"

"The courts," she said. "But even if the birth mother changes her mind, she just can't walk in and say 'Sorry, I was just kidding.' "

"Why not?"

"It doesn't work that way. Remember, I said she signs away her rights. But if she can come in and petition the court and prove that she signed those papers under duress or as a result of fraud, then she's got a shot. Otherwise—too bad, so sad."

"What kind of fraud or duress?"

"Well, the obvious one, like, 'Give me your baby or I'll kill you.' Or if money changes hands. In Ohio, it's a no-no to buy and sell babies."

"Just in Ohio?"

"There are several states in the union where it's perfectly legal to just buy a baby. But Ohio isn't one of them."

"How many states overlook kidnapping?" I said.

"That's where we have the problem, isn't it?" She sipped at her

Perrier; we had decided it would not do to show up tonight with alcohol on our breath.

"So what happens when the six months are up?"

"Ah," Suzanne said. "Then the adoptive family goes to court. In Ohio it's probate court, in other states it's called family court or some other kind of court. And at that time the adoption is made official and binding, and it's their kid, to have and to hold until after it turns adolescent, starts wearing a purple Mohawk, and runs around with a nipple ring and tattoos."

"And the birth parents?"

"Out of the picture. Generally adoptions these days are open. In other words, the birth parents know where their kids are, the adoptive parents know where the birth parents are. The whole secrecy thing that has been in operation in the last two hundred years has shown itself not to work very well. But that doesn't mean the natural parents are in the kid's life in any way; that's a matter of personal choice."

"Where'd you get all this?" I said.

Her blue eyes twinkled. "I have my sources, Milan. So it seems to me that our job tonight is to see whether these people, with Willy Clemons to guide them, have done it the right way, or adopted this baby through the back door."

"Our bigger job is to see whether the baby is the one I'm looking for."

She nodded, and put her fork down. "Shit," she said.

"What?"

"Milan—these people think it's *their* baby."

"I don't know, Suzanne. Maybe it *is*. Selfishly, though, I hope it isn't."

"Why?"

"Because then I can get off this damned case and get back to earning a living."

We finished dinner and went outside to ransom the car from the valet. I steered it onto nearby I-271, and we headed south.

Hudson is a pleasant place to live, an Andy Hardy kind of spot that fairly drips Midwest. On the road between the freeway and the town itself, a few industrial parks give way to rolling farmlands that then morph into streets of picturesque, well-kept century homes, in turn leading into the commercial district with its trademark clock tower, the quaint Learned Owl Bookstore, and the historic Inn at Turner's Mill. Although the township is only thirty-four miles from Public Square, most Hudsonites don't consider themselves Greater Clevelanders the way many of the other suburban dwellers do, and often go for months without ever visiting the big city. It's a pretty idyllic place in which to raise a child.

Even one that was kidnapped and sold.

The name Willy Clemons had given over to Suzanne that afternoon was Groom. Evelyn and Lawrence Groom lived in a large, charming, light gray center-hall Cape Cod Colonial about six blocks from the clock tower. Snow covered the grass and the bushes, of course, and hung prettily from the bare branches of the sugar maples on the lawn, but the circular driveway in front of the house had been meticulously plowed. An Ohio State flag was caught up by a stiff breeze and snapped proudly from its mounting on one of the pillars supporting the small overhang that sheltered the front entry. It was dark out when we arrived, but the cheery yellowish light coming through the windows of the house glowed happily. One of winter's nicer features, I think, is how nice and warm it looks inside other people's windows.

Evelyn Groom answered the door. Blond and handsome rather than pretty, with a kind of windblown, go-to-hell air about her, she made us feel welcome immediately with her broad smile. She wore form-fitting cinnamon-colored suede pants and a bright blue man-tailored shirt.

Once inside, she led us past a formal living room that looked as though no one ever did any living in it, and into a big, sprawling family room off the kitchen, where she installed us in matching barrel chairs. The television set against the wall looked bigger than most of the movie screens at the local multiplex, and many components of an expensive sound system were connected to two enormous speakers that, turned to full volume, could probably blow out a wall. On a marble coffee table the size of a tennis court, bowls of nuts and other assorted munchies had been set out, I supposed in anticipation of our visit.

In one corner was a gleaming new playpen, and scattered all over were the appurtenances that invariably accompany the arrival of a brand-new baby in an affluent home. On an end table was a little electronic speaker, its red light glowing softly, which I assumed was monitoring any sounds that might come from the baby's room. I tried with only partial success to swallow the galling knowledge that if the Takalos could have afforded such a device, their little Andrew would be asleep in his own crib, and perhaps Joseph Ettawageshik might still be alive.

Waiting for us in the family room was Evelyn Groom's husband, Larry—tall, bluff, and robust, in a chocolate brown sweater over a white shirt and tan Dockers. After he offered us drinks, which we declined, he told us he was the executive vice president in charge of sales for a large retail grocery chain that was headquartered in Solon but had outlets all over the eastern part of the country. Both he and his wife looked to be around forty, the kind of healthy, in-shape forty of people who aerobicized at Bally's several times a week.

"What about you, Evelyn?" Suzanne asked. "Do you work, too?"

"I own an antique store in Macedonia," Evelyn said, meaning the Macedonia southeast of Cleveland and not the one in the Balkans that boasted Alexander the Great as its favorite son. "Of course I hardly go in anymore since Chad came—maybe twice a week, just to pay the bills." And she beamed broadly, sitting down on the leather sofa next to her husband and taking his hand.

Chad. They had named their new baby Chad. Chad Groom. A strong, no-nonsense name. Not very Indian at all.

"He must take a lot of your time," I said.

"It's amazing. I had no idea." The bluebirds in her heart were making her face glow. "But it's worth it. Larry and I had almost given up on having children, so this has been such a blessing . . ."

"How difficult was it, Evelyn?" Suzanne leaned forward, knees on her thighs, wringing her hands a bit. "How long did it take, the whole process?"

"Well, that's the amazing part," she said.

Larry cut in. "We'd been trying to adopt through the usual channels for two years or more. We ran into nothing but problems, runarounds, bureaucratic red tape. And there just didn't seem to be any white kids available."

"It was very frustrating," Evelyn said.

I nodded sympathetically. "I can imagine. We've been going through pretty much the same thing."

"So when we went to Ms. Clemons, it was almost as though she was our last hope. We'd been disappointed so often before . . ." She trailed off.

"But she was able to get the ball rolling quickly?" Suzanne said.

"Oh, yes. I think from the time we first walked into her office until the time they brought little Chad to the door, it was no more than eight weeks altogether."

"Seven," Larry corrected her.

"Seven weeks," I shook my head. "Amazing. Was it in your mind to adopt a Native American child at the beginning?"

"No," Evelyn said. "It just never occurred to us. But Willy said that if we really wanted a baby quickly, that was the way to go. And we'd been trying for *so* long . . ."

"Did you specify boy or girl?"

"Well, it didn't really matter to me, but Larry had his heart set on a boy." Evelyn leaned conspiratorially toward Suzanne. "You know how men are about having sons . . ."

"He's going to play football at Ohio State," Larry cut in. "I've already decided. That's where we both went to school, you know. Maybe he'll be a classic Buckeye running back. Or a strong safety, depending on how big he gets." He fairly beamed with pride.

"That's terrific," I said. Just specify the size and color baby you want, and it's delivered directly to your door. Like ordering from the Lands' End catalog. "How did they happen to find a child for you so quickly?"

"Oh, I don't know," Evelyn said. "We just left it all to Willy. She's a miracle worker."

Some miracle. If you can't buy one, steal one. And, I thought, remembering Joseph Ettawageshik, throw in a little murder on the side. "It usually takes a lot longer than seven weeks, doesn't it?"

Larry grinned. "Willy Clemons cut through all that red tape for us. Like we said, she's something else."

She sure was, I thought. "And so then what happens? In six months you go to court and then the adoption is final?"

Evelyn Groom frowned just the slightest bit. "Oh no. The adoption is final right now. That's what Willy told us. We have the paperwork."

I gulped hard, knowing that's not the way it works; the Grooms were being led down the garden path, too. "That's good. That's—great, Evelyn." I wasn't nearly the actor Suzanne was.

"And the birth parents?" Suzanne said. "No problems with them?"

"Oh, no," Evelyn assured her. "The records are closed. We don't even know who they are, and they don't know who we are."

I felt as if I had swallowed an ice cube, cold and lumpy in my stomach. I couldn't think of anything else to say. Once again, Suzanne saved the moment.

"Well, this is certainly the easiest and most carefree adoption I've ever heard of," she said. "Sounds like it was a good move, going to Willy Clemons."

"Oh, it was!"

"Leon and I have lots of talking to do, but right now my gut instinct tells me to go for it." Suzanne smiled dazzlingly. "If it goes half as well as it did for you, we'll be thrilled to death."

Evelyn said, "I can only wish you and Leon the happiness that we've found, Suzanne." And she squeezed her husband's hand again. "I hope we've given you all the information you need. And all the encouragement."

"You've been very generous," I said. "Thank you both. There is one more thing . . ." I cleared my throat and looked down at my loafers. The Grooms looked at me expectantly. "I was wondering if it would be possible for us to just have a quick peek at the baby."

"Oh, Leon," Suzanne gushed at me. "I was going to ask, but I didn't want to impose . . ."

"It's no imposition," Larry Groom assured us. "As long as you promise not to wake him."

They led us up the stairs and down a long hallway to a roomy yet cozy bedroom. A Mickey Mouse nightlight glowed near the baseboard, but there was also a small table lamp burning. The wallpaper featured a light blue sky with multicolored stars that twinkled. Larry stayed out in the hall, but Evelyn led us inside, a silencing finger to her lips, and we all three hovered over the expensive white crib, draped with mosquito netting like a bed in a hunting camp in Kenya.

The baby was lying on his back, face turned to one side. His light brown cheeks were fat and smooth, pink mouth a perfect bow, and his jet black hair fell across his forehead like Moe Howard's of the Three Stooges.

"Here's Chad," Evelyn Groom whispered proudly, her adoring eyes never leaving the sleeping child. "Isn't he darling?"

"Oh, he's precious!" Suzanne breathed.

Evelyn, with the ravishing smile of a pre-Raphaelite madonna, leaned down and kissed the top of the child's head. "Babies are so soft," she said. "Their hair is like cotton candy." She breathed in through her nose. "And they *smell* so good."

I studied the child's face carefully. To one extent or another all babies, no matter what their ethnicity, are beautiful. I tried to memorize the tiny features anyway. "He's a little angel," I said softly.

And sadly.

After we took our leave of the ecstatic Groom family, Suzanne and I repaired to the lounge of the Inn at Turner's Mill, not far from the house; I think we were both in dire need of a drink. We sat at the far end of the bar in morose and uncomfortable silence, while the Mike Petrone Trio supplied smooth, tasty jazz licks at the other side of the room.

After our drinks had arrived, I took a photocopy of Andrew

Takalo's photograph out of my pocket and spread it on the bar. We both studied it carefully; there could be no doubt it was the same baby who slept peacefully less than a mile away, the one Larry and Evelyn Groom had named Chad.

"God damn it," I said finally.

"My sentiments exactly." She sipped moodily at her drink. "Sometimes I hate my job."

I nodded. "They seem like really nice people, the Grooms."

"They're so happy, so thrilled," Suzanne said. "They're going to be absolutely destroyed."

"Shattered," I agreed.

"It's a dirty shame."

We sat quietly for a while.

Then she said, "You know, Milan . . ." and left it in the air.

I waited until she was ready.

"There are a lot worse ways for a kid to grow up than with loving, well-to-do parents in a beautiful suburb like this."

"There are indeed." I fumbled in my pocket for my cigarettes, hoping she wouldn't ride this particular train of thought to the next station. My hopes died aborning.

"It seems almost criminal to take that kid out of that lovely, loving home and send him back to live in a shack with parents on welfare."

"There isn't any alternative."

"I wish we could come up with one."

"Suzanne, what the hell are you saying?"

"I'm just thinking of the good of the baby."

I shook a Winston out of the pack and ignited it. "That doesn't wash, and you know it. If it did, then only rich people should have children."

She raised one cynical eyebrow.

"Come on, Suzanne, the Grooms are intelligent people. They had to know something wasn't kosher about this adoption."

"They didn't know the baby was kidnapped, Milan, I'd bet my life on that."

"No," I said, "and I'm sure they didn't know an old man was

murdered because he found out about it, either. But basically they went out and hired a crooked lawyer to buy themselves a black market baby."

"You have no sympathy at all for them?"

"Sure I do," I said. "I know they're so thrilled with becoming parents that they're probably in complete denial about how it all went down so easily."

"Wow." She shook her head and waved an impatient hand in front of her face to dissipate my cigarette smoke, looking at me with a disapproval that had nothing to do with my tobacco habit.

"What?"

"You're a hard man."

"Right is right and wrong is wrong, Suzanne. There's no such thing as a *little bit* wrong."

"Oh, bullshit!" she said, and two people several stools away at the bar turned and looked at her. "My God, hasn't anyone ever told you that the world is *not* black and white."

"It should be."

"Shoulda-woulda-coulda, Milan. It's not!"

"That baby belongs with his natural parents, Suzanne, and you know it."

"I know, I know. It's just that the Grooms love him so much."

"So do the Takalos. You aren't seriously suggesting . . ."

She shook her head almost violently. "I'm not suggesting anything. Just kind of thinking out loud."

"Well," I said, "tell your thoughts to shut up."

CHAPTER NINETEEN

Lieutenant Florence McHargue and Detective Bob Matusen and I were sitting in McHargue's cramped little office the next morning, and neither of them said very much while I told them the story. She just sipped her tea thoughtfully while he efficiently scribbled notes. When I was finished, Matusen looked at his boss, wisely deferring to her to make the first comment.

She kept him waiting for more than a minute—kept us both waiting.

"It seems pretty clear," she said when she had evidently decided she'd left us hanging long enough, "that there might be a connection between all this and Joseph Ettawageshik winding up in the Cuyahoga."

"I thought so too," I said.

Without looking at Matusen, she said "Maybe you ought to go have a chat with Willetta Clemons, ASAP."

"She might have ordered the murder done, Lieutenant," I said, "but I'll lay odds she didn't do it herself. The old man was twice her size; even if she could have cut his throat without a struggle, there's no way she could have dumped him in the river without muscle."

McHargue looked at me through her blue-tinted glasses and waited for me to elaborate.

"Maybe the little guy with the cockeye and the redhead with the ethnic name," I said.

"The Bohunk name."

I tried not to smile. "Well, it sounded Bohunk to Marie Fightmaster, anyway. It could be something like Schultz or Schwartz for all we know."

"I guess we'll find out," McHargue said.

"What about the baby?"

"What about him?"

"How do we get him back to his parents?"

She looked at Matusen, then back at me, and her chest rose and fell with a deep sigh. "*We* don't," she said softly.

I started to protest but she held up a hand. "I know, I know. But first of all, this is the homicide bureau, and all I care about is who killed Ettawageshik. I don't have the personnel or the budget to chase kidnappers. Secondly, I'm an employee of the city of Cleveland, and that's where I get paid to police. Not only was the kid snatched in another state, the adoptive parents don't even live in this county. So even if you go down the hall to missing persons, you're going to get the same answer. The kidnapping is not in the Cleveland P.D.'s jurisdiction."

"It's departmental policy, Milan," Matusen told me. "You were a cop, you know how territorial local agencies can get."

"I sure do."

"So," McHargue finished, "if you want to get that baby back with his birth parents in Michigan, you're going to have to take care of it yourself."

I felt my shoulders slumping. I had hoped that now Andrew Takalo had been found my job would be over. But there's no rest for the weary, I guess. Or is it no rest for the wicked? I never have known exactly how that old saying goes. All I knew was that at the moment I was a hell of a lot more weary than wicked, and I wasn't getting any rest at all. I wasn't even getting paid. Maybe the quote should be, "no rest for the sucker for a sad story."

"I can't just walk into the Grooms' house and walk out again with the baby on my hip, Lieutenant. So how do you suggest I go about that?"

"Kidnapping is a federal squeal. If I were you, I'd talk to the FBI."

"Oh, crap." I sighed.

She smiled. "Don't you get along with the fibbies?"

"Let's just say that every time I've had to deal with the federal government in the past, the experience has been less than happy. Remember that drug business out in Lorain County last fall?"

"Ah, yes," she said, nodding, her face turning sour with the memory. "Special Agent McAleese. A real Tiny Alice."

"Tiny Alice?"

"You need to get back on the street, Milan," Matusen said. "A Tiny Alice is a tight-ass."

"Oh," I said, making a mental note.

"But McAleese is DEA, not FBI."

"It's alphabet soup no matter how you slice it, Bob. Besides, all G-men go to the same tailor for their tight suits."

"I wish I could help you out," McHargue said. "But my hands are tied. I know you understand."

"Sure," I said, and stood up. "Would it violate departmental policy if you were to let me know what happens with Willetta Clemons?"

McHargue thought about that for a minute. "I'll do what I can," she said.

I nodded, jerked my chin at Matusen by way of a good-bye, and started for the door.

"Mr. Jacovich." McHargue's voice was low and tight, as if she were straining to get the words out.

Mister Jacovich? I was coming up in the world, at least in this office. I looked back at her.

Her gaze was somewhere over my left shoulder. "Thanks," she said. "I appreciate your help. I mean that. Right from the beginning when you came in and told us about Ettawageshik sitting on the bench. I want you to know that the department is grateful."

I was more than stunned. My relationship with Florence McHargue had always been spiky to say the least, and that was on the good days. About all I could manage by way of a reply was, "Sure, Lieutenant."

On my way downstairs from her office, I thought of several things I could have said instead. Shoulda-coulda-woulda, as Suzanne Davis might have observed.

So I hied myself over to the Federal Building, was kept waiting in a chilly, sterile government-issue anteroom for almost an hour, and then told my story all over again to an FBI tape recorder that sat in the middle of the table, its red light glowing ominously, almost malevolently, like some sort of infernal machine in a cheesy 1950s horror flick. Also present to ask the occasional question was Special Agent Sylvia Melina, whose tailored blue suit was not quite as tight as those of some of her male colleagues. More's the pity; she was certainly the most attractive FBI agent I'd ever seen, jet black hair done up in a pre–World War II style that had evidently come back again, and black, flashing eyes. She was a trifle overweight, but she carried it well.

And that made me think about Connie again; maybe in my subconscious I was letting go of the relationship. I was starting to notice the charms of other women.

It took me four tape changes and the better part of two hours to tell the entire story, and then I had to give Melina the phone numbers of the Takalos and the Fightmasters and Eddie Ettawageshik in Michigan. And of course she wanted to talk to Willetta Clemons as well, and to Suzanne Davis for corroboration. I had a twinge of guilt about involving Suzanne as I had; it had started out with her as a simple favor, pro bono, and turned into an elaborate masquerade in Clemons's office, another in the Groom home, and now a grilling by the FBI.

Sometimes it isn't easy to be my friend, I thought to myself; that was something I needed to work on.

I had to wait another hour or so while an FBI word processor typed up a transcript so I could read it and sign it. The federal bureaucracy doesn't take any chances; it crosses all it's *t*'s and dots it's *i*'s to add to the government's great wall of paper.

"I'd like to know what happens to the baby," I told Melina.

"Why?"

"Because I spent a lot of time trying to find him, and because I've grown fond of his family, and because I'm doing my duty by coming in here and talking to you and figure that's the least I can ask for."

She was thoughtful for a bit. "We'll see," was the best she could offer me. My guess was that ever since George Bush asked us to read his lips about no new taxes, representatives of the U.S. government are pretty careful about making promises they aren't sure they can keep.

When I got back to the office it was nearly three o'clock. I called Eddie Ettawageshik and told him what had happened. He sounded overjoyed, and thanked me profusely.

"No thanks are necessary, Eddie. Maybe if someone else is in trouble sometime you can help them out."

"I will," he said. "You can count on it." But he kind of left the end of the sentence up in the air, as if he wasn't quite finished.

I waited.

"Now if I could only find out what really happened to my granddad . . ."

"Eddie," I said, "the Cleveland police are working on that. I can't really stick my nose in. It's a capital case. I'm not allowed to."

"Oh, sure," he said with a notable lack of conviction. "I understand that." But it didn't sound as if he did.

"I'd lose my license."

"It's okay, Mr. Jacovich."

"I've got the feeling that when the FBI finds the kidnappers, they're going to have your granddad's killers, too. Just be a little patient."

He was silent.

"The good news is that the one thing we could do something about, we did—finding Andrew. And he's alive and well, so that's a lot to be thankful for."

"I know," he said. "I didn't mean to sound ungrateful."

"You didn't," I lied. "And I'm going to let you have the pleasure of telling Wanda. Go over there, Eddie, don't do it on the phone."

"I'll go *right* over," he said, and sounded a little bit more cheerful before disconnecting.

I phoned Suzanne and let her know that the FBI had things in hand and would be contacting her, and that since the Grooms' adoption was in no way legal, Baby Andrew would be back in the bosom of his family within days.

"Great," she said tonelessly, as if I'd just told her someone had broken into her house.

"It's what's right, Suzanne."

"Right for who? You?"

"This isn't about me. Or you."

"No," she said, "it's about a baby growing up in a shack instead of a mansion. It's about a baby growing up to do day labor instead of carrying the football for Ohio State." She cleared her throat. "I know. I know what's right. Why do I just feel so shitty about it?"

"Because right and wrong isn't situational. It just—*is*."

Her sigh through the receiver was like a sudden rush of wind in tall trees. "I'm glad you can cuddle up to that at night, Milan."

Before hanging up, we made the usual polite noises about getting together soon, but I had the feeling we would not. Not for a long time, anyway. Making hard choices sometimes strains the warp and woof of a friendship.

So an old man was still dead and his killers were still walking around, at least for the moment, and affluent, loving, capable Evelyn and Larry Groom were going to lose their newfound son, while practically indigent Frank and Wanda Takalo were going to regain theirs. I knew what was right, too, but like Suzanne Davis, I felt shitty about it as well.

But at last it was over. Finally Andrew was found and on his way back to where he belonged, and the Odawas of Cross Village were out of my life and I could get on with running my business.

And that prospect left me with little joy as well. Because it meant making another hard choice, that of once more putting professional ethics against what was right.

I walked around the office for a while, smoking a Winston, watching the gulls scatter and then band together to talk things over in midair and then part again, dipping down to the surface of the ice-choked river and then up into the sunlight with a flash of the white undersides of their wings.

Then I bit the bullet. I sat down at my desk, dialed the TroyToy number, and asked to speak to David Ream.

Chapter Twenty

My first thought was to meet him at the Winking Lizard, where I knew he was comfortable and familiar. But I decided that at five-thirty in the afternoon the raucous, festive Lizard on Miles Road, the original and flagship restaurant of what was now becoming a chain, was a trifle too noisy to allow for the kind of conversation I was planning. So instead I asked David Ream to join me at the Lion and the Lamb out on Lander Circle. It was on his way home from Solon anyway.

The venerable Lion and the Lamb in Pepper Pike boasts one of the last true piano bars anywhere in western civilization, and while for the last twenty-one years Joey Sands could be counted on for mellow jazz four nights a week, here in the late afternoon it was quiet, save for the inescapable piped-in music in the background.

It hadn't been easy getting Ream to agree to the meeting. I'd used no subterfuge, though, giving him my real name over the phone, even though good old Leon Kobler had almost gotten me out of the habit, and when I told him it was urgent that I talk to him that day, he'd said, "I'm afraid your name isn't familiar to me, Mr. Jacovich."

"Perhaps the name Helen Moise is more familiar to you then, Mr. Ream?"

He'd sucked in his shock audibly. There was a very lengthy silence, and then he'd said tightly, "Where do you want to meet?"

I recognized him when he came in, of course. We sat at the piano bar, empty at this hour, away from the handful of men and women in business suits who had straggled in to sit at the L & L's big circular bar for a few quick belts to wash away the treacheries of the day. On the mirror behind the piano was posted a garish notice about an upcoming St. Patrick's Day party.

Ream was wearing a suit too, perhaps the same one I'd seen him in at the Winking Lizard, baggy, nondescript gray tweed with a muted knit tie of monochromatic maroon over a shirt of discreet white and gray stripes. His mouth was pinched and nervous, and he blinked his eyes a lot, regarding me as if I were a visitor from the planet Jupiter. I imagined the closest he'd ever been to a private detective before was watching reruns of *Magnum, P. I.*, on Nick at Nite.

"Thanks for coming on such short notice, Mr. Ream," I said after I'd collected our drinks from the bartender.

"I didn't have much choice, did I?"

"We all have choices."

"Yeah, right," he said. "What is this, some sort of weird blackmail scheme, mentioning Helen's name on the phone like that? What do you want from me? Money? Well, you've picked the wrong guy, because I don't have any money." He dug a finger around the edge of his collar. "I could come up with three, maybe four thousand, but that's my absolute limit . . ."

"I don't want your money, Mr. Ream," I said. "I just want to talk to you. I'm even buying the drinks." I gave him one of my business cards. "I'm a legitimate private investigator."

He looked at the card, then at me, then at the card again. "What is it you're investigating?"

There was no getting around it, so I just let him have it right off. "You."

He recoiled as if I'd slapped him. "Why me?"

"Because Armand Treusch was paying me to do it."

His Adam's apple worked strenuously, and I had to give him a lot of credit for a man who walked through life being beige; he could have loudly and falsely proclaimed his purity. He didn't. Instead he lifted his glass of beer and chewed at it. "I see," he said quietly.

"But my investigation has taken some strange turns, and I wanted to talk to you before I do anything. As a courtesy."

"Some courtesy."

I lit a cigarette, and he glowered his disapproval at that. Let him, I figured. We were in a bar, not the Cleveland Clinic.

"Let's get the basics out of the way first," I said. "You're double-dipping, aren't you?"

He gave me a puzzled frown, but it wasn't very convincing.

"Come on, you're an accountant, you know what that means. You're taking a salary from Armand Treusch, but along the way you're digging into their TroyTrike production secrets and funneling them back to Helen Moise at Consumer Watchdog, who is also paying you."

The skin on his face sagged as if it was being melted off his bones by a high, intense heat. His breath was a series of short, desperate gasps, and he turned so pale I feared for a moment he was going to have a heart attack.

"Are you okay?"

He gave the question some consideration, got himself under control, and then nodded brusquely, reaching for his drink again. When he set it down the glass was more than half-empty, and he exhaled noisily, a sigh that was more of a moan. "You don't understand," he said finally.

"I understand better than you think. I've talked to Helen Moise."

He seemed to get smaller on the bar stool, his already slumping shoulders practically disappearing, and he lowered his head, not looking at me. "I don't think I want to have this conversation," he said, but it came out like a plea for mercy.

"I think you do."

"Why should I?"

"Because I want to help you."

"Who asked you?"

"Nobody, Mr. Ream, I'm just dealing myself in." I smiled at him to take the sting out. "I do that sometimes."

His eyes closed and then opened again; it was too protracted for a mere blink. "Some things you can't help."

"I know what happened to your little girl," I said. "I'm sorry. Really sorry. I have kids myself . . ."

Now he raised his chin a little, more in surprise than anything else. "You've done some homework. You know a lot."

"I know enough that I don't like what TroyToy is doing."

"But . . ." He looked around as if the walls might be listening. "Army is paying you."

"Was," I said. "I quit."

"Oh. Well. Um—*I* can't pay you."

"I don't expect you to," I said. "This is my dime."

"As you pointed out, I'm an accountant, so I know damn well you can't make a living that way."

"I'm independently wealthy," I told him. "I've got enough in the bank so that I can live very nicely until, oh, say a week from Thursday at about two o'clock in the afternoon."

My attempt at humor was unsuccessful; either he didn't think it was funny or, more probably, he didn't get it. "I'm not sure why we're here, Mr. Jacovich. Exactly what is it you want from me?"

"I want to know all about your relationship with Helen Moise. I want to know what you know. About TroyTrike. Where are they, what are they doing, how close are they. The whole enchilada."

He wagged his head from side to side. "I can't do that. How do I know you're telling me the truth? How do I know you're not working for some other toy company? How do I know you're not going to go right back to Army Treusch and tell him what I tell you?"

"You don't," I said. "You'll just have to trust me."

"That's asking a lot." His eyes narrowed and grew suspicious and flinty. "I mean, I never heard of you until you called this afternoon. I don't know you, why in hell should I trust you? After all, you were working for TroyToy, and you're double-crossing them. How do I know you won't double-cross me?"

"How do you know the bartender didn't slip a cyanide capsule into your beer?"

He started, frightened. "What?"

David Ream obviously had the sense of humor of a cantaloupe. "Joke. Look, Mr. Ream, why do you think I called you? I've already turned down your bribe, and I already know about you and Consumer Watchdog. If I was going to blow the whistle on you to Treusch, I would have done it a long time ago, and you'd be out of a job, if not staring at a lawsuit. Treusch likes to sue people."

"I don't know," he said. "I'd need to talk to Helen first. Before we get into anything about TroyTrike, I mean."

"Why?"

"She's paying me. I owe her a certain loyalty."

"Treusch is paying you, too."

"That's different."

Sure it was. David Ream practiced selective morality. We all do, I guess; after all, Treusch had been paying *me*, too.

"How did you get involved with Helen in the first place?"

"She's a friend of a friend of a friend," Ream said. "You know how those things work. She heard what happened to my little Caitlynn, and that I had quit my job to take care of her."

"How is Caitlynn doing, by the way?"

He seemed amazed that I cared. "She's—coming along. The . . ." He blinked his eyes again as if it was hard for him to even say the words. "The brain damage—the permanent brain damage—will be minimal."

"That's great," I said. "I'm very glad to hear that."

He gave me another quizzical look. "Thank you."

The silence hung between us, suspended from a cobweb thread. "Helen Moise," I prompted gently.

"Oh. Yes. Well, she brought me in to do some tax stuff for her. Her ex-husband settled a lot of money on her, it's very complicated. And," he added, "I'm afraid it's confidential."

"That's all right, I'm not interested in how much money she has. So after you finished the tax stuff . . . ?"

"Well, we'd done a lot of talking while I was working on her books. I mean, I did most of it at home so I could be with Caitlynn, but I spent some time at Helen's house almost every day, and she's quite an open, talkative person. She told me about Consumer Watchdog, that she was going to be getting into the area of products that were hazardous to children, and she knew that was something that would interest me. Because of Caitlynn, you know."

"Uh-huh."

"So of course that kind of hooked me, and when she asked me to sign on as a consultant, I did." He smiled ruefully. "Especially since I needed the money. You know?"

"A consultant."

"Yes."

"And what did you consult on? I mean, before you went to work full-time at TroyToy?"

"Actually," he said, "I functioned pretty much the way you do. I investigated things."

"What things? TroyToy?"

"Oh, no. Not at first. Actually, when we got started, Helen was more interested in the food industry. Food and beverage, that is. You know, the snacks and drinks that are marketed directly at kids and have so little nutritional value? Well, I was trying to find out which of them might actually be *harmful* to kids."

"Where did Helen find out about these harmful products in the first place?"

"She didn't," he said. "That was *my* job. To hunt them out."

"You mean," I said with a certain wonder, "that Helen doesn't wait until someone makes a complaint? That she actually goes around *looking* for people and companies to screw over?"

He went on the defensive. "I don't see it that way—as screwing them over. I see it as being an advocate for the public who isn't very well informed about most things like this." He allowed himself a small smile. "The name of her outfit is Consumer Watchdog."

Helen Moise was getting more and more interesting to me by the second. "Is that what happened with TroyToy?"

The smile grew rueful. "No. She knew a lot about TroyToy from the beginning. That's why when she heard about the opening for my job, she jumped right on it."

"How did she hear about it?"

"I believe from Armand Treusch."

"She knows Treusch personally?"

"Oh, yes," he said. Then his brows knit together and I could see he was wrestling with whether or not to tell me something.

"How?" I said. Just a tiny prompt.

"Well . . ."

More wrestling.

"Um." His pale face turned color; I think he was actually embarrassed. "Up until about five months ago when he broke it off for some reason, she was fucking him."

I was glad the stools around the piano bar had backs on them, or I just might have fallen off mine. Helen Moise was not a brave crusader righting wrongs; she was a woman scorned.

"Mr. Ream," I said, "has it ever occurred to you that you're being used to settle a score between Helen and Army?"

He shrugged. "What's the difference? It's for a good cause."

"Which is?"

His eyes flashed for the first time since we'd sat down. "Keeping TroyTrike off the market."

"Then it's true, what Helen told me? It is unsafe?"

He nodded. "I have copies of the tests, the production records. It's just about enough information for Helen to take it public."

"And you don't care that Helen stands to make a lot of money out of the lawsuit."

"She's not doing it for the money, Mr. Jacovich."

"People don't do things like that if there's no money in it for them."

"Look at you," he said. "You're involving yourself in this, and there's not going to be any money in it for you."

"Yeah," I said, full of rue and regret. "Well, that's because I'm a dumb schmuck."

CHAPTER TWENTY-ONE

When David Ream finally left the Lion and the Lamb, he was badly shaken up, there was no doubt about that. His hands had actually trembled, and he was blinking rapidly. But it seemed when he walked out the door that he was standing a little taller, too, and his chin was set at a more determined angle. He wasn't the kind of man who could be completely comfortable with dishonesty or dissembling, and I think he was relieved to finally get it out in the open to someone, even to a man he wasn't sure he could trust.

He had uneasily promised me that he would get me copies of all his research and notes on TroyTrike by the end of the week. What I was going to do with them once I got them, I hadn't yet decided.

I didn't like Armand Treusch; I hadn't from the very start. The more I learned about him, the less I liked him. I certainly didn't want him making several million dollars from the pockets of parents of small children who were being unknowingly put in jeopardy by his cheesy practices and even shoddier materials. That I wanted to stop him was a given.

Helen Moise would do that quite nicely, I imagined, and enhance her reputation and her bank account at the same time. But then I didn't much like her either.

Rather than being motivated by genuine concern for the consumer, or by righteous moral indignation, Moise was a professional muckraker who went around hoping to find trouble and then cashed in on it in terms of both money and, what I imagined to be even more important to her, personal aggrandizement. Some people will do anything to get their names in the paper.

And then of course, in the case of Armand Treusch, she was gleefully driven by taking the revenge of a cast-aside lover.

I didn't want Helen Moise making her bones on my watch. Yet Treusch and his potentially lethal tricycle had to be shot down out of the sky. I was walking still another ethical tightrope, it seemed, and for the second time in two days.

That was too damned many.

Moving from the now-deserted piano bar to the regular bar at the L & L, I ordered another beer and took some time to think things over.

Except for the need to clean up a few odds and ends relating to other clients, I was basically out of work. I wasn't too worried about it; my business had flourished in the past year, and I was certain something else would come along soon, hopefully this time with a payday at the end of it rather than the fiscally unprofitable and ultimately expensive week I had just spent on TroyToy and the Ettawageshik-Takalo matters. But for the moment I had nothing requiring my attention and concentration except for my own personal life.

And that brought me to Connie, and a too-long period of silence that was rapidly coming to a head.

The Land of Limbo is not my favorite place in which to reside, and at the moment that seemed where our relationship was firmly planted. I've spent much of the past ten years since my divorce without a significant other, and I supposed I could do so again. Most relationships, at least the ones in my experience, don't end with a resounding crash and a shower of sparks; they simply dry up and blow away like the topsoil of Oklahoma in the Dust Bowl era.

You want to know the really tough part of being alone? Movies.

It sounds silly, but I am a big movie fan and always have been. And while the big studio films featuring explosions or coming-of-age angst leave me pretty cold, I still love films, especially the foreign imports and the independent variety so popular at the

Cedar-Lee Theater or the Cleveland International Film Festival, which was coming up in March. I just don't like going to them by myself, that's all.

So if Connie wanted to blow taps over our relationship, I could steel myself and eventually handle it. I'd simply rent videos and watch them by myself, drinking a beer and munching microwave popcorn. I just wanted to know where I stood.

It was nearly seven o'clock, and the dinner crowd was beginning to filter in. I knew Connie would be home from the White Magnolia by now, so I drained my beer and stood up with the idea of going to the pay phone in the long, narrow cloakroom off the bar. I took two steps and changed my mind.

If she wanted things to be over between us, so be it. I wasn't going to negotiate the relationship with her; either she wanted to be with me or she did not. I just wanted her to tell me.

And not over the phone.

I knew that her father and brothers would be at the restaurant, and that she would be alone so we could talk. If she was home, that is. And if she would talk to me. I climbed into my car, drove west on Chagrin Boulevard, and jumped onto the freeway. It took me about forty-five minutes to get to Connie's house on the west side.

She looked surprised when she found me on her doorstep. She was wearing a black sweatshirt with a colorful Bugs Bunny appliqué across her chest, and gray sweatpants, and her French braid had been combed out into a casual ponytail, secured with an ordinary rubber band. She put a nervous hand to her hair when she saw me.

"I'm not exactly dressed for company," she said.

"Serves me right for coming over without calling." I tried to smile. "Am I catching you at a bad time?"

It took her entirely too long to answer. "No," she finally said. "Come on in."

She draped my coat over the railing of the stairway going up to the second floor, as if she didn't expect me to be staying very long. The living room furnishings were eclectic; a big leather chair that I knew was forbidden to anyone but Leo, a sprawling sofa patterned in a Southwestern design, sisal area rugs covering a hardwood floor, and various wooden tables in several shades of brown or tan. The television was on—a *Frasier* rerun—and the detritus of Connie's dinner was on the coffee table.

We gabbed for a few minutes about not much of anything. I told her that both my cases had been wrapped up and that I was now pretty much a gentleman of leisure, and she lied prettily to me about how busy things had been at the White Magnolia. It was the kind of mindless conversation that doesn't quite accomplish anything except filling up time and space, and we both knew it.

And then came that awful moment where the polite, inconsequential small talk trails off into an awkward and painful silence that hangs in the air like one hundred percent humidity on a hot August night and precedes getting down to matters less than polite and more than inconsequential.

"Well," she said at last, not as cheerily as either of us might have hoped, "what brings you to the uncharted wilds of the west side?"

"I should think that would be obvious." I sat down on one end of the sofa. "Long time no talk, Connie."

"I know," she said. "It's my fault. I haven't returned your calls."

"I noticed."

"Sorry."

"Me, too."

"Well—we need to talk."

A shiver ran down my back. Every man knows what those words mean. When it comes to relationships, nothing good has ever been preceded by "We need to talk."

"Okay," I said. "Would you like to clue me in on what's going on?"

She was scanning the sky for passing aircraft, hampered by the existence of the ceiling. At any rate, she was not looking at me. "Nothing's going on, exactly."

"That's the trouble."

"What?"

"Nothing's going on. Between us. We're not being together, we're not even talking."

She sighed. "I'm just feeling very—conflicted right now. You know."

"I *don't* know," I said. "That's why I'm here. To find out. I thought maybe that if I called, you wouldn't pick up the phone. So I drove over."

"I probably wouldn't have picked up, Milan. Not because I'm mad at you, but I just don't quite know what to tell you."

"No easy answers?"

"Not easy at all."

"What's the problem then, Connie?"

She curled her feet up under her and leaned back against the arm of the sofa, as far from me as she could get. "I'm not sure I can explain it to you."

"Give it your best shot."

But she didn't. She just worried her bottom lip with her teeth. I waited for what must have been a full minute. Then I said, "So—what now? We just wait until it goes away?"

"No, that wouldn't be fair to either of us." She shook her head and reached back to give her ponytail a nervous flip. Then she sighed. "Okay. As you know, I come from a Marine Corps family. All the Haley men have *Semper Fi* tattooed on their hearts. I was just a little kid, but I remember so vividly my father being in Vietnam—I remember the day he came home."

I nodded.

"And then Sean and Kevin joined the Corps, too. They didn't stay in, of course, but they put in four years each. And it marked them. They're tough, hard guys sometimes. Not as hard as Leo, but . . ."

"And I was in the army and not the Marines and so you can't see me anymore?"

"Don't be silly," she said without rancor. "And stop interrupting."

I settled back.

"The point is, Milan, that I've spent my whole life with machismo. With big-shouldered men who knew their duty and did it, no matter what. I've seen how that can fuck up a relationship royally. Fuck up a *life*."

"And you're seeing me that way, too? As a kind of gung ho a-man's-gotta-do-what-a-man's-gotta-do guy?"

She looked away again. "I suppose I am."

"I'm not sure that's a fair assessment."

"Isn't it? When that Indian got himself killed, it was absolutely none of your business, but by God you *made* it your business, didn't you?"

"I did my duty as a citizen and went to the police about him sitting outside my apartment. And because I did, a grieving family is getting their baby back. I think that makes it worth it."

"To who?" she said.

"To just about everyone concerned."

She jerked a thumb toward her own chest. "Not quite everybody."

"You don't care?"

"Sure I care," she said. "I think it's wonderful. I think it's also wonderful that little Johnny Jones won first place in the science fair in Ames, Iowa, too. But I don't know him and I don't know your Indians, and the fact is that I'm more interested in *me*. In *my* feelings. In what *I'm* comfortable with."

I became aware of a curious process going on inside me. It wasn't in my head, exactly, and it wasn't even emotional. It was physiological. I could actually feel my body shutting down flat-lining. Almost as if my nerve endings had lost their power to feel. "And so I take it you're not comfortable with me anymore. With us."

One fingernail was idly scratching a spot on her knee I was sure didn't itch at all. "Not completely, no," she said.

"I see."

"Do you?"

"No."

"Milan, don't get me wrong. I'm crazy about you. You're a good, decent man, and I admire the hell out of you. I like you. In some ways, I really love you."

"Good. Let's hear some of them."

She laughed, but it was the laughter of the lost. "You're very intelligent and great to talk to. You're fun to be with, you make me laugh, and you're terrific in bed." She winked, and it seemed horribly inappropriate under the circumstances. "Of course, you know that already."

"*We're* terrific in bed. Together. When you're not there in bed with me I'm actually pretty dull."

She chuckled. "See, you make me laugh."

"Oh, I've got more where that came from," I said. "See, these two Jewish guys go into a bar . . ."

"Stop it."

"Hey, I'm leading with my strong suit here."

Her gaze was level and serious. "You have lots of strong suits. That's why it's so hard . . ." She hugged herself as if she'd gotten a sudden chill. "For another thing, you're so ethical that sometimes it makes my teeth ache."

That one bit hard. I wonder what she'd say if she knew about the ethical dilemmas I'd been wrestling with vis-à-vis Andrew Takalo and Armand Treusch. "And this is a bad thing?"

"It would be tough to live with."

That one sent my eyebrows rocketing toward my hairline. "Live with? I didn't think that was a priority of yours."

"It wasn't," she protested. "It still isn't. But someday it might be."

"So?"

"So I'm just telling you what I'm feeling, Milan."

"Which is that you don't want us to see each other anymore."

"No!" She leaned forward, tense, and then slumped back. "Just—maybe on a different basis."

"Just friends?"

"Oh, more than friends," she said. "I still want to sleep with you."

"I'm not sure I can do that, Connie."

"Sleep with me?"

"Sleep with you—casually."

"You don't believe in casual sex?"

"I'm quite fond of it, actually. Just not with someone with whom it used to be much more than casual, that's all."

She wagged her head from side to side. "I'm not sure I understand that kind of thinking."

"It's easy. We make contracts with people. Everybody, not just lovers. You're going to be acquaintances, you're going to be best buddies, you're going to be in love, you're going to screw once in a while, you're going to screw all the time with no strings attached, you're going to have lunch together every two weeks or so . . . It's not a stated contract, but it's understood. You following me?"

"I guess so," she said, but I got the impression that if she was, it was from a long way back.

"Now, when one party attempts to change the terms of the contract and the other party doesn't want to change . . ."

"The party of the second part?"

"Something like that. Well, then, that's where the trouble comes in, and you risk making the entire contract null and void."

She pursed her lips and thought about that. "So you're saying that you and I are null and void, is that it?"

"I'm saying that we've been hot and heavy for a long time, and I can't see myself scaling back to not so hot and not so heavy and every once in a while, and sitting home on the nights you're not in my bed wondering whether you're in somebody else's. Because that's what we're talking about here, isn't it? Non-committed, non-exclusive?"

"There's no one else in the picture, if that's what you're wondering."

"I was wondering, but in the end it really doesn't make that much difference." I inhaled and then blew a lungful of air noisily through my lips. "I'm sorry, I think we've come too far to do that. To step back."

"Are you saying you want to get married, Milan? I didn't think that was part of your game plan."

"It wasn't," I echoed her. "But someday it might be."

"And you don't think if we kept it kind of loose for a while but still kept a kind of a thing going . . . ?"

"No. I couldn't handle that. I could with someone else; I have. But not with you. It's been too good. Too intense. Too close."

"So it's all or nothing?"

"Not *all*," I said. "But not crumbs, either."

She slithered down in the corner of the sofa, looking very small and vulnerable. "You being you, I suppose I should have known that."

"I imagine that deep down, you did."

"You're such a stand-up guy, Milan."

"A stand-up guy. That's what some of my mob acquaintances say about me." My effort to keep the sarcastic edge from my voice was notably unsuccessful. "I'm touched you think so, too."

"Mob acquaintances," she murmured, and instantly I knew I had said the wrong thing, hammered in the final nail, sealed the package, stuck a fork in the relationship; it was done. "My very point."

"I'm hardly a gangster."

"Nowhere near. But you're hardly a picket-fence-and-rosebushes kind of guy, either."

"I might be," I said, my voice sounding small, echoing from far away and rattling around inside my skull. "If anyone would let me."

Chapter Twenty-two

My drive from the west side back to the east was only about seventeen miles, but it might as well have been from the far side of the moon. Plenty of time to think about things. Too much time—bitter time. Even when I crossed the Main Avenue Bridge and saw the downtown skyline bright against the inky sky, a sight that always filled me with unabashed hometown pride, it gave me no joy; the towers threatened me, the lights were pinpricks to the soul.

Maybe I needed to face the fact that I was the kind of man who just didn't function well in relationships. It came as a surprise to me; I've always thought of myself as a giving person, but the women who had come through my life in any sort of significant manner, the real affairs of the heart and not the libido who had cut a swath through my center and taken little bites of me with them as they passed, all apparently thought I hadn't given enough.

And that was really too bad, because it was the best that I could do.

I just don't do "casual" very well. Like any longtime bachelor, I've had my share of one- or two-nighters or six-weekers, but even though I have fallen away from the church, my stern Catholic upbringing eventually rendered them ultimately unsatisfying. What I really wanted was Somebody. A special Somebody; that's when I am the happiest. Years ago I thought I had found her when I married Lila, but that union had resulted in a divorce that left me adrift, confused, and self-doubting in my midthirties. I'd had only three serious romances since then, and all three women had decided what I had to offer them fell somewhat short.

I was no swinger, that was the trouble. Not like Marko Meglich, whose succession of inappropriately young, impossibly beautiful, and basically interchangeable women was for a while more like his career than his hobby, and who had been happy and almost boastful concerning his sex life. But just before his death even he had expressed to me a desire for something more meaningful.

At this point, driving home from Connie Haley's house, like Ol' Man River I was weary and sick of trying. My feelings weren't even hurt, really; when one is single and in the dating scene for more than three years, of necessity feelings develop rhinoceros skin. Vastly displeased with myself, it occurred to me that I hadn't really been in love with Connie, even though it was because I had wisely not allowed myself that luxury.

A man loves the woman in whose presence he likes himself the best.

So I wasn't sad, really—just disappointed and annoyed and frustrated, staring ahead down the long corridor of time to come at emptiness. Maybe it was better to date casually after all and expect nothing more; expectations are what really hurt, because few people live up to them. So from now on I would guard my heart behind a wall I'd have to erect carefully, brick by brick.

The familiar downtown touchstones loomed to my left: Terminal Tower, Key Tower, Jacobs Field, the British Petroleum Building. Now I would be adding my own self-built landmark to hide behind. The Great Wall of Cleveland.

I didn't even feel like having a beer when I got home. I just peeled off my clothes and dropped them on the floor beside the bed, lying there listening to the slowly dwindling late traffic outside on Cedar Road and falling asleep while studying the longtime crack in my bedroom ceiling that looked like the outline of Brazil.

The next day was a Saturday, and I didn't even have the refuge of work. I cast about for something distracting or engaging with which to occupy my thoughts. Gray and cold with a threat of snow that never materialized, it was no day to take a drive in the country, to putter around some of the quaint small towns of Ohio and wander through antique shops looking at treasures I had no reason to buy. I read the paper. I drank two pots of coffee. Then I walked down to Starbuck's on Cedar Road and drank some more, surrounded by young people with laptop computers who either found it more thought-conducive to work in the crowded atmosphere of an upscale coffee emporium or were hoping someone lovely and single of the gender of their choice would ask them what they were doing, start up a conversation, and perhaps strike a spark as well.

I went back home, caffeine nerves jangling like sleigh bells, and read a magazine, then read a mystery novel, with the TV tuned to a college basketball game whose outcome didn't interest me in the least, hoops being my least favorite sport.

I cleaned the apartment.

Smoked a lot.

Brooded.

My cupboard and refrigerator were both nearly bare, and at about three o'clock I went across the street to Russo's Giant Eagle to replenish them, wandering the aisles and noticing several attractive women who were all wearing wedding rings, stocking their carts with breakfast cereal and juice. I loaded up my basket with lettuce, chunky blue-cheese dressing and croutons, pasta sauce, potato chips, and small single-serving packages of meat—I might as well have been wearing a sandwich board sign reading "BACHELOR."

Later that evening I made myself a small salad, breaded and cooked a couple of pork chops, and baked a potato. After dinner I thought hard about going out for a big Saturday evening, but I didn't feel like driving down to the old neighborhood and talking to Vuk and his pals at the little tavern where I felt the most comfortable, didn't want to interact with a lot of people I might know at Nighttown, and I knew the elegant Velvet Tango Room just across the river would be full of beautiful, well-dressed young women who wouldn't be interested in me anyway, so I wound up watching three crime shows in a row on TV and falling asleep in my chair during the eleven o'clock news.

I was catching up on my rest, if nothing else. And at least while I was sleeping I was spared the necessity of thinking.

In the morning, the phone startled me awake, propelling me from deep and troubled slumber directly into a caffeine hangover, and I rolled over and reached blindly for it, catching a glimpse of the bedside clock. It was just a few minutes past eight. So much for lolling abed on a Sunday.

"Hello," I groaned, my voice crackling through the sand that had accumulated in my throat overnight.

"McHargue here." The police lieutenant bit the words off crisply; she'd obviously been awake a lot longer than I had.

"Good morning," I said with less than half a heart.

"How fast can you get to my office?"

"I'm not even awake yet."

"Well, splash cold water on your face. I have to talk to you."

"It's my day off," I protested, realizing too late that I was whining. "I'm spending Sunday with my son."

"You're spending *this* Sunday with me," she said. "At least the morning. After that, I don't really care what you do."

"What . . . ?"

"You'll find out. Forty-five minutes," she said. "Be here." The disconnecting click was like a nuclear blast in my ear.

I fumbled the receiver back into its cradle and lay back against the pillow, trying to marshall my thoughts; I'm not terribly lucid the first five or ten minutes I'm awake. After I had put my mind in gear I got up and staggered into the shower, which cleansed less than it awakened. Then I called Lila and told her I might be a bit late picking up Stephen, which got exactly the reaction I'd learned to expect.

"Don't you dare disappoint that little boy, Milan. He's expecting to see his daddy today, and I don't want him sitting here waiting and getting sad and thinking you don't want to be with him."

Lila had an endless supply of guilt to pass out like party favors, even after more than ten years of marital apartness, and was unfailingly generous in her distribution of it.

I dressed for my day with my son casually, in a sweater and cords. If Florence McHargue didn't like it, that would be too bad. Who dresses up to go to the police station anyway? I couldn't imagine what could be so urgent that she had to call me in on a Sunday morning.

Forty-five minutes later, I found out.

I walked into Lieutenant McHargue's office carrying a take-out container of coffee from Starbuck's, since I knew the only refreshment she'd have on hand was her flavored herbal tea. She and Detective Bob Matusen were waiting for me like the Unabomber jury, both of them grim and thin-lipped. She even had her arms folded across her chest judgmentally. She didn't bother greeting me.

"Sit," she ordered. I did so. I was getting off easily, at that; she might have told me to "Fetch."

When I'd settled into my chair she looked at me closely. "You look like dog crap. What's wrong?"

"Nothing that I want on the table," I said. "Personal."

Her eyes got steely. "All right, we'll let that go for the moment, because there are more pressing matters to discuss. You came in here the day before yesterday and gave me the deal on the Takalo baby. Now I want you to tell me every single move you made and who you made it with after you left this office."

"Sure," I said. "You want fries with that?"

Her tone was low and angry, sounding like hornets who have been disturbed from their slumber. "You can knock the smart-ass shit off, Jacovich, because I'm in no mood. Now where did you go?"

"Where I said I was going. To the FBI."

"You went there directly?"

"I didn't even pass Go," I told her. "And I sure as hell didn't collect two hundred dollars."

"You saw. . . ." She consulted a notepad. "Agent Melina?"

"That's right. As you suggested, I told her the whole story. The Takalos, the Grooms, Willetta Clemons. Agent Melina was pretty upset with her counterparts in Michigan for dragging their feet, and she assured me she was going to get on it right away." I took the lid off my coffee container. "Did she?"

"Yes, she called me right after you left her. What then?"

"What did I do then? I met with someone on another case that afternoon. Totally unrelated to the Takalos. Then I went to visit my—uh—a friend later that evening. And yesterday I didn't go out of the house at all except to the store across the street. What's going on, Lieutenant?"

"You didn't talk to anyone else about the baby? Or about the Grooms, or Willetta Clemons?"

"No," I said. "Why would I?"

"I don't know," she said. "Why would you?"

"I wouldn't. I didn't. As far as I'm concerned, it's ancient history."

"That's what you think," she said heavily. "What about Suzanne Davis?"

"I didn't talk to her, either."

"I mean, did *she* tell anyone?"

"I don't know," I said. "You'll have to ask her."

"I'm going to. She's on her way in here, too."

Matusen was standing against one wall, shifting uneasily. I had never seen him in McHargue's presence when he didn't look acutely uncomfortable. "Apparently Agent Melina contacted the Groom family and the Department of Social Services based on what you told her about the kidnapping," he said. "They were making arrangements to positively ID the Groom's little boy as Andrew Takalo, and then to return him to his parents in Michigan."

"That's good," I said. "And are the feds going after Willetta Clemons for kidnapping?"

"That was their plan," McHargue cut in. "Except that didn't quite work out. Because last night, someone put two bullets into her. She's dead."

The cleaning crew had found Willetta Clemons at her office desk, McHargue told me, at about nine o'clock on Saturday evening.

She'd been shot twice, once in the forehead and once in the chest at close range. An autopsy would determine which had been the killshot, as if that made any difference, but the medical examiner at the scene ascertained from the condition of the body that she had been dead for approximately six hours. That meant she had been killed midafternoon. Since it was a Saturday, the likelihood of anyone else being in her little office building on Prospect Avenue to hear the gunshots was slim.

"Of course," McHargue said, "we're going to take a close look at Evelyn and Larry Groom."

"What?" I said, almost coming out of the chair. "That's absurd."

"What's so absurd about it? They pay Willetta Clemons a goddamn fortune for a baby to adopt, she tells them it's completely legitimate, they take the kid into their home like the adoption is etched in stone and fall in love with it, and the next thing you know the FBI is crawling up their noses, telling them that not only must they give up their child, but that they might be looking at federal charges for buying him in the first place. I imagine they were more than a little pissed off, don't you?"

"Pissed off is one thing, murder is another."

"They often go hand in hand," she said.

"Maybe." I sipped carefully at my coffee; it was still hot. "I just don't see Larry Groom as a cold-blooded murderer."

"How about hot-blooded? Think about this scenario for a minute. Groom's whole world has suddenly fallen around his ears. So he calls Clemons on a Saturday and demands to see her in her office. He is not only enraged about losing the kid, but he wants his money back. She hedges, hems and haws, maybe even suggesting that he pound sand down a rat hole, and he loses it and pops two caps into her." She took off her blue-tinted glasses. "Or maybe it was his wife." She checked her notes again. "Evelyn. They haven't dug the bullets out yet, but the entry wounds looked like they were made with a small caliber. Like from a lady's gun."

I shook my head. "Couldn't happen. Evelyn Groom looked at that baby as if she was the Blessed Mother."

"All the more reason for her to come unglued, wouldn't you say?"

"You haven't met her."

"Well, I'm going to remedy that oversight very soon," McHargue said. "I've asked the Summit County sheriff's department to pick the Grooms up and bring them in to talk to me."

"Oh my God," I said on the exhale.

"What?"

"They're losing their baby. They must be shattered. And now they're being hauled in for questioning about a murder."

McHargue shrugged. "Shit happens."

CHAPTER TWENTY-THREE

My late parents, Louis and Marijanna Jacovich, were both born in Ljubljana, the capital city of Slovenia, which is one of the republics of the former Yugoslavia that managed to escape much of the horror that engulfed the Balkans at the end of the twentieth century. Papa was a big hard-muscled man who worked his entire adult life on the floor of the steel mills south of downtown Cleveland after emigrating here more than fifty years ago. He never learned much English, but that was somehow fitting because he never really lost his old ways; he embodied the old-country values and ethics of his homeland and managed to knock most of them into the thick, hard head of his only son and heir.

That meant, among other things, that I was taught from a very early age to take responsibility for my own actions. We don't see too much of that anymore; it's become easy and fashionable to blame our faults and excesses on outside influences, a lousy home life, poverty, ethnicity, or our beloved childhood dog getting hit by a car. I never learned how to do that; when I screw up, I admit it, if only to myself.

I guess that's what Connie meant by being a "stand-up guy." I am frequently wrong, frequently stupid, and if my father's example taught me to admit to it, it also has earned me some grief along the way.

And now I had to face the fact that in all probability Willetta Clemons was dead because of something that I did. Indirectly, of course, but that didn't make me feel any better.

It can be argued, I suppose, that Clemons was the architect of her own doom. It was she who had chosen the disgusting, illegal, and immoral business of baby-selling, and one who makes a conscious choice to live on the edge is almost predestined eventually to fall off.

But still, she had died in her office chair when a bullet smashed through her chest and another shattered her skull.

There was regret. There was horror. There was guilt, big-time.

It has been said by the purveyors of psychobabble, those who write the best-selling self-help tomes that all basically read like they were written by Norman Vincent Peale, that no one can really foist a guilt trip upon you; you have to be party to it and accept it. And I was putting the guilt for Clemons on myself and inhaling it like the bouquet of fine rich Beaujolais.

When I got back to my apartment, shaken, I called to cancel my date with Stephen. My current state of worry and angst was probably going to render me pretty unsatisfactory company.

In the way of all kids, he was cool with it; his mother was not. Over the years I've learned to tune out when Lila goes into one of her shame-on-you rants, but on this particular morning it was exceptionally hard not to snarl back. I managed to tune out while she was raging at me, not really listening to the words but to the inflections, the rising and falling at the end of sentences so I'd know when to respond. I didn't go into detail as to why I was not going to spend this Sunday with my son. She wouldn't have understood, anyway.

When she finally set me free of her tirade, I slumped into my chair in the den and pondered what kind of career I had carved out for myself that rendered my actions inexplicable to others, and sometimes even to myself? I'd lost Lila because of it, and later some other relationships that had been meaningful and important to me, most recently and painfully the one with Connie Haley.

Yet, for all its traps and trip-ups, I loved my job. When things work out right and I wind up helping people, I feel a real adrenaline rush and a satisfaction that keeps my belly warmed and my heart restful, and that makes the bad stuff that frequently happens bearable. I know I could have made a lot more money doing something else with my two college degrees, but that might not have provided me with the rush—and I can think of no sadder way to live one's life than working without joy.

So I terminated the conversation with my former wife feeling as raw and tender as a festering hangnail. The Sunday paper remained unopened and unread. I hadn't had time for breakfast before hustling down to police headquarters that morning, but I no longer felt like eating. I made a pot of midday coffee that didn't taste very good at all. I turned the radio on to mellow classical music on WCLV, their usual Sunday brunch broadcast emanating from Nighttown just down the street, but it didn't soothe me or bring me peace. Instead I stalked the confines of my living room like a captive lion in a small zoo cage, lacking only an angry tail to switch.

Just after two o'clock Suzanne Davis called me. "I'm on the car phone," she said. "Just got finished with a session with Lieutenant McHargue and I need to be gentled. I'm right in front of the Third Division on Payne. You busy?"

"Come on over," I told her, "the coffee's ready."

"I'm gonna need something stronger than coffee."

"That's on, too."

She arrived fifteen minutes later, the unnatural paleness of her face emphasized by a black sweater, black plaid skirt, and black tights. She stood in the doorway of my apartment for about thirty seconds, her blue-gray eyes wide and frightened, and then moved into my arms for a hug, putting her cheek against my chest. Her black, wavy hair smelled of coconut shampoo.

"Ah, damn, Milan," she said. She wasn't crying, but her shoulders were shaking under my hands.

"I'm sorry I got you into this, kiddo," I said, patting her back.

She straightened up and glared at me, her doubled fists on her hips. "You didn't 'get me into' anything, okay? The last time I was seduced, I was fifteen years old; everything since then that has been strictly voluntary." She dropped her hands to her sides and moved away, walking past me into the living room and plopping down on the sofa with her legs splayed straight out in front of her like a small child, pushing her hair from her face with both hands. "On the phone I believe you mentioned something about more than coffee?"

"Sure," I said. "Vodka okay?"

"Vodka *very* okay."

"I have it chilling in the freezer."

"Good, then we won't have to dilute it with ice cubes."

I went into the kitchen and poured a few fingers of the clear icy liquor into an old-fashioned glass and then got myself a Stroh's. I had consciously avoided alcohol all morning and afternoon, figuring it was the kind of day when once I started, I wouldn't stop. But it wasn't from lack of wanting it, and now I had a good excuse, since it would seem downright ungracious of me to allow my guest to drink alone.

"Here," I said, handing her the glass. "Sip it, don't shoot it."

"Easy for you to say," she told me with a sad smile, but she resisted belting all of it down in one motion. She took a pretty generous gulp, though, and then exhaled loudly. "Wow, that's so cold it *stings*." A little of her normal color returned to her face, and she nodded her gratitude as I sat down on the opposite end of the sofa.

"Your friend McHargue is a real lulu," she said. "I've seen rabid raccoons with a nicer personality."

"Aw, I think she's kind of cuddly."

"Did you know that she's going after Larry and Evelyn Groom for Willetta's murder?"

"She told me. She says they have the best motive."

"They've got the motive but not the moxie. I don't see either of them as violent people."

"I don't either, Suzanne, but McHargue has to start somewhere."

She shook her head. "Maybe it had nothing to do with the Grooms and the Takalo baby. Maybe it was a random office robbery that went wrong."

"According to McHargue there was no indication of breaking and entering, no sign of a search."

"Maybe after he shot her he got scared and booked before he could take anything."

"You can't even sell that one to yourself, Suzanne. If you were an armed robber looking for a random score, would you go into a cut-rate law office on Prospect Avenue at three o'clock on a Saturday afternoon?"

"I suppose not," she said miserably, holding the cold glass against her forehead. "And that makes Willetta Clemons getting capped our fault."

"*My* fault," I reminded her. "You were just along for the ride."

She threw me a disgusted look. "Stop being so fucking noble, okay? It gives me a pain right behind my eyes."

"That's the frozen vodka."

"The vodka is all that's keeping me upright."

"Here's to staying upright," I said, and lifted my beer bottle toward her in a toast. She touched it with her glass, and the *tink* sound was somehow comforting.

We sat quietly for a while, listening to Rachmaninoff's Second Piano Concerto on the radio, lost in our own thoughts and our own culpability. Then I said, "Let me run something by you, Suzanne."

"Make it good," she said.

"Are we agreed that Joseph Ettawageshik was no random crime victim? That he was murdered because he somehow found out who had taken his great-grandson and was getting too close?"

"It's logical, sure. Not a for-sure-for-sure, but it makes sense. And we know who took the baby; it was Willetta Clemons. At least she was behind it." She leaned toward me, suddenly interested. "Probably those two guys that visited Marie Fightmaster and offered to buy her kid. The redhead with the eastern European name and the little balding guy with the cockeye."

"And Willetta didn't kill Ettawageshik and put him in the river by herself, either. She wasn't strong enough, for one thing. For another, throat-cutting isn't a woman's method of killing someone."

"Women have their own methods?" she said, lofting an eyebrow.

"When a woman kills with a knife," I said, "it's often on the spur of the moment, something she reaches out and grabs, either out of anger or in self-defense. And when she does, she stabs . . ." I made a downward stabbing motion with my fist. "She doesn't sneak up behind and slice." I pantomimed that, too, and Suzanne unsuccessfully tried suppressing a shudder.

"So you think the redheaded Bohunk and the bald cockeye killed Joseph Ettawageshik, too?"

"That's my educated guess. Unless there's a whole lot of other people involved in this baby-stealing racket, which is unlikely. There isn't *that* much money in it, and even if there were, the fewer people who know about it, the less chance of someone getting shitfaced and bragging in a bar."

"So . . . ?"

"So," I said, "maybe it went down this way. I blew the whistle on Clemons, and the FBI came after her, and Cleveland homicide had started looking at her with fondness, too, for old Joseph. The whole scam was beginning to unravel. But she was the only one, let's say, who could identify her little helpers—the ones who actually did the kidnapping and the murder. And they went into panic mode and killed *her* too so she couldn't roll over on them."

Suzanne took a fistful of rich black hair and moved it behind her ear, where it stayed for approximately eight seconds before falling into her face again. "Well, if you're going to look elsewhere besides the Grooms for doing Willetta, I suppose that's a decent supposition."

"I'll bet I'm right. I've been running it around in my head all day long, and it makes sense to me."

"To me, too," Suzanne agreed. Have you shared this little flight of fancy with McHargue?"

"Not yet," I admitted. "I just came up with it."

She nodded thoughtfully, and looked at her watch. "She might still be in the office. Why don't you call her?"

"Lieutenant McHargue and I have gone round and round before," I said. "Last fall. When she gets an idea in her head about a perp, she clamps down on it like a pit bull and doesn't let go until she's run it into the ground."

"Wow, mixing metaphors," Suzanne said.

"I didn't know my paper was being graded. Besides, I can just picture myself telling her that her suspect has sort of an eastern European name and red hair and that's all I know about him." Now it was my turn to shudder. "I don't think I could survive the barrage of withering sarcasm."

"So what's your suggestion? Go through the entire ethnic community in Greater Cleveland until you find a six-foot-tall redhead and then ask him if he's got a cockeyed buddy with male pattern baldness?"

"Sure." I sighed, and leaned back against the sofa heavily. "That shouldn't take more than four or five years."

She nodded and finished the vodka, then held the glass out to me for more.

"Are we going to tie one on tonight?"

"Probably," she said.

I carried the glass out to refill it. When I brought it back to her, she took it with a curt little thank-you nod. "I wish to hell there was some way we could get into Clemons's office for a look," she said. "I'll bet the answer is in there somewhere. Go through her files, her Rolodex, her phone records, checkbook stubs . . . See if we could find anyone with an ethnic name."

"Not much chance of our being able to do that, Suzanne. It's a crime scene. Yellow tape all over the place, and probably a guardian angel in a blue uniform watching over it."

"I know. How about her apartment, then? You said it's right across the street. We could sit here drinking until the middle of the night and then just sneak over there and loid the lock . . ."

I looked at her, and she colored, grinned sheepishly, and ducked her head.

"Okay, I'm shot down. Lousy idea anyway." She crossed her ankle over her knee and wiggled her leg nervously.

We subsided into silence again, for nearly five minutes. Then Suzanne laughed. "We're like a couple who've been married to each other for thirty years and we've run out of things to talk about."

I grunted an agreement, and the clock ticked some more.

"You want to get something to eat?" I said.

"So we can sit in a restaurant and not talk? I don't think so. I should probably head out to Lake County pretty soon anyway."

"It was a thought," I said.

"I'm going to finish my drink first, if that's okay. This one and maybe one more. Or two."

"Sure, fine. And after that some coffee; I'm not letting you drive all that way with a snootful."

"That will blow the rest of your day."

"There's nowhere pressing I have to be."

"Me, neither," she said, and worked on the vodka.

I fired up a cigarette. Rachmaninoff had segued into Rimsky-Korsakoff; WCLV was doing Russians this afternoon, it seemed, and Suzanne's vodka was just going along with the program.

"Suzanne, do you have some free time tomorrow?"

"Early in the day I do," she said. "I have to be back in my office for a client meeting at three-thirty."

"Want to do something for me?"

She made a wry face. "Why stop now?"

"Except I insist on paying you for your time."

"Then I won't," she said.

"I don't want you working for nothing. I wouldn't feel right."

"Milan, everything is not about you. I'll put in the time, and you can buy me dinner again." She pinched an inch of flesh at the waistband of her skirt. "Knowing you is playing hell with my girlish figure."

"No, it isn't," I said, and the compliment made her smile for the first time since she'd walked through the door. "Okay, then. I want you to find out every scrap of information you can about Willetta Clemons. Court records, birth records, financial records, whatever there is on paper."

"What am I supposed to be looking for?"

"I don't know, that's the damn trouble. But maybe you'll recognize it when you see it."

"Kind of like Columbus sailing off into nowhere hoping he'll find the Spice Islands."

"Exactly like that. Will you do it?"

"Best effort," she said, and she clinked her nearly empty vodka glass against my nearly empty beer bottle again.

After we'd both polished off our drinks, she said, "Milan."

"Present."

"Why?"

"Why what?"

"Why are you doing this? You're not getting paid—you never were, for that matter. And you're out of it now, out of it clean."

"Not clean."

"No?"

"No." I stubbed my cigarette out. "I was trying to do the right thing. For the Takalos, for Eddie Ettawageshik, for the baby. But I screwed up somewhere along the way, and because of me, of what I did, Willetta Clemons is dead."

"So you feel like you owe her?"

"No," I said. "Gone is gone, I don't owe her anything. I owe *me.*"

She frowned, trying to figure me out.

"I'm not out of it clean at all, Suzanne. And I want it to be clean before I put it to bed for good."

She nodded.

"You understand what I'm getting at?"

"I'm afraid I do, Milan," she said. "Cleanliness is next to godliness."

Chapter Twenty-Four

Okay, subtle dig duly noted.

Maybe, as Suzanne suggested, I do have a God-complex. What can I say? In my job, where on occasion I hold the enormous power of justice and the well-being of others in my sweaty grasp, it just happens sometimes.

Besides, I *like* being in the right. Who doesn't? It beats being wrong, hands down. And when I am in the wrong, as frequently happens, I want to fix it.

So Suzanne and I both drank a little too much that Sunday afternoon and evening, and afterward I did manage to get a lot of coffee and some food down her throat before I sent her on her long drive home. Then I fell into bed, half-smashed and emotionally exhausted, and slept through until seven o'clock the next morning, awakening to a mouth full of teeth that felt as if they were all wearing gym socks.

I drove beneath a drippy sky full of threatening clouds and got down to the office before nine, adjusting the thermostat upward to sixty-eight degrees as soon as I walked in the door. Outside the temperature was just above freezing, not unreasonable for the upper Midwest, but it was the damp, unforgiving kind of cold that makes your bones complain of feeling their age.

I was going through the notes in my Eddie Ettawageshik file, trying both to deal with my severe case of the guilts and to figure out if I could have done something differently that might have meant Willetta Clemons would still be alive, when the telephone rang and Holly Butcher's voice crackled through the receiver. In the background I could hear the sounds of the *Plain Dealer* newsroom, but her cold and angry words knifed through it.

"The lawyer who got killed Saturday," she said. "Clemons. She specialized in Native American adoptions. That's too much of a coincidence. Is this something you're involved in?"

"A little around the edges," I admitted.

"God damn it, you promised me a story!"

"That was before somebody got murdered, Holly. The police would skin me alive if I gave you anything."

"Well, I'm going to skin you alive if you don't," she warned. "I trusted you. I only spilled my guts to you because you're a friend of Ed Stahl's and he asked me to do it on a favor basis. But this is a newspaper, not Information Central for private dicks, and now I'm sitting here red-faced and bare-assed while some other reporter is getting this story off a lousy police blotter."

"I'm sorry," I said. "I couldn't know it was going to turn out this way."

"Sorry doesn't cut it. I'm feeling used and abused. The way I figure, you owe me. So sing out, pal, I'm waiting."

I thought of Larry and Evelyn Groom and the further damage public disclosure would wreak on their already shattered family dynamic. I couldn't do it to them, even though they had attempted to buy a baby. Wrong as it was, they had tried to adopt someone else's child out of their own need to give love, and even if I might be marked lousy at the *Plain Dealer* forevermore, I just couldn't throw their bodies to the media that way.

And then a new idea popped into my head. I fumbled for my first Winston of the day as I tried to organize it. "I might have something else you might be interested in, Holly. It's not a murder, but it's pretty hot."

"I'll be the judge of that," she said. "Wait a minute."

She rustled around at the other end, and then I heard a beep from her computer. I pictured her at the keyboard, phone tucked between her chin and her shoulder, typing fingers at the ready. I wondered what ever happened to the concept of reporters using notebooks. "What?" she said.

I cradled my own receiver with a hunched shoulder and struck a match to my cigarette, sucking the smoke in deep. "Have you ever heard of an outfit out in Solon called TroyToy?"

"Of course. Why?"

And then I gave it all to her. The TroyTrike story, unadorned. And I even threw in the involvement of Helen Moise and Consumer Watchdog, just to sweeten the deal a little. Holly Butcher threw in an occasional "Uh huh," or "Go on," and I heard the soft clacking of the computer keys as we spoke.

The longer we talked, the faster she typed, and I could hear her breath coming a little quicker as well. For an investigative reporter, the deliberate manufacturing and marketing of a possibly unsafe children's toy by a major toy company was even more juicy than the lonesome murder of a low-rent attorney. I was more than happy to trade for some goodwill at Cleveland's only major daily newspaper with the soul of Armand Treusch.

When I was finished, she said, "And where do I verify this?"

I didn't answer her for a moment. Another ethical dilemma stared me in the face. I was no more anxious to give up David Ream to the tender ministrations of Holly Butcher than I had been the Grooms; he'd had enough trouble.

"I'll only tell you if you promise not to use his name."

"I can't make promises like that. You know better."

"Then there's no deal."

"God damn it, Milan . . ."

"Listen," I said, "this guy doesn't want the publicity. There are some things that are private. I don't give a damn about the public's precious right to know." Without using names, I sketched in some details about Ream and his little girl, and Holly Butcher was silent for a minute.

"All right," she said finally. "Let's just say that I'll make every effort to keep the name out of the story. Is that good enough?"

"No."

"You're killing me, here . . ." Exasperated.

"Holly, ten minutes ago you didn't know squat about TroyTrike, and I've just dumped a big story into your lap, one that could easily go national. So don't sing me any sad songs."

"My editor will have my head."

"Your editor is going to take you out to dinner for this one, and you know it. But I need a few guarantees. Listen, Holly, this is win-win. You contact him, tell him I gave you his number, and he'll spill it all to you—that's been his only aim all along, to stop TroyTrike. He gets what he wants, you get a byline and national attention, and a bunch of kids might live to see another day. But his name never appears in the story. Agreed?"

"You've got it all figured out," she said.

"No, actually I'm making it up as I go along. But that's the deal. In the future I'll probably be in a position to throw other stuff your way, things that Ed Stahl is too busy to fool with. But if you double-cross me and use this guy's name and hold him up as a target for every cuckoo bird and scam artist in northeastern Ohio, making your life miserable and difficult at that newspaper is going to become my lifelong hobby. Take it or leave it."

She thought it over some more for about twenty seconds. Finally she drew in a breath and let it out with the words "I'll take it."

And she did.

So that was that. As far as I was concerned, Armand Treusch and his tricycle from hell were behind me, and Helen Moise was not going to make a buck from it, either. Well and good.

And little Andrew Takalo would soon be back in the bosom of his family where he belonged. He might have been a hell of a lot better off with his adopted family, but that wasn't—*couldn't* be—a consideration. Right was right.

The godliness thing, again. Okay, I plead guilty.

That should have been the end of it.

Except that whoever murdered Joseph Ettawageshik was still out there walking around, and probably the same person or persons had killed Willetta Clemons. Officially, that was none of my business; I had no more client, paying or otherwise, and it was the job of Florence McHargue and Bob Matusen to catch killers.

But I knew in my gut that if it hadn't been for me, Clemons might still be alive. That made it my business.

So when my phone rang and the Caller ID readout told me it was Suzanne Davis, I almost jumped to answer it.

"Milan, you're not going to believe this," she said.

"Try me. I still believe in the Easter Bunny and the Tooth Fairy, so I'll probably believe anything."

"I'm at the library downtown; can I just run over to your office? I want to see your face when I tell you this."

"At this point in my life," I said, "anytime a beautiful woman wants to look at my face, I'm game."

"Ten minutes, then," she said, and hung up.

Because of the time it took extracting her car from the parking garage across Superior Avenue from the Cleveland Public Library, it was more like twenty minutes, but who's counting? She arrived at Collision Bend smart and breathless in her customary garb of black plaid miniskirt, black tights, and black sweater which suited her better than the suburban-housewife clothes she had worn as Mrs. Leon Kobler.

"Coffee?" I said.

She shook her head as she sat down across from me and plunked her briefcase onto the desk. "I'm wired enough." She fumbled the clasp open and pulled out a sheaf of photocopies.

"Do I have to read through all that?"

"Eventually. Let me give you the highlights." She cleared her throat. "You wanted me to look up anything and everything on Willetta Clemons."

I nodded.

"Well, I found out all sorts of stuff, but most of it wasn't really germane."

"Let's get to the germane part, then."

"You might have noticed when we visited her office that the door said, 'Willetta T. Clemons, LPA'."

"I did."

"That means Licensed Practical Attorney."

"So?"

"So that got me to wondering whether Clemons was a corporation."

"Most law firms are incorporated, even the small ones."

"Well, I looked up the corporation. It turns out that Willetta Clemons didn't even own her own law firm. She was just an employee."

I leaned forward, suddenly interested. "Oh?"

"That might explain the low-rent office."

"Yes. And a lawyer living in a rented apartment at Cedar Fairmount."

"There are two owners of Willetta T. Clemons, L.P.A. A Francis X. Bohannon—and Claudya Shanklin."

"Shanklin . . ."

"So," she went on, "I did some checking up on Francis X. Bohannon. Turns out he isn't an attorney at all. He owns a string of parking lots down in the southeastern suburbs—Streeterville, Twinsburg, Macedonia, and Cuyahoga Falls."

"Okay, so he's an investor."

"*And* . . ." I knew she was ready to deliver the killshot; Suzanne is nothing if not dramatic. "His home address is one of those tony developments out in Aurora."

"So?"

"The same home address as Claudya Shanklin. According to the records, she owns the house, but he apparently lives there, too."

"Ah."

"Could be he's her live-in."

"Everybody loves somebody sometime. What's so interesting about that?"

She sat back smugly. "You don't get it, do you?"

"Should I?"

"If I did, you should. Think about it."

So I thought about it. It took me about thirty seconds for the lightbulb to go on. "Bohannon," I said, and felt the blood pounding in my temples.

She grinned.

"Marie Fightmaster said the redheaded man who tried to buy her baby had a Bohunk name," I said, thinking out loud. "But it wasn't Bohunk at all, and she wasn't describing the *kind* of name it was. It was the way she heard it in her mind. It was Bohannon."

"You're a slow learner, Milan, but you get there anyway. What are the odds that Francis X. Bohannon is a redhead?"

"I'd say they were pretty damn good. Suzanne, you're a wonder!"

"I am, aren't I?" she said, dimples showing. "So what do we do now?"

"Right now, you hie your pretty butt over to Lieutenant McHargue and give her that sheaf of papers to mull over. It's not enough for her to make any arrests, but it will sure get her thinking. And thinking about somebody other than Larry and Evelyn Groom."

"And what are you going to do?"

"Shanklin and Bohannon must be in pretty much of a panic right now," I said. "I think I'll go out and rattle their cage."

Suzanne frowned. "If they're behind the killings of Willetta Clemons and the Indian, they aren't anybody to mess with," she said, wagging a cautionary finger. "You be careful."

"If I wanted to be careful, I would have become an accountant."

"Like David Ream?"

"Oh. Yeah," I said.

Nevertheless, after Suzanne left, I took my .357 Magnum out of the desk drawer, checked it and reloaded it, and slid it snugly into the harness holster I'd strapped around my shoulders.

Just being careful.

Aurora is in the same general direction as Hudson, southeast of the city, but not quite as far. The wind had come to rejuvenated life and returned to buffet us again as the sun was setting, and on the radio WMJI weather guru Shane Hollett was predicting another Alberta Clipper. Just what we needed, and Major League Baseball's Opening Day less than sixty days away.

Just what *I* needed to go running around in the suburbs.

Much of Aurora is given over to luxurious, sumptuously landscaped housing tracts with full-sized golf courses attached, the spacious homes selling in the mid six-figure range. I waited until seven o'clock to drive down there, figuring that Shanklin and Bohannon would be home from their respective offices by then.

Claudya Shanklin's house, all glass and flagstone and modern-looking dark gray siding, was on a winding road through one of the developments, each home the cornerstone of at least two acres of rolling green land dotted with ponds and wooded areas. Even in the dark—it was a little before nine o'clock—I could see that this was a beautiful place to live. Not exactly child-friendly; the lots were spaced too far apart for that. But the bucolic setting seemed like a lovely environment for unwinding after a long day's work.

I cruised the road twice, missing Shanklin's house on the first drive-by. When I finally pinpointed it, I could see that all the downstairs lights were on, and that a late-model Ford Windstar wagon was parked in the driveway. Its license plate was from Cuyahoga County, not Portage County, where Aurora was located. Apparently Claudya Shanklin had a visitor.

That was a complication; I didn't want to walk in there while Shanklin and Bohannon had company.

I drove around for a while, not wanting to park and wait. A high-ticket tract like this would surely have a security patrol making its regular rounds, and it wouldn't do to be caught skulking outside someone's house in a parked car. Especially with a .357 Magnum under my arm. Explain *that* to a security guard.

It was on my fourth pass that I saw a short, dark, balding man in a black suede jacket come rushing out of the house to leap into the Windstar, back down the driveway, and lay some rubber down on the road getting out of there. He seemed agitated, frightened, and in one hell of a hurry.

My first thought was that he'd done something to the house's occupants and that I should go inside and help. Then I realized that if it was the same man who had killed Joseph Ettawageshik and Willetta Clemons, I couldn't do much good inside anyway. So I followed him instead.

He headed out of the development for the main road and then turned toward the freeway, ignoring the posted speed limits. I kept up with him, hoping that if one of us got stopped for reckless driving, it would not be me.

I wondered if I should call the Aurora Police and tell them what I'd seen, but I discarded the idea rather quickly. I hadn't really seen anything that the police would want to know about yet, and if a zone car came roaring up their driveway, Shanklin and Bohannon would undoubtedly get spooked.

I kept close to the Windstar as its driver barreled it up the ramp onto the interstate heading toward Cleveland. I don't think he realized he had a tail; he'd have no reason to suspect one. Besides, he seemed far too intent on getting where he was going to even spare a look into the rearview mirror.

I activated my car phone and called Florence McHargue at her office; she wasn't there, of course, since she worked the day shift, but I left a message with the desk sergeant to have her call me on my cellular as soon as possible. Then I hung up, the better to concentrate on my driving; a person on the telephone at the wheel of a speeding car is a menace to himself and everyone else on the road.

When the Windstar took the turnoff from I-271 to I-90, I got the idea he might be headed for downtown. He was booking along at about seventy-five miles per hour, weaving in and out of the traffic as if the car itself were angry. The driver was evidently a man on a mission. No less than I was, though, and I kept his bobbing taillights in sight at all times.

To my right, the dark waters of Lake Erie churned, wind-powered waves throwing up peacock-tail sprays against the breakwater. In the wintertime the waters of the Great Lakes were as unpredictable and unforgiving as the Atlantic Ocean. And sometimes as deadly.

The mobile phone did its best imitation of a chirping canary and I snatched it up immediately, hanging on to the steering wheel with one hand.

"This is McHargue." The voice filtered through the receiver flat and metallic.

"Lieutenant, thanks for calling back so quickly. You talked to Suzanne Davis this afternoon?"

She sighed. "Yes. She gave me a lot to read."

"Did you enjoy it?"

"Shitty ending. You called me. What do you want?"

"Are you planning to pick up Claudya Shanklin and Francis Bohannon?"

"I have nothing to 'pick them up' for, yet. This is the millennium, we don't haul people in so quickly anymore. Lots of questions need answering first. And I can't arrest a guy whose name is Bohannon just because it happens to sound like Bohunk, which is a term I like only a little bit better than the 'n' word, by the way. But I asked the Aurora P.D. to stop by their place this afternoon and suggest to them that it would behoove them to come in and talk to me tomorrow."

"Well, I think that got their attention."

"What do you mean?"

I told her about the balding man running out of their house and heading for Cleveland at high speed.

"I see," she said. "We can discuss later just what you were doing hanging around their house. We *will* discuss it. But that's for another time. This guy, though—you think he might have capped the two of them?"

"I don't know. I did at first. Then I thought it over and came to a different conclusion."

"Would you like to share it with me?" Florence McHargue does sarcasm better than anyone I know.

"That's why I called. I think the man who was at their house is the other guy who went up to Michigan with Bohannon to buy an Indian baby."

"Is he cross-eyed?"

"I couldn't tell. It was dark out. He was short and balding."

"So are half the men on the east side of Cleveland."

"But they don't know Shanklin and Bohannon. They know that you're on to them, and I think this guy is their partner or associate or something, and they sent him off to cover their tracks in some way."

"What way?"

"I don't know."

"So what do you want me to do about it?"

"Nothing. I just wanted to alert you to that they're running scared and possibly ready to fly."

"Where are they going to fly to? She's got a law practice, he's got a thriving business. You think they'll give those up and go hide in Costa Rica or someplace?"

"If you were looking at Murder One, wouldn't you?"

"Hmm," she said. "Point taken. All right, I'll call the Aurora cops again and have them keep an eye open. I can't have them stake the house out—I don't have enough to go on. And I can't very well ask you to stake it out, either, if you were thinking about volunteering."

"I wasn't. I have other things to do."

"Like?"

"Right now I'm following the bald guy on the freeway."

Her intake of breath was harsh and angry. "God damn you, Jacovich, you have no right . . ."

"I'll contact you as soon as I know anything," I said, and broke the connection before she could answer, before she could order me to stop. Then I turned the ringer off so she wouldn't be able to call me back.

Ahead of me, the illuminated white circle and triangle of the Rock and Roll Hall of Fame blazed whitely in the darkness along the lakefront like a giant geometry problem, with the dome of the Great Lakes Science Center and Cleveland's new football stadium beyond it. I'm not fond of the hall, being no fan of rock and roll, but it's a spectacular building, and the view of it from the lake will take your breath away—if you're lucky enough to be offered a boat ride.

Not in February, though. Bad idea.

The Windstar exited the freeway at East Ninth Street and turned south. The streets were fairly quiet, so I had to hang back a bit to keep the driver from thinking I was following him. Unless the Indians or Cavs are playing at home, the downtown area is pretty deserted at night except for the bars and dance clubs of the Flats down on the east bank of the Cuyahoga.

I followed him all the way to Huron Street, where he made a quick turn and then aimed his car toward the ramp leading to the underground parking facility beneath Tower City.

I parked ten spaces away from him, making a mental note of his license plate and of exactly where he was leaving his car, and waited until he got out and started walking toward the entrance before I got out, too, unclipping the cellular phone from its cradle on my dashboard and slipping it into my pocket before following him toward the glass enclosure that led to the escalator up to the Avenue, the main shopping area. There weren't many cars in the garage at this hour. Most of them belonged to night owls catching the last show at Tower City Cinemas or grabbing a late supper at the Hard Rock Cafe on the second level. That made my tailing him more obvious, and I hung back and tried to act casual, but I'm afraid I didn't much look like I was going to a movie.

The bald spot on the top of his head was like a beacon under the lights, bobbing as he walked. I waited until he was almost at the top of the escalator before I stepped on, hoping he wouldn't make me, but he was so focused on his errand that he wouldn't have noticed me if I'd been wearing a clown suit and a red nose.

He crossed the fountain court quickly, went up the curved marble staircase, and headed for the elevators to Claudya Shanklin's office building.

I couldn't help feeling a little smug. I'd guessed correctly; he was obviously planning to go up there and pull some incriminating files. I couldn't very well follow him into the office, so I hoped he was simply going to remove them and not put them through a shredder.

I let him get into the elevator by himself, and then watched as the floor indicator clicked off numbers and stopped at Shanklin's floor.

I wondered how long he'd be up there.

I went back down to the fountain court, where I could see him when he came back.

The indoor fountain is one of Cleveland's greatest attractions for families. Programmed by computer, it sends multiple jets of water splashing and swirling and arcing, dolphin-like, through the air, illuminated by colored lights that change their moods every few seconds, waving and erupting in rhythm to whatever music is playing, while deliberate clouds of steam and fog rise eerily toward the high ceiling and then dissipate. Tonight it was Aaron Copland's lively ballet suite, *Rodeo,* booming mightily through several huge speakers scattered around the court and setting up a vibration just behind my breastbone. It was magnificent and thrilling and moving.

And extremely eerie as well. Because at this late hour there was no one in the huge space the size of a basketball arena except me. The little kiosks and rolling stands were shuttered and shrouded, the stores were all closed, and there were no security people in sight, no maintenance workers, no stragglers to watch the fountain go through its spectacular paces like a sad and lonely prima ballerina dancing her pliés and *tours jetés* to a spookily empty theater.

I pulled out my cellular and called the police again, to leave a message for Lieutenant McHargue.

"Is this Jacovich?" the sergeant who'd answered the phone wanted to know. It wasn't Billy Dockerty; he worked the day shift.

"Yes," I said.

"Lou said if you called again I should patch you through. Hangonaminnit." He made it all one run-together word.

I was put on hold, waiting through a series of beeps and buzzes until I heard McHargue's flat, low tones.

"Jacovich, where are you?"

"In the Fountain Court at Tower City, Lieutenant. Can't you hear the music?"

"Jacovich," she said, making it a warning. In the background I could hear a TV set, the canned laughter of a sitcom. In McHargue's case, recorded chuckles were mandatory, because I'd certainly never heard *her* laugh.

"My guy—the one I followed from Shanklin's house—he's upstairs in her office. My guess is that he's going to get rid of some files that would probably wrap your case up very nicely."

"Damn! You think he's erasing them from the computer?"

"I would, if I were he," I said, embarrassed at not having thought of that before, "but even a high school hacker could probably retrieve them from the hard drive." Just as no thought ever really disappears but goes floating off somewhere to become part of the continuum, no computer file is ever truly erased from a hard drive if someone with computer savvy wants to get to it badly enough. "My guess is that there's hard copies, too. Computers have been known to crash."

"Thanks for the lesson, Bill Gates. Okay, I'm sending a zone car over there to intercept him."

"Don't have them come blasting into Tower City like a SWAT team. It'll just spook him and he might run. He's wearing a black hip-length suede jacket and chinos, and he's been driving a dark blue Ford Windstar van with Cuyahoga County plates. It's parked in the second row from the front, section E. Have the uniforms wait down there for him."

"Yes, *sir!*" she said nastily.

How sharper than a serpent's tooth is a thankless homicide dick.

"I'll keep an eye on him when he comes down, just in case he doesn't go to his car."

"Where else would he go?"

"No place, probably."

"I don't want you keeping an eye on him, Jacovich. I'll send one of the officers up to the Fountain Court. To *relieve* you," she added.

"He seems to be in a bit of a panic. I'm afraid if he sees a uniform in here, he's going to bolt. Can you send a plainclothes guy instead?"

"How many suits do you think I have riding around in zone cars?"

"I'm just telling you we'll only cause trouble if we spook him."

"Where'd you get this 'we' shit?"

I finally got annoyed. "Lieutenant McHargue, I don't give a good goddamn what you do, I'm just telling you what's going on. And my take is, you'd be a hell of a lot better off sending an officer in here who's not wearing a uniform. If you can get one here in time."

"Sure I can, Jacovich," she said. "After that I'll turn loaves into fishes." She clicked off.

I waited, enjoying the fountain, or at least enjoying it as much as I could while waiting for a murderer to reappear, the music now the stirring martial strains of John Philip Sousa's "Stars and Stripes Forever," preternaturally loud with no warm bodies around to listen to it and absorb the sound. At one point a cleanup worker appeared, pushing a wheeled trash cart toward the food court, but he soon disappeared and I was alone again.

After about three minutes, I saw the guy from the Windstar up on the second level, coming from the elevators. He started down the staircase clutching a thick sheaf of file folders to his chest.

I was still playing it cool, trying to look as if I were waiting for someone to come out of the movies, but I looked at him anyway; it would have been bizarre not to, since he was the only other human in sight. Our gazes locked, and the blood pounded in my temples.

He gave me a curt, casual nod, the way you do to a stranger whose path you cross when there's no one else around—and then all at once his face became alert, frowning, the muscles at the corners of his eyes visibly tightening, and his pace slowed. He looked around to see if anyone else might be observing, and tucked the files he was carrying under his left arm, putting his right one into his side jacket pocket. His course altered slightly so that he was walking directly toward me.

The flesh on my back tingled. He had indeed noticed me following him in; with no one else in sight he probably couldn't avoid noticing, but had paid no attention at the time. Now, seeing me again, his suspicions were aroused. I knew I'd been made.

I set my feet solidly on the floor beneath me and nodded at him, trying to look pleasant. "Evening," I said, raising my voice to be heard over the music.

"Howdy," he answered, with the manner and inflection of a city boy to whom the word was unnatural. "Out late, aren't you?"

"I'm waiting to pick my kids up; they're at the movies."

"Ah, yeah. Kids." He licked his lips, unable to conceal the tension that must have been plucking at his nerves like banjo strings. I was fairly convinced that he, and Francis X. Bohannon had been the ones to attempt to buy the Fightmaster baby. For all I knew they had murdered Joseph Ettawageshik and Willetta Clemons, because he did indeed suffer from exotropia, or a wandering eye. Talking to him face to face was disconcerting; his right eye was directly on me, but his left one seemed to be scoping out something above him and to the side—at the moment it was pointed upstairs at the entrance to the Hard Rock Cafe. "What movie are they seeing?"

"I'm not sure," I said, caught out. "Some Disney thing."

"Disney."

I offered up a reluctant smile.

"Say," he said, "you wouldn't happen to have the time, would you?"

"It's . . ." I raised my left hand to look at my wristwatch, a reflex action that saved my life.

I caught the blur of his hand coming out of his pocket, saw the flash of light on the knife as it arced toward my throat, and raised my left hand higher for protection. The blade dug into the foam filler of the sleeve of my heavy cold-weather system parka and caught there, never making it through to my skin. If I hadn't had my forearm up it would have sliced neatly across my throat.

I lurched to my feet and let my forward momentum carry the punch I threw at him. It was aimed at his throat, a sure way of disabling him momentarily, but at the last moment he pulled back a bit and it hit him on his neck just beneath his jaw, which was fortunate for me because there was no bone to bruise my hand. It didn't land solidly, but it hit him hard enough that he stumbled backward and tripped, almost losing his balance and making him drop the files. They scattered all over the marble floor next to the fountain.

By the time he'd regained his equilibrium enough to come at me again with the knife upraised, my .357 Magnum was in my hand, its large muzzle pointed at his middle. "Don't," I said.

He stared at the gun with his right eye, the good one, and stopped, frozen like a statue for a surreal moment of suspended animation. Then he turned and ran toward the Down escalator.

I could have dropped him with one shot, but that didn't seem right somehow, even though he'd just tried to cut my throat—probably the same as he had done to Joseph Ettawageshik. So I sprinted after him, the Magnum at my side. We ran around the end of the fountain and then he was clattering down the moving stairs.

I got to the top of the escalator when he was halfway down, and my cop training kicked in. "Freeze!" I barked.

He stopped, turning to look back up at me with one eye while the other scanned the high-vaulted ceiling of the Avenue, and surprisingly there was a gun in *his* hand now, too, a shiny little silver one that looked like the head of a poisonous snake at the end of his arm.

Some might characterize it as a "lady's gun."

"Don't!" I warned him again, but he began to raise it anyway.

I dropped into a crouch, held the Magnum steady with both hands, and shot him through the chest.

The bullet's impact blew him backward off his feet and sent him tumbling down the escalator steps, turning one complete somersault along the way. He reached the bottom and stopped, but the moving stairs kept disappearing under him, rocking his body gently so that he looked like a man trying very hard to turn over in the middle of the night without completely waking up. It was a macabre death dance, and it gave me the shudders.

I quietly allowed the escalator to carry me down to where he was, and gingerly stepped over him. I looked down at his rhythmically moving body, feeling sick to my stomach. Up until two minutes earlier he had been a complete stranger to me, and now he was dead and my weapon was still smoking.

He was not the first man I had killed without knowing his name; but the others had been a long time ago in a far-off world where killing was the order of the day, and mine had earned me a Bronze Star.

Two uniformed policemen, probably dispatched by Florence McHargue and having just arrived in time to hear the shots, came pounding through the glass doors from the parking structure with their weapons drawn and ready. Both were African-American, and one was about ten years the other's senior.

"Drop it!" the younger one barked when he saw me holding the Magnum.

It clattered on the marble floor where I dropped it. I raised my hands in the air. "I'm Jacovich," I said.

The two cops looked at each other and relaxed their shoulders, but they didn't put their guns away until they had taken mine.

Bright, shiny fresh blood stained the escalator stairs just before they disappeared into the floor.

CHAPTER TWENTY-FIVE

The good news, as it turned out, was that I wasn't going to be charged with first-degree murder; even Florence McHargue didn't dislike me enough to try to make that one stick, and she backed up my story when the inevitable questions started being asked. Besides, the cockeyed killer's weapon proved it was clearly a case of self-defense.

But that didn't mean I could simply go home and sin no more. Nothing is that easy.

The next week was a long one, and I spent most of it with my feet to the fire. I had to tell my story so often that I got sick of hearing it. To McHargue, of course, and to her superior, the commander of the Third Division. To the deputy Safety Director of Cleveland, who wasn't very happy about a shoot-out in Tower City. To the FBI, who really didn't care that I shot someone but were very anxious to hear about kidnapping and baby-selling across state lines.

Ordinarily I would have had to tell it to the press, too, numerous times. Every TV station in town called me, and Channel Twelve even sent a camera crew to my office; I wouldn't let them in the door. I decided I wasn't going to feed the media frenzy on this one. Larry and Evelyn Groom were in enough trouble with the federal government without my making public spectacles of them to boot.

Besides, if anyone deserved the story it was the *Plain Dealer* and Holly Butcher, and she was so busy filing daily updates on the TroyTrike debacle that I figured she had enough on her plate already. As I had suspected, that story made the wire services, and within three days Butcher had received an offer from CNN that she was still mulling over. I had never seen her, but it turned out she was just over thirty and attractively telegenic.

And she did what David Ream hadn't yet been able to do; she derailed the production of TroyTrike. She mentioned Consumer Watchdog, too, so Helen Moise was left twisting in the wind with no one to sue and no way to recoup all the money she'd paid Ream as a consultant. Ream lost his job, which was no surprise to him or anyone else, but he got another one with a software company out on the west side. I spoke to him several months after it had all blown over and was pleased to learn that little Caitlynn was coming along nicely, responding to therapy, and that eventually her brain functions would be at least ninety percent normal. She would laugh and play again. And so might a lot of other kids who might otherwise have choked or suffered crushed skulls due to the shoddy workmanship of TroyTrike.

Ensuring the laughter of children is supposed to be Job One in this crazy world of ours; too often it isn't. At least I could feel good about that part of it.

While I dispensed a lot of information about the shooting and the kidnapping of Andrew, I got some back as well, reluctant courtesy of Bob Matusen, who took the risk, I think, because he was feeling sorry for me. If McHargue had known he'd told me inside cop-shop information she would have skinned him alive, busted him back down to patrolman, and had him patrolling the East Fifty-fifth Street drug ghetto on the graveyard shift.

His name had been Frank diPiazzo.

The cockeye, the guy I shot.

Forty-one years old and never married, he was a native of New Jersey who was well-traveled in the eastern half of the country. He'd done time in Missouri and Minnesota for shakedowns and minor racketeering, and in Indianapolis for running a string of underage hookers, and New York City authorities believed that his fingerprints might be on an unsolved killing and another disappearance in Queens, but no one had ever been able to nail him down on those so he had skated. Jack of many trades was Frank diPiazzo, and all of them dirty.

Rumor had it that he was mob-connected but not mob-made, for which I was thankful, lest the next body found floating in the Cuyahoga be mine.

He had marched through Ohio starting in Cincinnati, where he ran some nickel-and-dime cons on both sides of the Ohio River, thence northward to Akron, and finally to Cleveland, where he had hooked up with Francis X. Bohannon and helped him establish his parking lot empire with a little strong-arm extortion stuff, later working as his bagman.

But the Native American baby-selling racket was too slick and sophisticated to have been dreamt of in his philosophy. That one came directly from the fertile legal mind of Claudya Shanklin.

In her perfectly legitimate practice of adoption law, Shanklin had figured out the tremendous demand for non-African-American babies, and had decided to set up her own little black market ring for placing Indian infants into well-to-do homes. But since she had to stay respectable-appearing and above suspicion, she needed a front to do the dirty work.

That's where poor little Willetta Clemons had come in. An underachieving graduate of an undistinguished law college, Clemons was too untalented, low-key, and frumpy to catch on with a glittering downtown law firm, too poor to finance her own private practice, and too inept to run it in any case. She seemed tailor-made for the role of employee, and so Claudya Shanklin and her lover, Francis X. Bohannon, had set her up in the dinky offices on Prospect Avenue, where half her billable hours were given over to legitimate adoptions and the other half to the baby-buying enterprise that stunk to high heaven.

Shanklin dispatched diPiazzo and Bohannon as her advance men, to seek out newborn Indian kids and negotiate with their families. The little cross-eyed mobster was the smooth talker, and Bohannon was there so things would look legitimate; who would distrust a tall, open-faced, redheaded Irishman?

But it was a middle-aged, infertile couple in Birmingham, Michigan, whose desperation to raise a child speeded up Shanklin's timetable and led her to the idea of kidnapping where negotiation failed. The first baby, a five-week-old girl, had been spirited away from a Navajo reservation in Arizona in the middle of the night. Five others had followed, the last of whom was Andrew Takalo.

Bohannon and diPiazzo did the dangerous, hands-on stuff, Shanklin took care of the necessary paperwork, and Willetta Clemons did little more than handle the money and hold hands with the adoptive parents. For that she was paid the handsome stipend of forty-five thousand dollars per annum, plus bonuses. Not big money by Cleveland-lawyer standards, but enough to keep her in her cute little apartment just across the street from the bench in front of the ice cream shop where Joseph Ettawageshik had spent his last day on earth.

The knife with which diPiazzo had tried to take out my Adam's apple was tested by a forensic lab and found to contain microscopic blood particles between the blade and the hilt, the DNA of which would eventually be matched to Joseph Ettawageshik.

And when the Cleveland P.D. ran a ballistics test on his gun, which they accomplish by firing a bullet into a tank of water and then fishing it out by means of a dowel rod with a lump of Play-Doh stuck on the end, they found it more than a 99 percent probability that it was the same weapon that had fired the fatal shots into Willetta Clemons.

"What I don't understand yet," Suzanne Davis said, "is how Joseph Ettawageshik found out about Clemons in the first place."

We were sipping Bardolino and eating linguini with clam sauce at a small table tucked into a little bay next to the front window of La Dolce Vita, a *rustica* Italian bistro on Mayfield Road in Cleveland's Little Italy, just steps away from the hospitals, museums, and the Case Western Reserve campus of University Circle. When we came in, genial owner-chef Terry Tarantino had come over and sat with us for a few minutes until the food arrived, showing us pictures of his beautiful little girl before he was called back to the kitchen.

"Nobody will ever know that, Suzanne," I answered. "But my guess is that somewhere along the way diPiazzo and Bohannon left some sort of a trail in the Indian community that led Joseph to Willetta. And he was sitting across the street from her apartment in the snow waiting to catch sight of her. Probably to make her tell him what had happened to his great-grandson."

"You don't think he had any other agenda? Like to kill her himself?"

"I doubt it. But he was a proud old man, and I imagine he was determined to get little Andrew back on his own, without help from the authorities. He probably believed they wouldn't help him, anyway." I made a face. "That turned out to be a fatal error."

"So why did they kill him?"

"The same reason they eventually killed Willetta Clemons; to keep things quiet. They sure as hell didn't want to go to prison for the baby racket they were running, which is where Shanklin and Bohannon are surely headed. And now with a few more embellishments."

"Is the county prosecutor charging them with murder?"

"There's a pretty good case to be made that diPiazzo did the actual killings, but they can nail the other two with accessory to murder and inciting to murder. And most certainly they'll be looking at Uncle Sam hard time for child-selling and kidnapping. If their sentences run consecutively, they'll be inside until they're old and gray. Till you and I are, too."

"Matusen told you all this?"

I nodded. "The files that diPiazzo dropped all over the floor at Tower City when he ran had most of this stuff in it. For the rest, even though Shanklin is keeping her mouth shut and hiring a high-profile defense attorney to try and keep her bony ass out of the penitentiary, Francis X. Bohannon is singing 'Danny Boy' to the cops like an Irish nightingale."

Suzanne blinked, surprised. "I thought they were lovers."

"Love doesn't have much to do with it when you're looking at fifty years in the slammer. He figures if he rolls over on her, he can do himself some good."

"Isn't true love beautiful?" She deftly spooled some linguini into her mouth and washed it down with a sip of wine. "Did he say why they got rid of Clemons?"

"They were nervous about her. She was perfectly amenable to kidnapping children for profit, but she was starting to make loud whining noises about killing the old man; they couldn't afford to let her get any louder. And when you and I came into the picture, they went into panic mode. With Clemons dead, there was no one who could connect the three of them to the baby ring and the Ettawageshik killing. According to Bohannon, diPiazzo handled that little chore all by himself."

I looked out the window at the foot traffic on Mayfield Road; despite the cold weather, there are always pedestrians on the streets of Little Italy. Couples out for dinner, young guys from the neighborhood just chilling, the old men born in Italy who had lived on the hill for fifty years and never learned much English, for whom the street action on Murray Hill is their only social life. Things were being set to right in the death of Joseph Ettawageshik and the kidnapping of Baby Andrew, but I was deriving precious little gratification from it.

Suzanne looked at me closely, and her big blue eyes got very serious. "And you're still feeling like shit for shooting diPiazzo, aren't you?"

"Have you ever killed anyone, Suzanne?"

She shook her head.

"If you had, you'd understand."

She touched the back of my hand lightly. "He was a murderer, Milan, and a kidnapper."

"And he needed to be stopped, so I stopped him. Still . . . You suggested a few days ago that I have a God-complex, Suzanne, but it falls short of making judgments about who gets to live and who doesn't." I sighed and pushed my plate away half-eaten; just talking about it had robbed me of my appetite. Terry would pack it up for me to take home and eat another day.

"That's not the only thing about this case that stinks," I said. "Willetta was just a dumb kid who was in way over her head. She deserved to be punished, but she didn't deserve to die. Larry and Evelyn Groom did wrong, too, trying to buy little Andrew, but now they're probably looking at a government rap for it. At the very least their lives are going to be shattered—all because they had all that love to give to a child. And as for the baby . . ."

"The baby is back where he belongs, Milan, with his mother and father."

"Yes, he is," I said. "I'm not sure I did him any favors, though. The Grooms could have given him a better chance in life."

"That doesn't make it right," she said. "You said so yourself. So sometimes the right thing is the hard thing. You know that."

"Yes, I do," I said. "And the Takalos are overjoyed. That's one good thing that happened here."

"So why aren't you overjoyed, too?"

I could only shrug. "Give me about eighteen years, until Andrew becomes an all-state lacrosse player with a full scholarship to the University of Michigan, and maybe I will be."

"What if he just grows up learning to hunt and fish and play darts?" she said. "Will you be overjoyed then, too? What if he just grows up happy and laughing?"

I sighed. More laughter of children.

Suzanne clucked her tongue. "Jacovich, you really are the most soft-hearted sucker I know. You look tough and act tough, but you're just like a crème brûleé—a hard-baked crust on the outside but squishy and sweet when you cut through it." She squeezed my hand affectionately. "I like that in a man."

"Don't be eyeing me as husband number four, Suzanne," I said, forcing a rueful smile. "I've been told often by a lot of people, and very recently at that, that I'm lousy husband material."

She looked absolutely stunned for a moment, then threw back her head and laughed lustily. Some of the other people in La

Dolce Vita looked over to see what was so funny. "Wow, Milan. What an ego! This may break your heart, but the thought never even occurred to me."

And then she cocked her head to one side like a puppy listening for the sound of the can opener on the Alpo. "Although now that you mention it . . ."

I held up both hands in front of me in mock terror, my forefingers making the sign of the cross. Other than the generous supply of garlic in the linguini, it was the only way I knew to ward off vampires.

I had talked to Connie Haley once more, the day after the shooting. She'd called because, even though I was refusing to talk to the press, there was no way I could keep my name out of the newspaper.

"It scared hell out of me when I read that, Milan," she said. "Are you all right?"

"No broken skin or bones," I said. "I'm a little distressed, though."

"I can imagine." She didn't say anything for a minute. Then: "See, Milan, that's what I meant the other night. Your shooting people, getting shot at . . ."

"I know what you meant."

"I still want to be your friend, though."

"Sure, Connie, you can never have too many friends. Maybe some night we'll go out drinking together and pick up a couple of women."

She laughed. Then her voice got serious and low. "I'm sorry. Really I am. But I'm just not comfortable with it."

"You're not?"

"No, I'm not. I—can't handle it, that's all."

"Connie—did it ever occur to you that this isn't about *you*?"

Another long silence. "That's just it. I wish it were."

And then we said our good-byes and good lucks and see you arounds, and that was that. Three dead, four in desperate legal trouble, and another of my relationships went down in flames. The Joseph Ettawageshik case was taking its toll in casualties; any more and we'd be needing a triage nurse.

As for TroyToy, Holly Butcher was true to her word and kept David Ream's name out of her stories about the tricycle from hell. She kept mine out, too, for which I was thankful. Otherwise I would have been getting more ink than the mayor.

So I closed out the Treusch file as well, updating my computer disk. Two cases of exploiting children, in very different ways, and I hadn't earned the first nickel on either of them.

I hoped that by the end of the year business would have improved enough that I'd be able to use the tax write-offs.

And I figured that would be the end of it. Until two weeks after the diPiazzo shooting, when I got a surprise call at the office from Cat McTighe.

"Remember me?" she said.

"Of course I do. How are you?"

"Just lousy, thanks to you."

"What did I do?"

"I'm out of a job. Because of you and that *Plain Dealer* reporter, TroyTrike had to cease production, at a cost to Army Treusch of about a million dollars in lost development money. And of course the income projections for next year just about dropped off the end of the table. So he did some belt-tightening and downsized the whole company. I got caught in the fallout."

My eyes were suddenly tired and stinging, and I rubbed them roughly with a knuckle. There seemed to be no end to the collateral damage I had wreaked in the past few weeks. "God, Cat, I'm sorry."

"Me too," she said. "But I'll find something else. The days when people got hired directly by the boss are over; every company, even the little ones, need human resources people, if only just to handle the tons of government paperwork."

"I hope you do. Let me know, okay?"

"In the meantime, though . . ."

"Yes."

"I think you owe me another dinner. If for no other reason than I can't afford to buy my own."

I reached for a cigarette. It was March, now, and while in Cleveland that in no way means spring has arrived, outside my windows the river had thawed and the gulls darkened the sky by their sheer numbers.

"Cat . . ." I said.

"I know, I know, you're seeing someone."

"Well actually, not anymore, but . . ."

She waited, although from the rhythm of her breathing at the other end of the line, I couldn't say it was waiting patiently. I marshaled my thoughts while I scrabbled around in my desk drawer for a match.

"I'm going through some personal stuff right now, Cat. I'm not a good bet for a relationship at the moment."

"Who said anything about a relationship?"

"Well . . ."

"What are you, Milan, a commitment junkie?"

I had to think about that for a while.

"Look," she said, "I'm a millennium-type woman, and when I want something I just go after it and worry about forever later. I don't need a dozen roses every Monday morning, I'm not looking for happily-ever-after. I'm just very attracted to you, I'd like to spend some time with you, and frankly I want to go to bed with you. Now what's so terrible about that?"

While I seriously considered the question, I found a book of matches—from the White Magnolia, Connie's father's restaurant. I tore one out, struck it, and lit my Winston. The smoke seared my lungs, and I expelled it like a sigh of relief.

"Not a damn thing," I said.